To Aileen

PISTACO

A Tale of Love in the Andes

Lynn F. Monahan

Enjoy your life's
journey,

Lynn
9/28/17

i.e.

in extenso

Pistaco
A Tale of Love in the Andes
By Lynn F. Monahan

Edited by Michael Coyne

Interior layout and typesetting by Don Bashline; cover design by Patricia A. Lynch; author portrait by Mariana Monahan

Cover photo copyright © Robert Frerck/Robert Harding. Used with permission.

Copyright © 2017 by Lynn F. Monahan

Published by In Extenso Press

Distributed exclusively by ACTA Publications, 4848 N. Clark Street Chicago, IL 60640, (800) 397-2282, actapublications.com

Library of Congress Catalog Number: 2016921219
ISBN: 978-0-87946-982-5 (hardcover)
ISBN: 978-0-87946-981-8 (softcover)
ISBN: 978-0-87946-649-7 (ebook)
Printed in the United States of America by Total Printing Systems
Year 25 24 23 22 21 20 19 18 17
Printing 15 14 13 12 11 10 9 8 7 6 5 4 3 2 First

♻ Text printed on 30% post-consumer recycled paper

A note from the author about dialogue in Pistaco

The characters in a story taking place in Peru would normally speak Spanish, the country's principal language, or Quechua, the tongue of the Inca empire still spoken in places like the fictional village of Urpimarca, where *Pistaco's* main action takes place. Most of this book's dialogue, whether Spanish or Quechua, is rendered in English, though I have kept a few phrases of those languages to help retain a sense of the atmosphere of the Peruvian highlands.

A glossary of Spanish and Quechua words and phrases appearing in the book is appended after the last chapter for the reader's convenience.

Pistaco is a work of fiction. Aside from references to a few historic figures mentioned by name, any similarity to actual people, living or dead, is coincidental.

For Elsie

All sin is rooted in the failure of love.

Thomas Merton

1

June 1985
Urpimarca, Peru

A hushed voice from the street blurted out its message in a tone of urgency.

"Dile al padrecito que ya vienen los terrucos. Que no salga!" Tell Father the terrorists are coming. Don't come out!

The young priest recognized the voice of Don Javier, the mayor of Urpimarca. One of the few men in the village respectfully addressed as "Don," he was a man deferred to even in unofficial matters by most people in the community.

Father Steven McMahon had been called upon to anoint Magdalena Quispe, who could no longer lift her frail frame from the earthen platform covered with blankets of llama wool that served as her bed. The priest prayed with Señora Quispe's daughter and eight-year-old grandson. Her son-in-law, Angel, waiting outside, repeated the mayor's warning. The one-room house of unstuccoed adobe with its packed dirt floor and walls blackened by years of wood and kerosene smoke barely accommodated those already inside.

Don Javier stayed outside. Angel and a neighbor entered and stood silently. The priest didn't turn to acknowledge them, tending to the old woman, who, though awake, seemed unaware of what was going on around her.

"Recemos," the priest said. He prayed the Our Father in Spanish and the daughter and son-in-law repeated it in a dissonant murmur, reciting the prayer in Quechua, the only language the old woman knew. The neighbor tried to keep up with the priest's Spanish, mumbling the last words of each line a fraction behind the priest, producing an echo in a language he spoke rarely, and only when outside the village.

Father Steven knelt by the grandmother and held her hand. He made the sign of the cross while her other hand followed in midair. He asked God to give her comfort and rest.

"Señora, tengo que irme," he told her. The daughter translated that the priest had to leave. The grandmother nodded her head and blessed the priest with the sign of the cross, as he had her. She said something in Quechua that he recognized as a blessing that mingled two universes, two visions of the divine, one Christian and the other handed down the millennia from her Andean ancestors.

As Steven turned from the woman, Angel said in Spanish, "Padre, the terrucos are in the square looking for you. They have three prisoners. They plan to make an example of them."

"What do they want with me? Do they want a priest for the prisoners?" The question seemed ridiculous to him even as he asked it.

"They aren't looking for your blessing, Padre. They are looking for your hide."

Angel handed him a poncho and a chullo to pull down over his light brown hair.

"You won't be noticed in these. Come on. Let's get you up to the cemetery."

The colorful wool cap with its pointed peak, tassel, and earflaps gave him the look of a campesino. The poncho was black with fine blue lines, the color villagers used for funerals. Outside the house in the bright sunshine, they hefted a large canvas bag filled with sticks and straw onto Steven's back. It was almost as

2

tall as the priest and twice as wide. He had often seen farmers and poor laborers doubled over at the waist, balancing such loads on the flat of their backs like burros tottering beneath their enormous packs.

"Why would I carry such a thing to the cemetery?" the priest asked.

"Don't worry. Outsiders pay no attention to such people. They are invisible to them," Angel said.

True, no one would expect a gringo priest to behave like a burro or a llama.

They headed up a dusty path to the road that led to the cemetery on the hill opposite the village. The men apologized as they walked, uncomfortable at subjecting the priest to such indignity. Shining Path guerrillas had for a while been railing against the church and making threats against anyone who accepted material aid from nuns or priests. They had warned religious workers not to fund or supply soup kitchens, health clinics, or agricultural projects. You could pray with the people, but in the convoluted logic of the Maoists anything that alleviated temporal suffering was a salve, an attempt to pacify the poor while doing nothing to change a system that left them in misery. The church in Lima continued to send medicine, enough to provoke the guerrillas' rage, but not enough to meet the need.

Steven had another, more important, mark against him. He was an American.

He shifted the load on his back to keep it from slipping. It wasn't heavy so much as it was incredibly bulky, and his breath was labored as he waddled in this unnatural position. He stopped every few minutes and knelt in the dirt to avoid standing conspicuously. The bottom of the bag rested on the ground as he stretched his back and adjusted the load. The track was hardly wide enough for a small vehicle, if one had come along, an unlikely event. After years of government neglect, the dirt road into

3

the village was largely impassable. No one who lived here owned even a truck, and only an occasional vehicle belonging to a government agency or to mining engineers came anywhere near the pueblo. Steven had left his 1965 Beetle an hour's hike from the hamlet, as far as he could safely drive along the crumbling road.

Angel and the neighbor walked ahead of him, pretending they didn't know him. They pressed on. The chullo and poncho were stifling in the late morning sun. The wool made his head itch. Sweat ran down his cheeks. His clothing stuck to his back. He stopped to wipe his dripping forehead. A bit of red caught his eye in a bush just off the trail. He rested and watched a vermillion flycatcher, its head and belly brilliant red and its back and wings dull black. The little bird made him think of Lima, though he saw the flycatcher frequently in the campo. Just this morning one had been singing on the school patio. In Lima the bird did a strange thing. It camouflaged itself. At first Steven assumed the chocolate-colored flycatcher he had seen in the city's wide parks was a different bird, until a Peruvian ornithologist told him it was just the vermillion flycatcher engaged in a form of natural selection. The brown bird was a dark morph, a rare variation that occurred naturally in the species. But in Lima, where red birds made such inviting targets for children, who frequently killed them, the darker, less conspicuous form prevailed. On the other side of the bush, a dark gray thrush with a bright yellow beak and yellow legs landed and in a swoop of crimson the smaller bird disappeared into the brush farther back from the road. Steven resumed his slow trek.

After about half an hour he could see the cemetery ahead, looking from this distance like a city itself. Many of the tombs were topped with concrete rectangles, the headstones shaped like little houses with crosses on the roofs. On one side of the cemetery stood a large square structure, looking like an apartment building, with niches where the dead were laid in rows, four graves high and ten graves long, their entries sealed over and the names of their occupants and dates of their deaths etched into concrete.

When they reached the graveyard, Steven loosened the bag ends tied around his chest and rested in the shade beneath the wall of niches. He pulled off the cap, his hair soaked and darkened with sweat. The other two men dropped to their haunches. They peered around the corner.

"Padre, I don't like this," Angel said. "We're too exposed here. Farther up on the hill is a hut for animals. It's nothing but a lean-to and isn't easily seen. They won't know it's there. We can go up through the trees."

"Let's go," the priest huffed. He quickly retied the bundle and the men helped him position it as he rose. They walked with him now, watchful as they moved, helping prop up the bag as the priest grappled up the slope into the trees above the graveyard. The ground in the stand of eucalyptus trees was deep with the decayed remains of long narrow leaves, the air rich with their scent. They hiked deep into the grove. The ground here was open and free of other plants, naturally inhibited by the oily detritus of green and silver fronds. While the lack of undergrowth offered little cover, Steven found the fragrance of eucalyptus oddly comforting. Everything in the Andes smelled of it. Eucalyptus trunks timbered the country's many mines. The rafters of houses were fashioned from it and most meals were cooked over its red embers. The highland people boiled its leaves for medicinal vapor and even the local honey tasted of its flowers. An introduced species native to Australia, the immigrant tree thrived in the semi-arid mountains. Successive governments heavily promoted reforestation with eucalyptus, planting saplings so abundantly that it had become indispensable to the common people.

"It's safe to get rid of that thing," Angel said, slapping the pack on the priest's back. "We need to move more quickly."

They dropped the bag behind a clump of trees and headed through the grove. Beyond the trees the open hillside was furred with tufts of coarse grass that made for uneven walking, though the priest, freed now from his burden, felt as if he were running. They crossed a couple of small ridges, the tops of gullies and defoliated washes that fanned downhill, crouching at the top of each rise to check their trail for signs of pursuit. After about forty minutes they came upon the lean-to of eucalyptus poles, still covered with papery bark peeling in fine strands. The hut, topped with thickly leafed branches, sat in a fold in the hill and was scarcely distinguishable from the surrounding terrain. The three men crouched to enter and huddled together once inside. Steven stripped off the chullo and poncho.

"Padre, I will go now and come back for you when the terrucos are gone," Angel said after a brief rest, using the pejorative for terrorist. "Cesar will stay." He slipped out.

The two men settled into the leaves and dry grass on the shelter floor. Above the earthen bank that half blocked the front of the hut they could see a glimmer of hillside.

Cesar said little. Steven was familiar with the sometimes discomfiting silence of Quechua men. Already taciturn by nature, they could be virtually mute around strangers. Cesar was probably embarrassed by his poor Spanish and kept what he had to say in that alien tongue to a minimum. Steven knew only enough Quechua to mumble a few prayers, a smattering of the liturgy. He remembered visiting a family that wanted him to attend a sick elder. "She is ignorant, Padre," they apologized. They meant no disrespect. It was just that the old woman couldn't speak Spanish, so must be, to their thinking, ignorant. Steven chastised them lightly, protesting that it was he who was ignorant for not knowing their tongue. Her son smiled and told him, "That's fine, Padre. That's fine. Don't worry."

"I'm not worried," the priest replied. "I'm frustrated."

They stood in two different worlds, he and the Quechua, separate islands, and the wide stream between them was Spanish, a language that was neither his nor their native tongue. He managed Spanish pretty well, thanks to his Latin studies in seminary and some intensive Spanish tutoring before he left the States. Quechua, on the other hand, was a mountain more formidable for Steven than the Andes themselves. He could ask them their stories in Spanish, persuade the families he visited most often to talk of the rhythms of their lives and their venerated customs, like paying the earth, their annual blessing of the fields, when they would burn an offering of food to the mother of the world, Pachamama, and spill a drink of corn brew, chicha de jora, in fervent hope of a good crop. But he was never really taken into their deepest confidence. Something was always held back, something they declined to share with him. He was never sure whether they did not think it worthy of him, a priest, a fair-skinned and educated foreigner, a Yankee, or whether it was he they found unworthy. The mother and father of their own mythic truths, their Adam and Eve, their Moses, were children of the bottomless Lake Titicaca. They wandered the fragile crust of this earth with a golden rod the creator had given them to plunge into the ground and where it sank founded a civilization, without edicts of forbidden fruit or tablets replete with commands. Steven wanted to know what life—past, present, future, morality, love, hate, everything—looked like, felt like from here, from their side, their view from the great depths of shadowy antiquity, echoed through a timeless tongue, now obscured beneath a superficial veneer of Spanish language and modern culture.

A gunshot brought him back from his reverie with a sensory rush—the odor of eucalyptus, llama hair, sweat, a brilliant wash of sunlight, all sharper in the sudden silence behind the reverberating crack of gunfire. Another shot rang out.

Cesar shifted onto his haunches. "From the village," he said. Steven nodded. They exchanged a glance, and the priest assumed his own eyes reflected the same apprehension he saw in Cesar's expression.

Three more shots echoed across the hillside, spaced a few seconds apart.

The priest pushed his forehead to his entwined fingers and prayed.

"Don't worry, Padre, they won't come here," Cesar said, his voice tight, his breath short. "I'll go to where I can see down the hill. I'll be right back."

Cesar brushed by him and squeezed out. Steven felt fear well up in his chest, in the tautness of his arms and legs, in the burning in his stomach, fear for himself and for what might be happening in the village.

A few minutes later, Cesar returned and spoke into the lean-to from outside.

"Nothing. I think we should wait for Angel. I'm going off just a little way. I will warn you if anyone comes."

After a moment's hesitation, Steven pulled the poncho and chullo back on and went out to join Cesar. The hut now seemed vulnerable. He found Cesar lying on the ground atop an arroyo that sloped to the land below. He was looking across the open hillside in the direction they had come, toward the eucalyptus stand now out of sight behind the undulating ground. He nodded at the priest, who crouched beside him. Neither spoke. Nothing stirred.

For the next few hours the two men kept watch from this vantage, too nervous to return to the cover of their refuge. They spoke only once, agreeing that if Angel didn't come by nightfall the priest would stay in the lean-to and Cesar would go down to find out what had happened. They waited. As the high sun passed through late afternoon, shadows defined the choppy terrain, accenting the texture of the surrounding hills and the terraces where potatoes and quinoa grew across the valley.

Steven stared in the direction of the village, straining not to linger on what the shots might mean, pushing away the worst possibilities. The shooting could have been nothing more than boyish impulsiveness, the targeting of flycatchers. Or hungry rebels slaughtering a lamb, a pig, or an alpaca, collecting their war tax on a village where cash was an uncommon currency. What he couldn't stop thinking about were the people in the village. He focused on Don Javier, the perennial mayor, chosen time and again by the village. Usually such an honor rotated among the men of a hamlet. Here it inevitably rested on Don Javier, occasionally lighting upon the shoulders of another who showed signs of responsibility and sagacity, only to return like a falcon to the falconer the following term. Against his will, Steven pictured the teacher. He didn't want to think of her, not now, not while he was in hiding and she was still in the village. He hadn't asked Angel about her and now he realized why. How could he run if she was in danger? Perhaps there was no reason she should be. He was the foreigner, and they were singling him out. Panic coiled inside him. The rebels' behavior had been vicious and erratic before, so it well could be now. Wait. Pray. But his prayers felt haunted, his petitions seemed mocked by some obscure peripheral presence, something beastly and demonic that sought to thwart him now when he most needed grace. What stymied his prayers? Was it the logical fear and anxiety of hiding from men who wanted to kill him, or the prosaic—and chronic—doubts that had nagged and unsteadied him for so long? Shamefully long.

What he found emerging from darkness was neither of these, nothing so logical or immanent or tangible. It was folklore, a legend of horror. It was a beast that lurked in the deepest recesses of the Andean highlands. That his subconscious should invoke this monster just now both frightened and annoyed him. The Andeans believed in it without doubt and feared even to mention it. The Quechua word, so rarely spoken aloud, at first escaped him: pistaco. Yet Steven imagined the shadowy fiend in human form thirsting to suck fat from people who knew its ravaging only by the wasting away that followed its secret assaults. He recalled his own irrational terror when he had feared it was stalking him, alone at night in the mountains not far from here. He had embraced the local culture's apotheosis of evil. He continued praying.

The chill of mountain air began to settle in as sunlight retreated higher up the peaks, leaving the men in shadow. From a swath of sun across the top of the hill on their side, a condor lifted off, descending straight across their field of vision. Its great black back and wings glided downslope, parallel with the ground until the earth dropped off into a ravine and the bird soared over open land, the telltale, downy white collar around its neck fluttering ever so faintly ragged in the wind. It disappeared quickly into the gloom of the darkening valley.

Angel returned soon after sunset, still crouching as he climbed in the waning light. Steven could no longer see detail in the murky valley below the backlit peaks rising against the sky, still lit by a sun fallen below the massive ridge of igneous crust in which this valley was but a wrinkle. Angel emerged from the twilight and dropped quickly to their level, showing more caution than appeared necessary.

"The terrucos have left," he said in an expulsion of air as he squatted. His breathing, heavy and slow, marked the seconds as the other two sat waiting for him to continue.

"The guerrillas were furious," he said. "They demanded to know where we were hiding you. They gathered everyone into the plaza."

They told the people they were going to witness a trial, he said. Three beaten captives were forced to sit in the dirt, hands tied behind their backs. All of them kept their bloody faces turned to the ground. The rebels, about a dozen of them, were dressed like villagers. Three were women, two of whom wore wide campesina skirts and long dark braids. The man leading them had railed against the priest, against American imperialism and foreign interference. This, he said, was why the three bound men had been brought to this place.

"They were technicians working on a power project or something," Angel said. "They were foreigners, Padre. The terrucos said those men had no right to be here."

The priest waited.

"We have dead to bury, Padre."

Six Months Earlier

2

Father Steven came up on Villa El Salvador from the old Panamerican Highway on the south end of Lima, through what looked like a mission documentary on Third World poverty. He and his companion had driven through Ciudad de Dios, where Catholic missionaries had worked for thirty years, ever since the sudden spawning of a vast squatter city of shanties on the bleak desert beyond the southern limits of the capital.

Steven rode with Father Michael Roti, an American priest who was showing the newcomer the city neighborhoods and carrying on an unceasing monologue about geography, sociology, politics and ethnicity as he drove. They had started out from Pueblo Libre, where neocolonial architecture met the aging art deco homes of the middle-class. There highland immigrants set up makeshift food carts along the curbs. They grilled and sold skewered and seared chunks of marinated beef heart and chopped and fried fresh tripe, dishes with the sonorous names of anticucho and choncholi. The two priests started down the double-wide Avenida Brazil to Avenida Ejercito, across the top of sea cliffs and into once-elegant Miraflores, where an eclectic architectural patchwork of quaint hacienda rustic met plate-glass commercial, and finally out through Surco, where it all ran into blocks of Bauhaus. That was where Lima had once stopped, Michael said. Beyond that was a wasteland as sere and feature-less as any desert on earth, except it wasn't along any trade route, so it went unnoticed by all but miners and archeologists. Then, overnight, a pueblo joven mushroomed out of the barren sand.

"Pueblo joven is a Peruvian euphemism for shantytown," Father Michael explained on the morning they entered Ciudad de Dios. "In most of Latin America they're called barriadas. In Brazil they're favelas. They're not slums. They're not so grand as slums. They're all on land nobody wants."

"For people nobody wants," Steven said.

"Still, this place represents the best hope of these people. They've dreamt of coming here."

"Incomprehensible."

Ciudad de Dios, the City of God, was one of the original pueblos jovenes, a sprawling mass of makeshift straw mats and canted canvas that rose as if from the desert floor one morning in the 1950s. Now, rebar stuck out of unpainted and rarely stuccoed brick and concrete houses and storefronts, one- or two- or three-storied, grimed with dirt, dust, and exhaust, with laundry lines strung on the rods and draped with perpetually damp and forlorn apparel in the muted colors of the land. They passed a pile of garbage where two scrawny dogs, one tawny with matted fur and the other pointed like a Doberman, rooted for scraps. Just up the curb, two little girls in frayed, once-white dresses squatted and played in the sand before a house of coarsely laid brick and iron-barred windows.

"They don't see this place as all that depressing the way you do," Michael said. "For them this is the dream, a chance for a little piece of land of their own that they can build a house on, away from the slums downtown. Think about three or four families, each with a passel of children, living in three or four rooms in a building that went up before there was indoor plumbing. Then you can see why they come here. This is their land of opportunity. You're looking at the end of the rainbow."

Pueblo joven. Young town. A city smothered in grayness that enshrouded sky and ground and people, the disarray of concrete

16

buildings alongside the ubiquitous dry grass matting, dull and dusky, where even the clothing people wore was washed in water that only served to distribute the dirt more evenly among the garments. Only something new could look white here—and not for very long. The two priests drove on in silence.

Nothing could have prepared Steven for the view that stretched out before them when the car crested the grade above Villa El Salvador, the Village of Our Savior. Steven found himself staring at the blunt edge of civilization as he knew it. Just which edge—a beginning or an ending—he wasn't sure. Hovels crammed together across the parched sand as far as he could see, a jumbled assortment in varying hues of gray and dun and dusty beige, an infant town with nothing small about it, a teeming encampment of internal refugees.

"It's like a swarm or a hive of something," he said.

"A good analogy," Michael said. "At first glance, a hive may look like a bunch of bees swarming around in confusion, but an apiary is very organized. Honey bees cooperate with one another. There's division of labor. This looks random, but most everything in Villa El Salvador is intentional. The idea was to create a self-governing urban community based on Inca concepts of cooperation and extended family. This is a thriving social experiment in community organization."

Farther on they turned into Villa El Salvador along an artery of asphalt from which shot capillaries of sand. Up close the dwellings appeared to be at best concrete and brick with corrugated metal for roofs. At worst they were five straw mats making four walls and a ceiling, like a house of cards, stacked upon a packed sand floor. Here, out of this exodus of a quarter-million people in houses built on sand, they found Zoila, the young woman they had come to visit, on the fringe of the vast sand plateau whose height was revealed only in the broken escarpment plunging more than five hundred feet to the sea below.

Like scuttling crabs the priests sidled down the hill, keeping one foot lower than the other, the only way to prevent pitching headfirst into a somersault. They hopped down to a hut, the sand seeping into their shoes as it poured to rest at a warped hardboard wall that was the back of a house. They walked around to the front of the hut where Zoila sat on the threshold. Her two children played on a ledge that extended a few feet from the house, a precarious perch from which sand tumbled to the next shack below.

Down, down, down the bank sand crept to ever lower grades, each defined by another row of sticks, canvas, straw mats, plastic sheets, hardboard, plywood, bamboo caning, corrugated tin, and hammered-out oil cans, until finally it reached the tarmac of the Panamericana. Beyond lay the sea, foaming at the shore, then slate gray and unperturbed until it disappeared into mist.

Zoila smiled at Father Michael and stood up to shake his hand. The younger child, a girl about two, scurried to her mother, while the little boy, a couple of years older, looked up from where he plowed a plastic truck along the yard-wide shelf that was his playground. The mother was a slight woman, about five feet tall, with straight hair lightened almost to the color of the sand that surrounded her. She wore a pink sweatshirt, with a cartoon decal too battered and peeled for the character to be distinguishable, and yellow shorts that, above her bare legs and feet, looked threadbare, nearly sheer.

"Hola, Padre Miguel."

"Hola, Zoila. How are you?"

"Fine, Padre. And you?"

"Very good. Very good." He glanced at the children. "These two look like they're having fun."

Zoila shrugged. "We have no water," she said, waving a hand toward an orange plastic barrel on the other side of her house. "So we are waiting for the truck."

18

"Ah. When does it come?"

"Who knows? It comes when it comes. I have not seen it in a couple of days. You have to keep watching."

"Of course. Of course. Zoila, I'd like to introduce you to Padre Esteban," Michael said, converting Steven's name to Spanish.

"Hola, Padre."

"Padre Esteban is just down from the United States and I'm showing him where I work and presenting him to the wonderful people in Villa El Salvador."

"Gracias, Padre," Zoila said. "When I meet some wonderful people, I will tell them you are looking for them."

Michael laughed. "In the meantime, you'll be nice to my compatriot. Maybe we can convince him to stay and help me with the work here."

"You should," she said to Steven, who felt admonished.

"I don't know," he said, immediately realizing he sounded standoffish. He tried again. "I'm looking at a few different sites for my mission here in Peru." He looked out to sea. "Maybe one with a nice ocean view."

He turned back to Zoila and laughed.

"In the summer it's very nice here because the kids and I can just walk down to that little beach. But in winter it is very damp and foggy. You can't ever really get warm and the kids are sick a lot."

His joke had backfired.

She stepped off the hard-packed platform and her tan toes sank beneath the sand.

"Here we walk and walk and then we slip and go backwards. My husband has to keep carrying the sand that piles up behind the house around here to the front so everything we own doesn't slide down to the road."

"Zoila and her husband moved out here about a year ago from downtown, where they had a room in his father's apartment," Michael explained to Steven in English. "It's a typical situation of multiple families and multiple generations all packed together."

"Does he want to look around?" Zoila asked Michael.

"If you don't mind," Steven replied.

She marched straight along the hillside a few steps without coming back up to the packed earth, lifting her feet high each time, reminding Steven of someone walking in deep snow. She pointed and said, "Our bathroom." A yellow shower curtain hung in a circle on the sand a little away from the house.

"It's usually just a pit, dug into the dune," the other priest said.

While Michael stayed with the children outside, Zoila took Steven inside the house.

The door was fashioned from two overlapping panels of woven straw nailed to posts driven into the sand to form the front of the building. Her kitchen was directly inside the door to the left and was roofed with blue plastic. Light seeped in between the wefts in the straw and filtered through the translucent ceiling. Greasy dirt formed the floor. A single kerosene burner on a wooden table served as a stove, and three wooden folding chairs ringed the table.

A proper wooden door led to the bedroom. After the brightness of the kitchen, Steven could just make out the plywood and hardboard walls and ceiling that let little light or air into the windowless room. Mote-filled beams of light leaked in through faults in the seams at the corners of the room. Zoila clicked on a lamp. Steven's eyes widened at the improbability.

"Electricity?"

"Sí, Padre. We strung a cord over the top of the dune from another house that has power. It's only enough for the lamp and TV, but it's something."

"That it is."

The room was furnished with a double bed with a wooden headboard and footboard, a long three-drawer dresser, and a wooden stand supporting a small television. The center of the floor was covered with a large piece of dingy yellow shag carpet. The walls were unpainted and bare of any adornments.

Zoila sat on the bed, while Steven, seeing no other place to sit, remained standing. Her feet played with the end of the carpet, the nap brushing the dust from her nails but not the grains from between her toes. She bounced her feet up and down and rested her palms at her sides on the grayed bedspread and stared at the rug.

"This is good, something on the floor," he said.

"It's so the kids aren't playing on the ground, which holds a lot of dampness."

She planted her feet flat, her heels on dirt and her toes on carpet, but couldn't keep still for long and began wiggling digits up and down, showing their dark undersides. Dust a shade lighter than her skin coated her shins and calves, making the fine hairs seem thicker than they probably were. Her knees were rough and discolored, like a child's in summer. The length of her thighs betrayed the woman her simple apparel seemed to deny. Her tan legs became lighter high up and pale where the shorts rode up as she sat.

She spoke and Steven started, fearing his intimate observation of her in this stuffy bedroom could be read in his expression and hoping the dim light covered it.

"That's about it. Just one more room for my brother, who is sleeping because he works nights."

"Oh. Yes. Well, thank you."

She looked at him for what seemed like a long time, sitting there on the edge of her bed, as if waiting for him to say more, or perhaps to do something. He looked past her, trying to keep his eyes from the soft-looking legs and her young and daring face.

Steven's scalp prickled. She stood up. They turned and walked out to join Michael.

The priests drove back along the coast road, swinging first toward Lurin and passing the adobe ruins of Pachacamac, Peru's most sacred pre-Columbian site on the Pacific coast, a pyramidal mound so wind-worn and sun-bleached it could barely be distinguished from the hills behind it. The gold-lusting Spaniards under the Pizarros, Michael explained, were sorely disappointed to find nothing more than a wooden effigy of the god worshipped there.

When the sea was on their left, Michael pointed to the shacks on the long slope of sand. Steven could just make out Zoila sitting as she had been, waiting for water as the day grew toward noon and the sun began to burn off the morning haze. A twinge of desire embarrassed him again and he kept his face turned toward the window.

"These houses, if you want to call them that, near the road here where the land flattens, are a problem," Michael said. "Up there where Zoila and her family are is desert. This is real estate."

"Somebody wants it?"

"Someone could put a shop or a restaurant or a gas station along the highway."

"So?"

"So it's already owned and these folks trespassed and have battled with police trying to dislodge them. Sometimes people get killed in these land invasions. They stone the police until the cops open fire."

"But not up there or on the higher flats?"

"No. Believe it or not, when this invasion started they negotiated terms with the military in power then, a bunch of leftists who nationalized companies and instituted massive agrarian reform. The generals supported the poor and Villa El Salvador had their blessing."

"So the pendulum swings and this place isn't in such favor under a democracy?"

"Yeah," Michael said. "This place smacks too much of socialism or communism. The leftist military wrecked the economy. The powers that be are naturally suspicious of people coming down out of the mountains. And they are streaming out of the hills to be here, where they feel safer. Safety in numbers."

"In masses and masses, I'd say."

"There's so much need here, Steven. You wouldn't lack for things to do. I know you've said you might like to work in the countryside, but here the mountain has come to Mohammed."

"Right. To get away from political violence."

"A nice plan, huh? Unfortunately, the violence has followed them. You'll see."

3

Back at the mission house in San Isidro, a part of Lima known mostly for its banks, grand hotels, fine restaurants, and walled, stately houses, Steven sank into a worn chair in front of an unlit fireplace and looked through the local newspapers.

He had been in Lima less than a week, arriving the day after Christmas, at first thankful to be in short sleeves, escaping the snow of New England, and thinking he might like this city—an ecclesiastical haven from the colonial era, replete with abbeys, and monasteries, and convents, and churches, lots of churches. His first awakening had been the drive from the airport at midnight when the smell of garbage along the riverbank foretold the squalor he would witness a day later, when he went back to Jorge Chavez International to pick up some delayed luggage, which by then had been rifled through and his binoculars and some shirts stolen. Steven's rapid orientation to Lima also included being flea bitten from ankle to groin on a bus that spewed black smoke while the fare collector hung out the open door yelling destinations, half carnival barker, half extortionist. Another day, as he walked toward the Plaza de Armas to see the cathedral and presidential palace, his arm was jerked from behind him and he found himself eye to eye with a man whose left arm trailed back, caught by one finger under the unyielding strap of Steven's watch. In the foiled thief's other arm a little girl slumbered.

It was all new and exciting, if occasionally upsetting, and Steven was sure he would get used to the chaos that pervaded his strange new world. What did disturb him was the constant threat of violence. The legend was that Lima was no more dangerous than New York. That's what Steven was told before coming here. Okay, he could deal with that. Terrorism was confined, people said, and not really a major problem, no more than the Basque separatists were to Spain. One took a calculated risk. Steven would exchange a safe life lived in the insurance capital of America for an exotic port of call, alien, colorful, exhilarating, if maybe a little dangerous.

Here the violence was splattered in vivid color on newspaper pages. A vendor in a market stall lay sprawled over burlap sacks of potatoes, his mouth agape in a death grimace, his chest a blossom of blood. The director of a school was gunned down outside a classroom by young assailants who called her name before firing so she could see the faces of her assassins. They tossed a stick of dynamite, fuse sparkling, onto her dying body, the Shining Path coup de grâce, and blew her to pieces. These were too-familiar stories. Political assassinations. Car bombings. When he went outside, Steven found himself sidestepping soldiers guarding bridges and trying not to stare at them on buses, where they stood in front with arms wrapped over their Kalashnikovs.

He had read of the Shining Path before coming to Peru, this guerrilla group led by Abimael Guzmán, a fanatical and mysterious philosophy professor preaching Chinese-style communism to peasants in the Andes Mountains. Yet everything about coming here had happened so quickly that he hadn't really focused on it. The threat seemed remote, not something likely to break out where he would be working. The missionary priest who had encouraged him to come had never dealt with the rebels himself and had downplayed their significance. He had painted them as a small band of idealists with little popular support, mucking around ineptly in remote villages, trying to rally campesinos in a country that had already had one leftist revolution, a military junta that had broken up its feudal haciendas in the early 1970s. That the Shining Path remained isolated and ineffectual was also the official government line. So why were the guerrillas active now in Lima?

Steven closed the paper in dismay. He tried to read newspapers to help his Spanish, but had all he could take of gore today. He gave up and began sorting through a pile of books about Peru on the coffee table, photo editions highlighting the country's natural wonders and its cultural and historical heritage. One had wide color photos of archeological sites, the Nazca Lines, Machu Picchu, Cuzco, many others he had never heard of, places where the human spirit had resonated for millennia— a vast adobe city in the north destroyed by conquering Incas, a subterranean palace in the high peaks region associated with puma heads carved out of stone, and mushroom-shaped chullpas where the rich and powerful were entombed as much as a thousand years before Columbus set sail. A book of artifacts showed an array of tumis, ceremonial knives with their distinctive half-moon cutting edges that varied from crudely fashioned copper blades with a bluish-green patina to ornately jeweled human figures of honed gold. He had heard that Peruvians hung replicas of tumis in their homes for good luck, but it seemed to Steven that could not belie the blades' bloody origin as instruments of human sacrifice. Another book showed the jungle, with shots of red and blue macaws and yellow tree frogs, tiny buff-colored monkeys with dark heads, and jaguars with black, crude circles on their yellow coats. What attracted him most, though, was a book of black-and-white photos, dating from the 1920s and 1930s, of highland peasants and Indians.

In a way these pictures reminded Steven of Old West photos: indigenous faces, stoic, imperturbable, holding onto dignity, an expression he hadn't seen in the countenances over the pushcarts or in Ciudad de Dios or Villa El Salvador. In one, a family of three campesinos posed in traditional dress. The man, identified as the mayor of Tinta, Cuzco, wore a heavily embroidered poncho and carried a chest-high staff, wider at top than at bottom. His wife wore a dark, broad skirt and a shawl over her head, beneath a square-fringed hat. The boy mirrored his father, right down to the staff. The mayor stood erect, feet apart, hands clasping the stick, his mouth as straight as the chord of a circle. Yet something in his expression bespoke good humor and contentment. The son's expression was the same. But in the wife's face Steven detected something amiss, anxiety, apprehension. A foreboding.

He was brought to a halt by another photo of a couple dozen people, many including women holding dark beers, one man strumming a guitar, at a family fiesta in Cuzco, circa 1930. With the variety of faces and skin hues, it was obviously a mestizo clan, with two dark-skinned women in a lower corner holding babies. These he guessed to be nannies.

Steven flipped through this book of photos by a man named Martín Chambi with more than curiosity. Might not this way of life still thrive there in the mountains, where roads were scarce, unpaved and as often as not running across the tops of cliffs? Might not these Indians and these not-so-sophisticated mestizos be much like this today in the pueblos beyond the few cramped cities?

He turned to a photo of a man sitting on a hillside playing a cane flute, a llama tethered behind him, the musician and pack animal in stark contrast to the densely clouded sky and snow-capped mountains. It evoked in Steven a sense of the mystical. Here was something beyond. So did another photo of hundreds of campesinos in striped ponchos and pointed wool caps with disheveled earflaps, looking like pilgrims wandering the open

27

highlands beneath a mountain of snowfields.

These were the places he had imagined when he had embarked on this mission, when he fled his very personal temptation in a comfortable parish near Hartford. He had envisioned himself as an heroic figure, a rock, a comfort, a light in a dark world, serving the peons, beloved, venerated, a cassocked friar in the style of the old Spanish missionaries, a Junípero Serra. He fantasized at times of crossing remote mountain passes on horseback, bringing the Holy Eucharist and the great Good News of a better world to the spiritually undernourished. Then, somewhere between that vision of the mission and the frank reality of it, his dream faltered. He began to dismiss the picture of Peru he had painted as outdated and unrealistic. His new reality was to be a world of mass migrations, of unspeakable suffering, of poverty, of a Third World metropolis burgeoning with the unwanted.

So he had come to Peru resigned to working in Lima, where he had been told there was so much to do. What exactly he would do remained as much a mystery to Steven as to the men who sent him. He would be allowed some time to consider what he wanted to accomplish here. It seemed natural, and was probably presumed, that he would patch a hole in a poor parish and do here what he had done so well for a time in Hartford. He would offer quiet service to God in a poor parish in the heart of Lima. That was another reason he hadn't worried much about the Shining Path. It had been his understanding that they were far from the city, deep in the mountains, removed from where he expected to find himself. Today's trip, and today's newspapers, gave him second thoughts about his decision to come to Peru. Seeing the shantytowns had been traumatic. He found the desert overwhelming. If the violence was here as well, it changed his entire perspective. If staying in the city couldn't insulate him from this rebellion, he didn't have to limit his choices either. Events were running him out of safe choices.

On New Year's Eve, a couple of days later, Steven was invited to a dinner in a pueblo joven by Sister Maggie Kalinski, a Dominican sister who had spent forty years in Peru. His new colleague Father Michael, who had introduced them, testified that Sister Maggie knew Lima and the Peruvian people better than any missionary in the country.

"We're going to a pachamanca," she told Steven after flagging down a taxi and negotiating the fare. To Steven, Maggie looked Peruvian, with her long gray hair in a single braid down her back and a hand-woven bag in red and black over her shoulder—the only bright color accenting her white blouse and brown skirt. Although she was old enough to retire, she spent long hours running a women's center downtown.

"The invitation comes from one of the señoras I work with from Cono Norte," she said, settling into the cab. "You know it?"

"The northern pueblos jovenes. I've heard about them. But not paca…"

"Pachamanca. The food is cooked in the ground. You'll see. It's sort of like a barbecue pit, only it's covered up and bakes."

"Sounds good to me. Should we be bringing something?"

"Oh, no," she said. "This kind of dinner invitation in Cono Norte is not free. We're paying to go. The host puts it on and then charges people to come. Everyone has a good time and the host makes some money."

"How much is it?"

"You're my guest, so for you nothing. It works out to less than five bucks a person, no small change for Peruvians."

They rode out through the same kind of sprawl Steven had seen earlier. She called the straw-mat and scrap-lumber shelters they passed "chozas."

"Not quite so elegant as a shanty," she said.

The pueblo joven was off a long stretch of road with buildings packed together with scant attention to compatible use, factories next to convenience stores next to shops of inexpensive furniture next to gas stations next to restaurants next to fireworks studios with thin bamboo towers atop. They looked to Steven like they were made of Tinker Toys, and appeared about as sturdy.

"The towers there," Maggie said, "are advertising. They set Catherine wheels spinning and fire bottle rockets over the neighborhoods. Not as grand as what you see in the States."

"They seem to be blowing up a lot of things here these days. I don't know if I will ever get used to that."

Here and there, dummies slumped on chairs in front of shops or houses, their heads fashioned from cotton rags or burlap bags. Some were topped with a battered cap or hat.

"They represent the old year," Maggie said. "At midnight they burn them as a way of saying goodbye to the old and welcoming in the new."

The area they drove into turned hilly and Steven began to see switchback streets scaling the mountainsides. They turned into a mass of houses that crept like ivy up the steep slope. Following the vine out to one tip, they came to the last house on the lane. Anything beyond was too rugged to build upon. Where the sand stopped against the rock face so did the shacks. Most of these homes were far more solid than the dune dwellings he had seen in Villa El Salvador. They had evolved beyond the squatter stage and were in expansion mode, with some brick and mortar already piled to two stories, a few to three, with power connections running to every house. These people were here to stay.

The taxi left them in front of an as-yet one-story house where a group of men stood around a mound of sand. One man was pouring beer into a small glass held by another. The pourer smiled when he saw Sister Maggie. Handing off the bottle, he came over.

"Madre, it is an honor to have you at our house."

"Well thank you for including me. I've brought a friend and we brought big appetites."

"Very good. Very good. You will not be disappointed."

The man and Sister Maggie exchanged light hugs and kisses on the cheeks before the man ran to the door and called to someone. A few seconds later, a woman came out wiping her hands down a brown apron covering a black skirt. A similar greeting was exchanged between the women before Maggie presented Steven to the couple.

"Carlos, Juanita, this is my friend Father Steven, from the United States. This is his first pachamanca."

They greeted him with firm handshakes and much smiling.

"Watch what they're doing with the fire pit," Maggie said to Steven. She and Juanita entered the house, leaving him to fend for himself.

Steven and Carlos joined three men in the yard. After introductions someone passed the beer and glass to the host. Carlos turned the glass upside down and gave it a couple hard shakes. He filled it three-quarters full with beer and handed it to Steven.

"Salud, Padre!"

"Ah, got it. Thank you. Salud!" Steven raised the glass to his lips.

"Nah, nah, nah, Padre! Don't forget Pachamama," Carlos said.

"Pachamama?"

"Sí, sí. Like this." Carlos tipped the end of the bottle a little, letting a bit of beer splash to the ground. "Now you."

Steven tilted the glass and lost a third of his beer. The men laughed.

"Not so much," admonished one of them. "You'll get her drunk." They laughed again.

"You always remember Pachamama when you start to drink," the man said. "You wouldn't want to offend her. But she only needs a tiny bit."

"Don't give her a hangover. Just a taste," one man offered.

"Sorry."

Steven raised the glass to Carlos and the others and downed a heavy sip. He surveyed the pit ringed by the men. In it was a beehive mound of rocks with an opening on one side, a well-stoked wood fire burning in it.

"So this is the Pachamama?" Steven pointed with his toe, almost touching a stone. The men burst into laughter. The one who first chided him doubled over with mirth.

"No, no, Padre." Carlos put his hand on Steven's arm, as if needing the priest's support to control his snickering. "This is the pachamanca, not Pachamama, manca, ca, ca, ca, not mama." He broke into another peal of laughter. "Pachamanca is this preparation of food. Pachamama is Mother Earth."

Steven hung his head in exaggerated chagrin. Carlos patted him on the back.

"That is all right, Padre. You are new here. But we never forget to make our offering to the sacred earth, Pachamama, so she blesses us."

"I understand." He didn't really, not completely, though perhaps enough. The priest in him had to wonder if this Pachamama stuff merely personified Mother Earth or deified her. And if it was the latter, where did this earth goddess fit into their Christian pantheon? Did she outrank God the Father? Jesus? The Blessed Virgin?

"Is Pachamama more important than God?" he asked Carlos.

The man stepped back as if offended, legs astride, arms open wide, the brown beer bottle in his right hand, his belly in a white T-shirt hanging over his belt.

"Padre! Of course not! God is all powerful. But to each due respect. Salud." He raised the bottle, but didn't drink from it.

"Just making sure," Steven said before he sipped some more beer. He was glad Carlos hadn't taken his question as a rebuke. He didn't want to stumble into the role of a theological heavy disturbing working men just trying to enjoy a few drinks at a

32

party. He hadn't done his homework. Now wasn't the time to crib.

Steven nursed a little more beer.

"Drink up!" encouraged the one who had ribbed him. "We're waiting for the glass."

Steven drained the beer in a gulp and handed it across to the jokester.

"You shake it first, then pass it to your left," the man instructed. "Then you pour and after that hand the bottle to the drinker. He'll do the same when he's done."

"I understand," he said, and he did this time. Yet, as he followed the glass, he couldn't help but wonder how much saliva he would drink by the end of the night. Perhaps the alcohol killed the germs.

Day was just starting to wane when the wood had burned to embers. The men broke down the glowing dome with sticks and formed a radiating bed of stones. Juanita and a couple of other women hurried out with pans and bowls and everyone except Steven began placing meat and chicken directly onto sizzling rocks, then piled on potatoes, sweet potatoes, corn, lumpy pods of fava beans, and some sprigs and leaves of herbs. The women covered it all with layers of banana leaves, and over them spread heavy wool blankets while the men stood by with shovels. When the women were done, the men shoveled sand on top of the pile until all traces of smoke were gone. The women went back inside, while the men kept vigil around the hermetic mound. Carlos opened another beer.

As the glass made its rounds, Steven did his best to join the conversation and found the beer made both speaking and listening easier. He understood their stories without trying too hard, and as the beer rose in him he was even catching their jokes. At one point he noticed someone had joined the group with another bottle and a fresh glass, doubling the frequency of passes.

In the mellow mood that settled over him, Steven found himself in quiet awe. Here he was, only a week from the white clapboards of prim Connecticut, on a craggy desert hillside, a place so parched it looked like moonscape. He had gone to shantytowns where life was lived on biblical terms, waiting for water in houses of straw built on foundations of sand. Just the sight of these places would have given nightmares to most Americans, including a fair number of his brother clergy back in the States, and he couldn't in honesty dismiss his own shock, his own repulsion, his own depression in the face of the unremitting misery of it all. Yet here, sharing a glass of beer—that he half believed was being miraculously replenished—he was astoundingly at ease. Carlos and his guests were treating him with the utmost respect, including him as a new friend. Granted, he basked in the reflected light of their endearment for Maggie, and without her introduction he wouldn't be standing here at all. And he was pretty sure that had he been in his Roman collar they would have taken the beer elsewhere. He marveled at the hereness and the nowness of this singular moment, in this unique and alien place.

The glass came around again, and was at last deposited with him for safekeeping while the men attacked the underground oven. They scraped away the sand, and steam broke through like ash from the throat of an erupting volcano. They pulled the blankets back carefully in a cloud of smoke and vapor, and the remaining sand slipped cleanly away from the food. Both men and women quickly gathered the hot meats and vegetables into pans and baskets and onto plates as the last of the day's light slipped away.

Steven found a seat in the house. With its concrete walls and floor and spare furnishings it reminded him more of a Hartford basement than a living room. He sat on a wooden chair against a wall and savored a meal that alone was worth the journey to Peru—meat spiced with herbs he didn't know, with lyrical sounding names, marmakilla and paico, and the earthy flavor of vegetables roasted on stones, all fragrant from the smoke of the smoldering fire.

After a while guests who had finished eating got up and began dancing to music from a boom box. While dancing soon seemed almost obligatory, Steven managed to beg off enough that the señoras left him alone. He had way too little experience at parties and he certainly wasn't going to make a fool of himself plunging into salsa and the other Latin rhythms that he could neither name nor distinguish from one another. He avoided going outside, where he had astutely left the glass and where he was sure to be ensnared in another drinking circle. A beer and glass made an occasional circuit inside too, but far less frequently, and nobody cajoled him to "drain it!"

Maggie wound through the crowd, apparently looking for him, greeting other guests along the way.

"You're a stick in the mud," she said.

"You aren't dancing, Mother Maggie," he said.

"I am seventy years old and would pay dearly tomorrow if I tried. I used to dance till dawn. I even did some of the folk dances in the mountains, spinning around in my own pollera and everything. Probably what aggravated my hips and knees in the first place."

"I'm impressed."

"Yeah, well, after Vatican II, the first thing I did was get out of that habit."

Maggie pulled no punches.

"I'm trying to shake a few bad habits myself," he said.

Maggie laughed.

"You worked up there, in the highlands?" he asked. "I mean, in a village?"

"I did for twenty-five years. I still miss it. But as I got older, it got harder to take the altitude. That happens. Some people can

35

never work up there. Some of these places, like Puno, are over 12,000 feet above sea level. No town or city in the States even comes near such an elevation. If you're not born to it, there's no guarantee your body will let you stay there."

Steven hadn't considered that one might never adapt at all.

"It was wonderful," Maggie said. "From the bleakest outpost in the highest reaches of the mountains where you can't imagine what in the name of Our Dear Savior they live on, down to these lush valleys that are little paradises—or were before all the violence started."

"It's here too."

"It's worse all over."

"Part of me is so tempted. The countryside was more the mission I had in mind, but everyone wants me to work in Lima. They're desperate here."

"They're desperate everywhere. Listen, if you've got an option to work outside of Lima and want to, put your foot down. At least get out and see the countryside first. See some of the work there. See if you like it. More importantly, see if you have the guts for it. You can't really know until you try. Lima isn't going anywhere."

"That's true."

"Besides, anyone who has worked in the sierra will understand these people better. Most of them are first- and at most second-generation transplants from the Andes anyway."

Juanita, their hostess, came over and locked elbows with Sister Maggie.

"Padre, have some more to eat. You did like it, no?"

"Very much! But I am so full."

"There's plenty."

"Thank you. Maybe later. Peruvian food is delicious."

"Better eat up now if you like it. You won't find this so easily in Lima."

"No?"

"This we eat in the sierra, in Huancayo where me and Carlos come from. Limeños eat too much fish. Pachamanca is food of the mountains."

Sometime after eleven o'clock Juanita set a plate of grapes near Steven.

"Is everything good?"

"Muy bueno," he said, without reservation.

Beside him a señora, who was about Sister Maggie's age but with only a few strands of gray on her head, told him of her devotion to El Señor de los Milagros. Steven had heard of the Lord of Miracles, but the festival honoring that particular image of Jesus wasn't until October and he had missed the procession that he was told clogged the streets of downtown as nothing else could.

"I always wear the habit, the purple habit and white cord, the whole month of October, in devotion to El Señor," she said. Leaning closer, she whispered, "Padre, in October I go to Mass twice a day."

"I'm sure Our Lord is happy with you." He wanted to tell her not to be too hard on herself, that he was sure she was a good Catholic and that he had no doubt God heard her prayers, but she rambled on, oblivious to his attempts to reply.

"But I take communion only once a day, Padre," she assured him, and he had to smile and pat her hand. She took his hand and raised it to her lips and kissed the back of it. He hoped no one had seen. Then he noticed the moist rim around her eyes.

"You are very good to come here to us, Padre. In Peru, we suffer, but the Lord sends us good people like you and Madre Maggie."

He looked her full in the face. "So we can be with good people like you."

There was that after all. Whether he worked in the sierra or Lima, he would find people like this, with this fierce and honest religiosity. They might seem overly pious at times, yet this unflinching faith was part of what had made him want to come to Latin America in the first place. Here he would so easily find fraternity with the men around the pachamanca, embrace with them the traditions so accessible, so much a part of their being, like honoring Pachamama. He didn't need to traipse off to some remote and forbidding terrain. What he sought was right in front of him already. Maybe the mountains *were* coming to him. Perhaps as a migrant himself he should meet these migrants half way, as pilgrim meeting pilgrim.

The lights blinked and then went out. Murmurs and exclamations echoed in the sudden pitch darkness.

"Ayiii, a blackout!"

"Apagón! Aw, no! No lights!"

A match was struck across the room. Another lit elsewhere.

"I will look for candles," the señora said to Steven before wandering off into darkness.

"Those damned terrorists!" someone said.

"What have they blown up now?"

Guttering candles struggled to compensate for the vulnerabilities of ElectroPeru. The music resumed, toned down by the limits of batteries. A teenage couple who had held their place on the floor pulled out of an opportune embrace and resumed their dancing. Maggie appeared out of nowhere and sat in the vacated chair beside Steven.

"Maybe a good time to head out," she said.

"If you are ready."

"I was going to stay until after midnight, but my feet are killing me and we have to walk back down to the main road to find a taxi. Might be harder now that they've knocked out the power."

"Well, that certainly hasn't stopped the fiesta."

"These folks will be up all night, so if you'd rather stay, don't let me drag you away. No self-respecting Peruvian goes to bed

38

before dawn on Año Nuevo."

"I'm not much of a partier."

"You're a man of God. They'll let you slide."

When Steven and Maggie had at last said their good nights, Juanita instructed Carlos to walk their American friends down to the road. A couple of teenage boys said they would go too. Before they left, Juanita pressed a bag of grapes into Maggie's hands. "It's almost midnight."

"What's that about?" Steven asked as they began walking.

"Tradition," she said. "You have to eat twelve grapes at midnight on New Year's Eve for good luck in the year to come."

"One for each month, I guess."

"Something like that. Did you wear yellow underwear?"

"What?"

"You think I'm a sassy old nun, don't you?"

"Well…"

"It's another New Year tradition for good luck. Don't ask me where it comes from, but right after Christmas the vendors start selling yellow undershorts. Most of these people out tonight are probably wearing them. Don't tempt fate."

"Are you?"

"Father McMahon, are you really asking an old lady the color of her undies?" she said. "But I am expecting a spectacular year to come."

Midnight came with a sudden explosion of fireworks as they reached the road, where a cluster of people waited for buses and taxis. Everyone started hugging and patting each other's backs, many kissing on cheeks, young couples on the mouth, and all with "Feliz Año Nuevo. Feliz Año." Maggie handed out grapes to Steven, Carlos, and the boys. One of the teenagers flagged down a taxi, and they repeated farewells before the two Americans got into the cab.

"Feliz Año," Maggie said to the driver, who turned and repeated it to her and then to Steven. She offered him the last of the grapes. He thanked her repeatedly.

Firecrackers sputtered at the curbs and bottle rockets zipped in arcs over rooftops as they drove. Steven looked out the side window, away from the headlights, toward the hills.

Hundreds of beacons from burning dummies flickered in front of houses and hovels, like watchtowers flaring in the night. High up the mountainsides they were but faint twinkles, shrinking embers of the past, burning to ash to make room for the future, an annual rite of renewal, an assertion of hope that things had to be better this year, especially if the past one could be incinerated. Lingering troubles and misfortunes were dispatched in fires that lit up walls and doorways. By the road, the flames cast elongated shadows of celebrants toasting to a better year ahead and the passing of the old in human figures bound to chairs, their torsos and heads ablaze in breeze-fanned pyres.

"This is incredible," Steven said softly.

"It is," Maggie answered. "But if you want to witness what is truly incredible, go to the campo. You'll see what I mean."

4

Cori brushed her dark hair back with her fingers and lifted her face so she could inhale deeply, trying to draw enough air to get a good breath in the high altitude. All the way up on the bus from the town of Pisco she had felt progressively worse and now she worried about fainting from lightheadedness. She wondered how she would endure the three or four hours more it would take them to cross this dry highland they called the puna, well over 12,000 feet above sea level, to get to the city of Ayacucho, never mind where she would find the resolve to press on to the village of Urpimarca.

She had begged them to send her to the village. Anywhere, she had said. She would take any assignment teaching anywhere, coast, highland, or jungle. The official at the Education Ministry in Lima had said Cori's physical limitations made her unfit to teach. She would go where she was most needed, she argued. Teachers were always needed in the countryside. Too long on your feet, the administrator had said, and the posts were too isolated, hours of walking, far from passable dirt roads. Only after she had repeatedly pleaded and touted her strong academic record had a position been offered, a consolation job, a throwaway in a hamlet no longer deemed worth the cost of a teacher. She knew that by his tone.

It's dangerous, he told her. Nobody wants to teach there anymore, he had said. The village wasn't all that far from Ayacucho, but was small and isolated. The biggest problem might be the army, not the rebels. The military suspected that local teachers were guerrilla sympathizers. Cori hoped that as an outsider she might not face that problem.

What she hadn't expected was to be sick. Now she feared soroche, altitude sickness. She had never been so high up in the mountains before. What if she couldn't adjust to living in the highlands? What if her disability went beyond her fused femur and pelvis to a general weakness of constitution that had never been tested living so close to the sea in Lima? Maybe her excuses for not exercising, as difficult as it was with one immobile hip, were catching up with her and she lacked the physical strength to live in a place where the weak didn't normally live past infancy. What a place the mountains were, where she'd heard that children weren't counted as people until they survived to age five, when they could be put to use keeping track of sheep.

Near the window next to her dozed a woman with two long black braids trailing from beneath a bowler hat. Her polleras, the skirts Andean women wore in three or four layers of varying colors, fanned onto Cori's side of the bench. The bulk made the woman look heavier than one would expect from her face. On the campesina's lap sat a girl about six or seven, who wore a simpler version of her mother's dress, with the same style braids and a similar light brown derby with a wide band. On top of the hat, someone had stuck a wad of gum, probably some nasty boy— just the kind Cori was looking forward to having as her student. She tapped the child's arm and pointed to the gum.

"There's gum on your hat."

The girl grinned and nodded. She reached up to exactly where the gum was, plucked it off and popped it into her mouth.

Cori laughed at her own ignorance.

Behind her, voices grew insistent and louder than normal for a bus journey, especially with the altitude sucking energy out of

42

everyone. She turned. Three seats back and across the aisle sat a sandy-haired young man with light skin. An older man sitting beside him pushed a hat onto the young man's head. A woman behind them leaned over the back of his seat.

"You need to look Peruvian," she said.

"Okay. Sorry," the young man said in an unmistakably gringo accent.

"Listen," the old man said, "if the Senderistas stop this bus, they'll kill you." Around them passengers agreed. Most riders now seemed to be following the little drama.

"Foreigners should fly," muttered the woman next to Cori. "They've plenty of money."

Cori wondered how much the gringo understood. Very little probably. He seemed amused. Or was it veiled fear? She looked at him more closely, and he met her gaze. His eyes were a golden brown, sort of hazel, so unlike the deep brown of the campesinos and of most Peruvians she knew. What was he? German? They were notorious for trekking in Peru, intrepid adventurers. American? But alone? She tried to remember enough English from school to say something to him.

"Hello, you are American?"

He smiled and sat up straighter.

"Yes," he said. He leaned into the aisle and said something rapidly in English that she missed completely.

She shrugged her shoulders and gave him a helpless look. She wasn't going to be of much use. She might think of a few more textbook questions, such as how are you or what's your name, but she didn't want to make a fool of herself. Maybe she would try talking to him later if they stopped for a break. She hadn't the energy right now. Besides, her fellow passengers were fussing over him. A woman draped his chest and lap with a multicolored manta, the kind campesinas usually wore over their shoulders. With the old man's dark sombrero, he seemed to blend into the highlanders around him—as long as he kept his head down.

He should have flown. Cori guessed that everyone else on the bus probably wished they could afford to fly and save themselves the twelve- to fourteen-hour journey over these rutted dirt roads, the last of it over this exhausting and dizzying stretch of puna. Most of the passengers were mestizos and campesinos used to the puna, so altitude sickness, which could leave a person weak-kneed and vomiting, wasn't much of a concern for them. But security was.

Cori had ignored the apprehension on people's faces at the bus terminal in the coastal city of Pisco, where she switched coaches from Lima for the trip into the mountains. Who could be looking forward to the ordeal ahead? People don't mention their worst fears when they have no option. The gringo's presence, however, brought their justified anxieties to the surface.

Three bad things could happen—an accident, bandits, or terrorists. Buses regularly plunged off precipitous mountainsides. As often as not it was the driver's fault, speeding carelessly on curves, trying to race past another bus, or so hung over that he couldn't have driven even the straightest highway. Poor vehicle maintenance was another cause, particularly brakes that failed or steering that gave out as buses careened down the switchbacks. Highwaymen were a constant danger. Buses had no option but to stop, with a mountain of rock up one side of the road and a steep cliff off the other. Across the lonely puna the chances of witnesses were slim and the likelihood of police intervention was negligible. The police themselves were often the thieves. At least mountain bandits rarely killed their victims. The guerrillas, on the other hand, were merciless. Police, soldiers, and government officials now avoided using public transportation on routes the Shining Path was known to travel. The road to Ayacucho, the city whose name means Corner of Death, was one of them.

The gringo made everyone nervous. They recognized him as a bad omen, a magnet for trouble.

Cori turned her attention outside the bus, where a gray rock landscape was covered with brown clumps of feathergrass and an occasional cactus. An opaque layer of clouds hung close to the ground and here and there veiled a high peak or ridge. Everything seemed wet and uniformly lit. Even through the bus window, the clarity of jagged outcroppings and pervasive feathergrass surprised her. She attributed the crispness to a recent rain. Maybe it was just mist that made the ground damp, but she hoped it was rain. Mist was common enough in Lima, where it rarely poured, the closest thing to rain being garúa, the winter drizzle that did little more than make the dust and pollen encrusted sidewalks slippery. She was looking forward to rain in the sierra. The most rain she had ever seen had been a brief shower during an outing once to Chosica in the foothills of the Andes just outside of Lima. She wanted to stand in a real storm. She wanted to feel torrents of water drench her to the skin, and see lightning flash and hear heaven-shattering thunder. She had not witnessed such a rainfall in all her life in the capital, plunked down as Lima was on a wide, alluvial valley formed by three rivers cutting through desert on their way to the sea.

Her father had described the cloud-splitting deluges from his boyhood in a town in the central mountains. If he didn't mention it when he saw la garúa, which Limeños counted as rain anyway, the memory of deep, soaking rains showed on his face. He had somehow passed that longing for rain on to her. When she got to Ayacucho, she would walk down the street in the first rain that fell with her face uplifted, letting drops splatter across her forehead and cheeks.

Cori scanned the horizon, hoping she might spot a condor or perhaps even a vicuña. Both were synonymous with her country. Like most Peruvians, she had only seen them in zoos. The vicuña formed the center of the national shield. Sometimes children or foreigners mistakenly thought the emblem bore a llama, the vicuña's more common cousin. The Ayacucho region was noted for wild vicuñas, an animal whose wool is considered the finest in the world, a creature so endangered that the sale of its wool was prohibited. Spotting a condor was much more likely. It wasn't the national bird, ironically, as it was in most Andean countries. That distinction went to a flashy red jungle bird, the Andean Cock-of-the-Rock. As a teacher, Cori knew such things. She imagined herself in a mud-walled classroom in the mountains trying to explain her excitement to children who had seen condors for as long as they could remember. Would they think her daft to be thrilled about seeing the huge bird, just a vulture, a scavenger, a consumer of carrion? On the other hand, condors had been sacred to the Incas, so wouldn't the indigenous people she would be living among still revere them? She determined to get all of that straight. For the first time a whisper of doubt about her ability to teach the children of the sierra crossed her mind. The idea of appearing foolish to campesino children, who in all likelihood spoke very little Spanish, hadn't occurred to her before. And if she showed up sick on top of it all, the whole village might see her as a useless costeña, a girl from the coast, too rarified and precious to handle the rigors of high altitude, never mind to endure the lack of common comforts like running water and electricity.

After jumping for the only job she could squeeze out of the ministry, Cori didn't want to let self-doubt undo her. She hadn't even consulted her family when she committed to going to the sierra at a time when people were fleeing the mountains because of the violence. How suddenly she had left Wachi, too. She hadn't even said goodbye.

Wachi, I had to go. I am so sorry, but I had to. She told him now in her mind what she hadn't said before leaving. I couldn't let you talk me into staying. Someday you would have left. I'm sure of it, and then it would have been too late for me.

If only the doctor had not given her that dream, filling her with the hope of fixing her hip. She wished he had just told her what she had wanted to know. Could she conceive and carry a child? Instead he said her hip could be replaced with a prosthesis. Cori had soared higher than any condor flying over the peaks of Ancash, leaving even Mount Huascarán below her. She had walked out of the doctor's office as if the operation were already completed, standing straight and tall and stepping with the precision of a cadet, if only in her own eyes. For three days, the time it took to go for X-rays and her next appointment with the doctor, she had been perfect at last. Perfect! Just as she had been created, before an infection caused by a vaccination destroyed her hip socket in first grade. She told only her sister. She would wait until the surgery was scheduled to tell her parents—and Wachi. Yet she and her sister were already talking of wedding dresses and how she would promenade down the aisle to Wachi with the grace of royalty. For three blessed days the eighteen years of silent humiliation were gone. And then she returned to the doctor.

"I'm so sorry," he said. "The hip we can replace. The problem is the spine. The intractable problem is the spine."

The speed of her plunge was overwhelming. She scarcely heard his words.

"The spine is badly curved from years of offset hips. Your back is so misshapen that correction is pretty much impossible."

She felt she could hear the wind roar in her ears as she raced toward the ground.

"The risk is just too great," he said. "You are better off as you are than you would be in a wheelchair."

Impact was deep and muffled.

Outside, propped between her sister and a column, Cori broke down. She wept as never before. Just this time, she told herself. She would never hurt this much or cry this hard again.

Two days later, Cori strode into the Education Ministry armed with the knowledge that there could be no further loss after a complete defeat. She balked at the ministry's feckless effort to dismiss her as handicapped, standing her ground in the face of authority in a way she could not have done a few days earlier. She was implacable. The bureaucrat eventually understood she would not be denied. A post was offered. Even though it was a difficult one, one that wouldn't have been filled at all if she had not accepted, it was all she had hoped for. It was a new life, a way of never having to tell Wachi what had happened. She couldn't have faced him and still have kept her vow never to cry like that again. He would have been so supportive, and would have tried to reason with her. But her lot was not a thing to be explained. It was just to be endured. Only then, walking out of the ministry, did she recall that the doctor had never answered her original query. Could she conceive and carry a child to term? But she didn't go back or call. It didn't matter anymore.

The bus slowed. Cori looked up from her seat, hoping they were making a rest stop. When the vehicle jerked to a halt, she sat upright so she could get off as soon as the driver opened the door. She was in the front row on the right side and didn't want to make others wait as she limped down the steps.

Before she could get up, a man rushed into the stairwell and up the steps waving a pistol, first at the driver and then at the passengers. He settled on pointing it right at Cori's temple.

"Que nadie se mueva!" he yelled. Don't anyone move. Behind him the heads of two other men entered the stairwell. Unlike the first man, they wore black ski masks over their faces.

Even Cori's breath was stilled. Then she remembered the gringo. The pistol pointed at her didn't scare her as much as the possibility that this innocent man might be pulled off the bus and killed. Her lightheadedness worsened and her stomach churned. She felt like throwing up.

"The bus is too heavy, so we're going to lighten it a little," the gunman said, like a helpful attendant, a broad white smile gleaming from his clean-shaven, boyish face. "We're going to take up a collection—jewelry, watches, dinero—and you can give with or without blood."

Ladrones. Only robbers. Cori breathed again.

The two other men headed down the aisle, each carrying shopping baskets woven in tartans of red, orange, green, blue, and white, the kind many campesinas on the bus used to carry food and water for the trip. Cori heard the bay doors creak open and other men searching the cargo area. A woman seated across the row dropped her rings into a basket and folded her hands across her pleated burgundy pollera. Without a word, one hooded man grabbed her hoop earring with the swiftness of a campesino harvesting apples and ripped it through her earlobe.

"Ayiiii!" she screamed, cupping a hand to her right ear and doubling forward, as the man as efficiently snatched the other loop. It snapped at the clasp.

The murmur that had risen as the men began their collection stopped. Everyone stared toward the sobbing woman.

"With blood or without!" yelled the gunman, this time without smiling, and without moving the pistol from Cori's head. "We don't ask twice. All your jewelry and your wallets and then open your bags. Everyone has to donate."

He looked at Cori. He pushed the pistol to where it touched her skin. "No jewelry, mamita? Open your purse and your other bags." He kicked the duffle she had stowed partly under the seat and waved the gun, signaling her to unzip it.

When she had packed, Cori had divided her money, just enough to live on for the first weeks at her new job. Half of her cash was in an envelope in the bag she carried on board the bus, and the other half was in her purse, hidden behind her, pushed deep into the corner of the seat. That was all the money she had until she started to get paid, whenever that would be, and she had borrowed even this from her parents.

Her hands trembled as she reached for the bag on the floor. She shuddered as she bent over, not just for fear of losing her money or even because of the gun pointed at her. She felt like she was going to be sick. She took a few rapid breaths and tensed from her stomach to her toes.

"Please, I have only a little money," she said as she opened the bag. What she needed to say was she might vomit and needed to get off the bus. But behind her was her purse and the rest of her money.

The gunman grabbed the duffle bag and pulled it onto Cori's lap, pushing her farther back into the seat as he did so. With her deformed hip she couldn't sit quite upright and leaned into her seat, her left leg stretched out from lack of flexibility in that hip. It forced her into an awkward position, which now helped conceal her pocketbook.

"Why are you sitting like that?" the man asked.

"I can't bend my hip. It's not right. I have to keep it straight on that side."

He looked her in the eyes for a few seconds. "Poor you," he said, and then started picking through her bag. He quickly found the envelope, looked into it and put it in his shirt pocket while continuing to push his other hand deeper into her luggage, pulling out a couple of books and shaking them open before dropping them onto the floor.

"Your purse! Your documents!"

"My documents are in my pocket." She resisted the urge to deny she had a purse. She reached into the pocket of her dark blue sweater and brought out her national identity card.

He glanced at it and shifted his attention, but not the pistol, to the woman with the little girl. The señora dropped her rings and earrings into his hand along with a wad of colorful banknotes.

"All your cash," he demanded. The woman sighed. She reached a thick brown hand into the neck of her blouse and pulled from her brassiere a slim fold of bills.

"Gracias," he said with exaggerated politeness. Then he patted the child on the head. Without saying anything more he shifted his eyes to his accomplices, who were working from each end toward the middle of the bus. He stepped back near the bus driver and finally swung his weapon from Cori, who watched it arc away.

The gunman stepped farther into the bus and stood beside the American, who did not look up. One bandit had passed him so the gringo must have been fleeced already. The bandit leader paid him no special attention. The robbers returned to the front of the bus.

The leader pointed the gun at the driver. "You wait here fifteen minutes. You understand?"

The driver nodded quickly, his eyes fixed on the gun.

"There is a rest stop three kilometers ahead. You wait there one hour." The bandit lifted the index finger of his free hand up for emphasis. "After an hour you can move on. If I catch you before that, I won't be so nice." He let his gun hand fall to his side.

The driver looked only at the gun hanging next to the man's leg but nodded again.

Everyone was silent as the men stepped off the bus and walked away. When they disappeared around the next bend in the road, mutterings of indignation rose from the passengers. Some opened windows to look beside the bus, checking the luggage strewn on the ground during the search. The driver waited a long while before getting up and looking out the door.

"Stay on the bus," he told the passengers as he and his assistant got down. Everyone stayed, although many stood up and began checking what remained of their belongings. Voices, some angry and some tearful, bemoaned losses. Cori heard the busmen tossing bags back into the cargo hold.

51

"We'll check everyone's belongings when we stop ahead," the driver said, getting back into his seat. "There's a restaurant there."

The bus whined into gear and lurched forward.

"I've seen that guy somewhere before, the one with the gun," a young man a few seats away from Cori said. "In uniform."

His traveling companion pressed her flattened hand against his lips. "We don't know who is on this bus. Better keep your opinions to yourself."

At the rest stop, Cori sat at a square Formica table with a cup of mate de coca steaming in front of her. She stirred sugar into it. She felt lightheaded and coca tea would help her cope with the altitude. Around her, fellow passengers grumbled. A palpable mist cloaked the bus stop and spilled through the open door, which let in much dampness but little light. Someone sat down at her table. It was the gringo.

"No more English?" he asked.

She shook her head. If he wanted to talk to her it would have to be in Spanish. Maybe she could have recalled a little more English on a good day, but not now, not when she mostly felt dizzy. She sipped her tea.

"Okay," he said and then continued in passable Spanish. "You look pale."

She nodded. Of course she was. Another woman getting off the bus had been ashen gray. That was soroche, perhaps mixed with trauma. Cori figured she looked about the same. She drank more tea. A waitress brought some to the American.

"Are you all right?" he asked.

"It's just the altitude—and the scare, probably."

"That was horrible. You were very brave."

"Me? No. I was scared stiff," she said, laughing nervously.

"Me too, and I didn't have a gun in my face. I was worried they would hurt you."

"We were lucky they weren't terrorists, especially you. Foreigners are supposed to fly."

"I am more afraid of Aeropeor than of terrorists."

She laughed at his substitution of "peor," Spanish for "worst," for "Peru" in the name of the national airline, Aeroperu. It was an inside joke that he had caught onto quickly.

"It's not that bad," she said, thinking she would have loved to have flown had she been able to afford it.

"I'm sure," he said, "but I'm a nervous flyer, especially on airlines I don't know anything about. My friends don't speak highly of it. They say Aeroperu is a tragedy waiting to happen."

Cori considered telling him he was being condescending, something she had heard of Americans, but he seemed so innocently frank that she was sure he didn't mean offense.

"Did your friends recommend you travel by bus?"

He shook his head. "I can't blame them. It was my idea." He stirred his tea and watched coca leaves swirl around his spoon. They sat in silence for a minute before he looked up.

"I'm Steven."

"Mucho gusto. My name is Cori."

"That's sounds very American."

"It's Peruvian. It means 'gold' in Quechua."

"Really? You're a golden girl."

She flipped her dark brown hair off her shoulder with the back of her hand and gave a faint laugh.

What she thought as she looked into his eyes was, "Golden are you." They seemed to hold a glint of amber even in the dimness of the poorly lit building. She drank down her tea. She was feeling better already. She signaled to the waitress for another cup of coca tea.

"Your color is coming back," he said.

"Mate de coca is the best thing in the mountains," she said.

"It's got cocaine in it, I guess."

Cori shook her head in disbelief. Silly gringo.

"Not at all. They do get cocaine from this leaf but they have to treat it with chemicals first. This is just a tea from the leaf. It's strictly medicinal. People take it for altitude sickness and to settle their stomachs."

"So I won't get addicted?"

She looked at him askance. Was he kidding her? She couldn't tell. People always said Americans, for all their money, were gullible, and usually fat. But Steven certainly wasn't fat, and didn't look dumb at all.

"Seriously," he said, "we don't have this tea in the States."

"It isn't addictive."

"Okay." He smiled at her.

How trusting he seemed, and how endearing that was. Her compatriots weren't trusting at all. They weren't unfriendly, but caution with strangers seemed prudent. Peru was poor and had many social strata. But this man seemed to want company. Why not? He was alone. Too bad he's a tourist, probably taking the adventurous route to Cuzco. They might even explore Ayacucho together. She felt herself blush, and wondered if he noticed.

She fanned herself as a new cup of mate was set before her.

"Now it's getting a little warm, no?" she said.

"No, it's a little chilly. Maybe it's the coca tea. Too much... medicine."

He was insistent. He seemed to stare into her eyes. Or was it she who was staring?

"It's not a drug," she said. "It's just an herbal tea. If you are looking for something like that, I'm sorry. I can't help you."

"Oh, no! I'm not," he said. "I'm just thinking that coca must have some effect. Don't people chew this and get high on it up here?"

"The campesinos chew it in the mountains, but with something else that helps them get the stimulant out. They say it's like drinking coffee all day for them. That's all."

"Why did you think I wanted drugs?"

"You're a tourist. Everyone knows young Americans come to Peru looking for drugs."

"I'm not a tourist. I'm going to be working in Ayacucho."

"In Ayacucho?"

"Yes."

"Me too," she said. "How surprising. I'm going to teach in a village outside of Ayacucho. What do you do?"

"I'm a priest."

"Oh," she said.

The driver called for passengers to board the bus.

"What village are you going to teach in? I may get out there."

"It's called Urpimarca."

"I will try to remember that."

"Who knows, Padre. Ayacucho's not so big. Maybe we'll see each other again."

"I hope so."

On the bus Cori sensed the other passengers shared her anxiety. It was still a few more hours to Ayacucho. The landscape looked more desolate than ever. She missed Wachi. She would have to get used to that. Priests should wear their collars, especially when they are that nice and handsome. He was probably just being kind. She would be lucky if even she could find Urpimarca, much less a yanqui like him.

Outside the bus, on the slope of a crag, something moved. A large black bird pecked at a fawn-colored animal carcass. Cori guessed it was a vicuña, and feeding on it, *Vultur gryphus*, its unmistakable white collar ringing its neck, announcing it was an Andean condor.

5

S teven wanted to continue talking with the young teacher
when they returned to the bus. Instead he could only look
at her from three seats behind for the rest of the ride to
Ayacucho, and even then what he saw were glimpses of her thick
dark hair and the side of her face. He tried to read a book on
Liberation Theology that talked of committing oneself to the
poor and finding solidarity with the oppressed, as Jesus had, but
finally put it away because he couldn't concentrate.

Like most other passengers, Steven found himself anxiously
watching the road. Each time the bus slowed, one or two people
would stand or lean toward a window to see why. The older man
beside him, who appeared to be dozing, would open his eyes and
close them again when the driver accelerated after rounding a
curve or downshifting to climb a grade.

Steven longed for someone to talk to and had drawn what
little conversation he could out of his seatmate. As the bus
descended from the puna and neared the city of Ayacucho, the
man awakened and accepted back the hat he had lent earlier. He
told Steven he was a farmer who now lived close to town, where
it was safer. Steven suspected the conversation had gotten only
as far as each could manage in Spanish. The man was clearly
Quechua-speaking, and neither seemed to understand exactly
what the other was trying to say in what was a second language
for both.

So he found himself watching the teacher, drawn back to her time and again, a conversation on the tip of his tongue that was frustrated by her sitting down the aisle. He had found in his short time in Peru that people had a boundless respect for the clergy. As soon as they knew he was a priest they trusted him unquestioningly. What he had liked about the woman named Cori was her openness before she knew of his calling. As soon as he told her he was a priest, she had shut down. For one of the few times since taking holy orders he wished he hadn't told someone he was a priest. He had seen the change it engendered in people often enough and usually relished the lift in esteem that came with it. But this time he had felt disappointed. Cori had at first seemed happy that he was going to be working in Ayacucho, that she might have an acquaintance there. He could have pursued it, asked her if she was going straight to the village or might be in Ayacucho for a few days, but her reaction to his revelation had warned him not to. He had let the moment pass.

Anyway, he didn't need to open that can of worms. This was not the time to revisit old issues, to renew old doubts and longings, to resurrect what he had come to Peru to leave behind.

Steven had flirted with love in high school and again when he had taught briefly before ordination. His decision to enter religious life eventually ended both those early relationships, and accepting God's call to Peru was his current attempt to quench the fire of another.

He had volunteered for mission work after seeing the growing Latin population in his home diocese in Connecticut. He reasoned—and his bishop had agreed—that mastering Spanish was essential if he and the diocese were going to minister to its changing ethnicity. Parishes that historically had been Italian, Irish, Polish, or French Canadian were now drawing far more Spanish speakers than descendants of the immigrants who founded them.

Steven had been asked one Sunday to fill in at a traditionally French parish. He protested that he spoke no French. No problem. His Masses would be in English. The one French Mass of the day was covered. The church, an imposing granite temple with massive spires mimicking those of St. Anne de Beaupré in Quebec, sat smack in the middle of a barrio. The faces that stared at him from the pews and the voices that drifted up to him when they greeted each other at the sign of peace were Caribbean. As he said Mass, Steven felt for the first time that something alien to him was going on among the parishioners before him, that the spirit moving among them and the one moving him were not the same.

The speech of those who stopped to thank him for coming lilted in heavy Puerto Rican and Dominican accents. People lingering on the steps outside the church bantered in staccato Spanish. Children just paroled from their hour of confinement careened in and out of adult legs or tugged at hands and hems with pleas of "Vámonos." Steven accepted an invitation to stay for a parish festival. The women lavished him with balls of deep-fried mashed potatoes filled with spicy meat, and plantains mashed and fried, and orange-colored empanadas, and stewed goat. The men offered him beer with looks that said, "C'mon, Padre, aren't you a man just like us?" He ate until he could eat no more and drank more beer than was prudent. He felt wonderful, as if he belonged with this community, as if he had been adopted and their goal was to make the orphan feel welcomed, to show him what a loving family it was. He left amazed that he, the priest, who should have been welcoming them to God's house, into the holy family of the church, had been so welcomed by them, at once fêted and engaged as friend, treated like an honored guest and an equal at the same time.

When he was offered an assignment to Peru, he imagined pampas and gauchos. He had to check the big globe in the rectory before he realized he was confusing it with Argentina. He had settled back into the leather armchair in the study, and wracked his brain for something about Peru before remembering, to his great relief, the pre-Columbian civilization of the Incas and that wonder of the world, Machu Picchu.

The only other images of Latin America that Steven could evoke were Hollywood Mexican. Somehow it was what he had pictured for himself. Neither vision, he would learn, neither salsa nor ranchero, fit the startling reality of the Andes. But it didn't matter. Any country would have been fine, just so it was a continent away from a woman he could no longer resist.

When the bus finally made Ayacucho late in the day, Steven briefly forgot about the teacher. In the crush of people trying to get off and the others there to meet them, he worried he would miss the person who would take him to the monastery where the old American priest lived.

A man in the crowd held up a sign as Steven stepped down from the bus: "Father Steven McMahon."

"Buenas tardes, Padre," the man greeted Steven as the priest approached him.

"Buenas tardes. You'll take me to Father Jaime?"

"Sí. He is waiting for you. Bienvenido a Ayacucho!"

"Gracias."

As Steven climbed into a small station wagon, he looked around the street and saw the teacher duck into a white sedan. He could still catch up to her and get her address so that he might have at least one friend here. While he debated, the sedan lurched and sped up the street, weaving around pedestrians as if fleeing the scene of a crime.

Only meeting the young American priest had salvaged the trip for Cori, and she wanted to wait for him after getting off the bus.

59

When she saw someone greet him, she got into a small, white sedan with a card inside the windshield saying "taxi" and headed to an inexpensive hostel that friends had recommended.

The car was missing a front passenger seat, so Cori threw her duffle bag and rucksack there and sank into the rear bench. Its springs collapsed nearly to the floor, and she found herself looking up through the windows like a child. The driver threw the car into gear with a jolt and sped down the cobbled street. The vehicle seemed to have no shocks and the driver struggled to control it, throwing his arms and back into reining in the beast as it bounced over the bumpy pavement. Cori gripped a torn armrest with one hand and extended the other to keep from being tossed from side to side.

"Hey," she yelled to the driver. "What is going on here? This heap shouldn't be on the road. You're going to kill me." As the car lurched toward the curb, she added, "Or some poor soul on the street."

The engine whined as the driver downshifted and the car slowed to where he could better restrain it.

"Excuse me, señorita," he said. "I'm sorry. The steering is very bad. It's not my car. I only rent it to make some money. The owner won't fix it and I can't afford to. Don't worry, please. I will go more slowly."

After suffering a moment of her silent rebuke, he continued. "Imagine, I do this for twelve hours a day. I'm so sore after this that I just sleep all the rest of the time. It isn't easy to find another vehicle. No one has any money to buy cars and when they break down you can't get parts. Ayacucho has been abandoned, señorita. Because of the terrorists, los terrucos," he said, gritting his teeth, "nobody wants to come here. Nobody wants to invest. There are no jobs, and still people come in to get away from the guerrillas. They only think Ayacucho is safe because they hear so little news in the mountains. You are from Lima?"

"Sí, from Lima."

"Then you know. Some people here say it's not so bad, that the newspapers exaggerate and give Ayacucho a bad name. Let me tell you, it's worse."

Cori didn't want to hear more bad news. She had been telling herself since accepting the job that the media portrayed only the bad and never truly reflected daily life. Hearing no objection to his ranting, the driver went on with his complaint.

"Last week a houseful of people got killed in a barrio," he said. "A bunch of men, women, and some kids. Some were shot, some stabbed, and some raped. The police said the terrorists killed them, like in some sort of vendetta. But who ever heard of the guerrillas raping women? Where they run things there's no drinking, no gambling, no womanizing. They go into a village and find one mean, drinking, wife-beating carouser. They shoot him dead in the street and everyone else starts behaving. They tend to their crops all day and stay home all night. The señoras do not even sell chicha anymore. Do you know chicha?"

"Chicha de jora? Corn beer, right? I tasted it once, but you can't really find it in Lima."

"You can find it easily in the market here in Ayacucho. But when the Shining Path goes into a village it dries up just like when the Pentecostals convert a place. The only difference is that in one the people fear hell, and in the other they are afraid of being hacked to pieces by communists."

He pulled to the side of the road as the car neared a congested intersection. Somewhere ahead music played, a typical Andean rhythm associated with festivals.

"The procession," the driver said, turning and smiling at her as though he had himself provided entertainment to compensate for the rough ride. "If you have come to Ayacucho for Carnival, you are just in time. The violence hasn't ended this tradition yet."

The dancers came down the street dressed in embroidered

white skirts and blouses that seemed to deepen the bronze of their skin. Each wore a white, high-crowned hat with a stiff flat brim and black band. Bright mantas of pink, green, orange, blue, red, and purple stripes on a white field were draped over their shoulders and tied in front in the style of Andean women. Each swayed to the music of a trailing band of male musicians dressed in complementary Stetsons and white ponchos.

As the twirling women passed the taxi, Cori rolled down her window for a better view. The driver's warning—"Señorita, careful"—registered before she could close it again or duck.

Foam sprayed across her face and onto her blouse, then into her hair as she belatedly turned to protect herself. The driver slouched and pulled his jacket collar over his head as one of the dancing women turned a can of shaving cream in his direction.

As the woman stepped back into the passing parade, the driver sat up laughing and shouted, "Quickly, señorita, roll up your window."

Cori cranked madly, but not before a cloud of baby powder caught her in the face and another dancer, plastic squeeze bottle in hand, squealed in delight. Other gyrating women tossed token sprinkles of talcum to the rhythm of music and smiled at the spattered and well-dusted woman behind the closing window.

"Carnival! I forgot about Carnival!" Cori said, her own laughter bringing tears to her eyes and leaving long drop tracks down her powdered face, giving her the look of a tragicomic clown. "In Lima they just toss water," she said in a pant, catching her breath and pulling out a hankie to wipe her face.

"They do that here, too," the driver said. He started the engine as the last guitarists, brass players, and drummers passed. "So watch yourself when you go out of your hotel."

The very next day, after sleeping off the rigors of travel and rising near noon, Cori was doused by revelers while walking down the street, followed by more foam and talc. It didn't matter, because right after that she was caught in her long-yearned-for thunderstorm. It rinsed away not only the foam and talc but the growing anxiety that had begun to gnaw at her. The rain refreshed her as she had expected it would. Fear, doubt, and homesickness washed away. The heavens opened up and cleansed the familiar self-pity she felt and was fleeing on this personal exodus, the crippling sense of herself as a defective person, flawed and malformed. That was enough to keep her going, on to the village of Urpimarca.

6

Early one morning the following week, Cori completed paperwork at the Education Ministry's Ayacucho office and took a bus reeking of diesel fumes to Huamanguilla, the last bus stop on the route to Urpimarca. She found a car to take her as far as the driver dared to go. The road eventually grew so rutted the car was in danger of bottoming out. The driver ground down to first gear and drove the last half mile with one pair of wheels on the berm, one on the center hump between the ruts.

"So sorry, señorita" he said, bringing the car to a halt. "This road is impossible. You'll have to walk from here. Just follow these ruts and you'll come to it."

"I was warned," Cori said. "How much farther?"

He shrugged. "Who knows how far a place is until they have been there?"

She counted out the fare and took her change.

"Vaya con Dios," the driver said. Go with God. Cori nodded.

"Sometimes," she smiled. "When possible."

She pulled her things out of the car and watched as the driver crept back down the road in reverse. She threw her bags over her shoulders, turned and started toward the village with the hobbled gait that had been hers since first grade.

The school in Urpimarca was a one-story, dull yellow building of plaster on adobe with a rust-stained, corrugated metal roof.

The plaster and paint contrasted with the huts of bare adobe that she'd passed along the way, simple earthen structures that seemed to rise from the very ground they stood upon. The chipped plaster of the school exposed in places the same core of dirt and straw brick used for the houses.

The school only went to the fifth grade. Cori knew that more education than that was considered an extravagance in the campo. A handful of children would continue to study, usually living with relatives in larger towns that could afford the luxury of a secondary school. Campesinos expected their children—at least their sons—to learn just the basics. Girls seldom went beyond elementary school. Most remained at home, helping their mothers and waiting until a suitable husband could be found, often when they were only fifteen or sixteen.

The children in Urpimarca had gone a year without a teacher and Cori wasn't sure how consistent the school year had been before that. Rural teachers were notoriously lax. Because of the isolation, teachers in the campo had to live where they worked, at least during the week, but many left so early on Fridays and got back so late on Mondays that children were often schooled just three days out of five. Cori took a deep breath. That would not be the case at her school. She tested the front door of the school and found it locked against her.

Cori had expected a better reception. More accurately, she had expected some kind of reception. She hoped a village that had gone without a teacher for so long would embrace their new maestra, even one with all her shortcomings—a novice, a Limeña, and handicapped. Instead they seemed to withdraw into their dirt houses. Little faces sneaking a peek out of the cracked doors of their huts were jerked back into obscurity. It seemed as if the village parted before her, leaving her a clear path to the school. Or were they offering unhindered passage through, a not-too-subtle message to keep going?

After dropping off her things and stretching to ease the pain in her back and legs, she set out to explore her new home. The school sat on the village plaza, a stretch of bare dirt broken by a cement wall forming two quadrangles, one two feet higher than the other. The schoolhouse stood on one corner of the upper half. Behind it a brush-covered knoll rose into a stand of eucalyptus. Cori limped up the rise to see how much farther the village extended. A dirt path led to a pasture of deep grass on the side of the hill. Before her the horizon stretched for miles across the wide plains of Ayacucho and the rocky Wari region to the city and cordillera beyond. Insects buzzed in the high grass, and gusts of wind wafted at her ears. The rest was a stony silence.

To the left in the panorama before here she could just discern the white point of an obelisk to the south. She realized it marked a place familiar to every Peruvian schoolchild, the site of the Battle of Ayacucho, where the outnumbered troops of Simon Bolivar under the command of José Sucre won a great victory against the Royalists in 1824, the beginning of the end of 300 years of European domination of Spanish South America.

Low in the center of the landscape the haze of Ayacucho made but a blur on the horizon. Ayacucho was now at least a half a day's journey away, assuming she was lucky enough to catch a ride once she reached a drivable section of the road, much longer if she wasn't. The city, and all the things there that were familiar and important to her, tugged at Cori as her disappointment at the lack of a reception took grip, awakening the fear and loneliness she had fought all along her journey.

This view would be her blessing. Even if her acceptance was less than she hoped for, this was a beautiful, idyllic place. Still, she worried she would not be welcome at all. She hoped the behavior of the villagers was just Andean shyness, their natural reticence, a wariness of strangers to be overcome in time. She would soon have the children to herself all day. She would win them over and they would surely open many doors for her.

She tried to reassure herself that everyone must be working in their fields or at the market, or maybe even away somewhere recovering from Carnival. The glances from the shadows must have been the children or the aged, naturally leery of outsiders. When evening came, she thought, the fathers and mothers would surely welcome her, and unlock the school and her lodgings there. Then she pictured herself huddled by the classroom door, wrapped against the cold in her light shawl, passing the night like a derelict. She shook off the image.

Turning to go back to the village, she noticed a chapel. Squat and stuccoed white, it sat higher up the knoll, partially screened by trees. How odd that the church would not be in a central place of honor. The chapel didn't seem to belong to Urpimarca at all. Cori doubted it would fit more than a few dozen people. Still, it looked cared for, which she found encouraging. If the village had a chapel, it might draw a visiting priest, perhaps an adventurous young foreigner.

A path by the chapel led around the side of the hill. Cori guessed it would loop around to the square and would be an easier route back than tramping through the high field grass again. The trail ran straight at first, narrowed into brush and came out along the top of the steep ravine forming the back of the hill. The sides of the ravine were terraced for crops, like steps down the slope, each narrow step retained by a stone wall. It was clear that going right would take Cori back to the plaza, so she headed that way. She had gone only a little way when she stumbled over a wide piece of flagstone set unexpectedly into the path. The stone sat at the foot of a walkway to the right and led to a huge house that loomed above her and the ravine. The building, larger and grander than any in the village, startled her. The plastered walls had once been painted white, and the massive door was intricately carved in a floral and leaf pattern. Wooden balconies jutted from four broad upstairs windows. The clay tile roof was gray with dirt, moss, and lichens. A few window panes were broken and some missing altogether. She stifled an urge to run from the specter and an opposite desire to creep up the spur that led the twenty yards to the door. She stood mesmerized by the strange beauty of the forlorn structure. It reminded her of the aging mansions in the older neighborhoods of Lima, now rapidly disappearing, either razed for new development or hidden by high walls topped with iron spikes or broken glass. She moved on, but her curiosity lingered. This anachronism wasn't going anywhere. She would learn its story soon enough.

Back at the school she found her packs untouched. She walked to the wall dividing the common and sat on it, facing houses tossed across the hillside. Urpimarca was little more than a cluster of mud huts and fields, almost certainly part of a grand hacienda before being broken up during the land reforms of the military dictatorship in the 1970s. The leftist generals who had given the land back to the people had most likely ordered the building of the school and the community center set diagonally across the square from each other. The house on the hillside must have been the old manor. That both calmed and unsettled her. The building was a soothing link to her Peru, Spanish-speaking and educated, the world beyond these hills. These campesinos, on the other hand, had been here on the hacienda, had obeyed and served the hacendado, and were now owners of what had been his land. That was just. They were here before the estate, before the Spanish. The language they spoke, Quechua, was the tongue of the Inca empire. It was as if they floated on the surface of this land and were stirred by waves of tumult, only to be, when all settled again, still bobbing more or less where they had been before. Through conquest and revolution, battles and coups d'état, the campesinos remained much as they had been for centuries. Their lives were altered little by the changes—a few new tools, iron to work the land, horses, sheep, and cows in addition to llamas and alpacas, modern clothes and somewhat different food, new music, the guitar, the trumpet, a few trinkets. But their enduring attachment to the land never changed.

This was where Pachamama, Mother Earth of the Quechua people, met the sky, and where the indigenous blood was purest, the least diluted by the raping Pizarros, where the Castilian and criollo of Lima were as foreign as the English or the Americans, where even Spanish was an immigrant tongue. All she identified as truly Peruvian she would find here.

As she watched the houses through the shimmer of late summer heat, Cori felt that she had arrived at last where she was meant to be. She closed her eyes and leaned back, letting the sun fall on her face. *Everything will be fine. Everything will once again be exactly as it is supposed to be.*

Late that afternoon she sat up. She squinted in the sunlight at a man walking unhurriedly down the road toward the plaza. As he passed the houses he waved to those inside or spoke without pausing. A little girl ran out of one doorway. He patted her head and sauntered on. As he neared the plaza, Cori could see he wore a dark fedora and a sage suit jacket with unmatched dark trousers. His white shirt was yellowed around the collar and he wore heavy work shoes.

"Rimaykuyki. Imaynallataq kachkanki?" he said in Quechua. *Hello. How are you?*

"Allimllam kachkani," she said. *I am fine.*

"Qanchu kanki musuq yachachik," he continued. *Are you the new teacher?*

She answered in Quechua and knew immediately from his expression that she had faltered. He nodded, not to her it seemed, but as if in confirmation of a conclusion already drawn.

69

He looked toward the school and her bags. She tried to explain that she had no key, but her vocabulary was too limited. She substituted Spanish words and mangled her sentences. She winced, a teacher sounding as illiterate as her pupils. She swallowed the next syllable as she spoke it and struggled to regain her composure.

"You'll have to work on your Quechua, señorita," he said in Spanish. "You will need to meet your students more than halfway." He took a key from his jacket pocket, walked to the school, unlocked the classroom door and pushed it open.

"We didn't know just when you were coming," he said. "No one told us. I am Javier Huanta. I am the mayor."

Cori spoke just her name.

He gestured for her to enter, and then followed behind her. Inside was a single large room with walls painted light green to about eight feet up, where plaster gave way to earthen blocks. Long eucalyptus beams supported a ceiling of corrugated metal. The room had no desks. Instead, unpainted wooden benches ran four rows deep and filled half the room. Faded charts with the alphabet and numbers hung on one wall. A small wooden table and a chair were pushed against the far corner of the room. A green chalkboard was mounted on another wall. There was no chalk. A row of rusty metal-framed windows faced the plaza. A weathered overhang covering a shallow veranda muted the sunlight from that side. Windows lined the other side of the room. A row of trees outside those windows blocked what would have been the sweeping view of the countryside she had seen from the hilltop.

Señor Huanta walked to the back of the room and opened another door. "This is the office. You can sleep here. There's a bed."

The office-bedroom held a small table for a desk and an armed wooden chair that looked as though it once belonged at the head of a dining room table. Along one wall was a low twin bed. Perpendicular to it was an ill-used armoire.

He opened a door at the back of the room. "The kitchen is across the courtyard," he said, indicating an outside patio paved with rough flagstone.

"That's good, señor," Cori said.

"You must be hungry after your journey."

"Yes, but I brought something with me for now."

"Fine. If you can come to our house this evening, we can offer you something hot to eat and we can talk."

"That would be lovely. Thank you," she said, feeling a rush of gratitude.

"We feared we would have no teacher again this year."

"Here I am."

Señor Huanta seemed to size her up.

"Yes," he said. "Here you are for now. You should get some rest. I'll come for you later."

He pressed the key into her hand and wandered back through the classroom and out the door.

Señor Huanta returned a few hours later and led Cori back the way she had come on her entrance into the village. His house lay along the main road to the square. She noticed now that it was newer than surrounding ones. The adobes were square at the corners, retaining the sharp edges of the wooden molds into which they had been pressed. The unfired bricks had been laid smoothly to two stories and were capped by semi-circular clay tiles, dull brick orange and clean of moss. Crowning the house near a black chimney pipe were two terra-cotta bulls. Between them was stuck a bouquet of plastic flowers.

The door was unpainted lumber with an inset brass lock and no knob. A shank of rope with a knot at the end hung out of a pencil-thick hole. Twisting the key in the lock, Señor Huanta gave the door a push with the palm of his hand to open it and stepped in, turning to beckon her inside.

71

The open door lit a large rectangular room half the width of the house, bare of furniture save a wooden bench against the wall to the right. The walls looked the same inside as out, unplastered and unpainted. Only a calendar from last year adorned them, with a photo of a red and white tractor-trailer, the name Hermanos Mantaro stenciled in gold on the cab door. The floor was dirt. Out of it rose an earthen platform two adobes high, running around three walls. A brown woolen manta lay on one spot of the platform. Señor Huanta pointed to it and asked her to please sit down. The house smelled of the earth, of eucalyptus smoke, and something cooking.

Señor Huanta went through a dark doorway next to the wooden bench. Cori heard him speaking Quechua with a woman. She assumed they were in the kitchen. That their words were muffled by thick walls and in a language that she spoke poorly made little difference. The tone was enough. The woman was bothered, abrupt. Since breakfast Cori had eaten only an apple, some cheese, and a few crackers. She was famished from the hike to Urpimarca. She had two packets of soup mix in her bag. One would hold her over tomorrow, when she would have to find where to buy food here.

Señor Huanta entered and sat on the wooden bench. He still wore his hat. He folded his hands between his knees and looked straight ahead for a minute before turning in Cori's direction.

"Where are you from?" he asked.

"Lima. I arrived in Ayacucho earlier in the week."

"By motorbus? Or did you come by airplane?"

"By bus, via Pisco."

"Ah. That is a long journey and a rough one."

"We were robbed. Men with guns," she said.

"That is too bad. I hope no one was hurt."

"No. Not really."

"On the puna?"

"Yes."

"The puna is big and lonely. Almost no one lives there, just vicuña. The thieves take advantage of the isolation. The police can't really patrol it."

"Someone said the robbers were probably police themselves," she said. "Or soldiers."

"That would be terrible," he said. Cori concluded from his tone that he was being ironic.

She recalled the leader of the robbers, a robust and well-groomed man with erect bearing. She could easily imagine him in the green of the national police.

She considered what this mistrust of police meant. In Lima, people associated police with bribery and shakedowns. Anyone with a car knew that getting stopped by an officer meant opening their wallet. It was the same when police stopped public buses to check passengers' documents. Still, as useless and annoying as they were in everyday life, police were at least some protection against the rising violence. She doubted that the national police bothered with places like Urpimarca. Life here would be ordered by the natural rhythms of the sun and the rain and the land.

The woman called from the back of the house and Señor Huanta excused himself.

A few moments later he reappeared. He held a steaming bowl in his hands and returned to his seat on the bench. Behind him a woman in a wide, light-blue skirt, long braids, and a hat very similar to his own carried another bowl, which she offered to Cori. The woman's face did not match the haranguing voice. Her eyes were bright and showed no resentment. Though she was far from young, her cheeks were taut. The creases around her eyes were few but deep.

Cori took the hot bowl and set it on the bench beside her. The woman left the room and returned quickly with two faded red plastic cups, setting one beside the man and one beside the guest. She then brought the same for herself, soup and a cup of what appeared to be juice, and sat on the same adobe shelf as Cori, but nearer Señor Huanta. She did not introduce herself, nor was she introduced by Señor Huanta.

A few tiny shreds of meat in the broth were unidentifiable, but potatoes, carrots, fava beans, onions, and pieces of cabbage were abundant, as were grains of wheat, barley, and quinoa. Bits of cilantro floated on top alongside small globules of grease. Cori stirred the soup with a bent spoon and thanked the couple in Quechua.

The woman smiled and told Cori to eat, making a gesture of bringing food to her mouth.

They ate together in silence.

The soup was so much better than cheese and crackers that Cori didn't miss the conversation that she might have expected during a dinner at which she was the guest. She was still weary from the long walk. Her hip hurt and her feet ached. Her hosts, most likely up at dawn and out working in the fields all day, seemed tired too. When they had finished Cori set her bowl beside her, following Señor Huanta's lead, while the woman held hers on her lap. The unspoken rule of silence remained in force for a couple of minutes more.

Eventually, the woman said something to Señor Huanta that Cori didn't catch. It was about her, she was sure. He nodded with such conservation of effort that his response could easily have been missed.

"Señorita, do you know why there was no teacher here last year?" he asked.

"I assumed," she said, fearing she sounded like a child explaining why she didn't know a lesson, "that no one was available. The shortage of teachers in the campo is no secret."

The woman got up and gathered the bowls and went through the dark doorway muttering. Cori caught the Quechua verb for knowing. She guessed the woman was saying that Cori should know the answer to that question.

"The last teacher, Señor Cespedes, disappeared."

A chill went through Cori. She weighed his words, not sure what he meant. She waited for him to go on. He took a long time.

"Many parents didn't like him. Others adored him. He was very political and told people they were trapped in poverty and ignorance as part of a worldwide plan to keep the rich fat and happy at our expense. He compared it to the Inca system. You know how when the Inca ruler died his successor didn't inherit his palaces and wealth? That stayed with his ayllu, his family and court. All the old Inca ruler's palaces, his fields with their crops, his llamas, even his wives, were dedicated to serving him in death, to serving his mummy. A cult of the dead, this teacher called it. He said we were like that, an ayllu supporting the corrupt old order that maintained North American imperialism at our expense. He promised a new order based on equality for everyone, Indian campesinos just as well as white Limeños. He painted a very pretty picture. Some people in the village thought he was brilliant and believed what he said."

"You didn't," Cori offered.

"No. We are subsistence farmers here. What we grow, we eat. None of us sells more than a little of our production in the market, and then it is only to buy clothing or cooking oil or a few household items, like pots or kerosene. We barely support ourselves on this land. How are we supporting imperialists? Perhaps when the hacienda was still here, but not now. Most of the parents here believed all this politics had little to do with us. Why didn't he just teach our children to read and write and do mathematics so they don't get cheated when they go into town?"

Cori wondered whether her predecessor spent any time teaching the children or devoted all his energy to re-educating the villagers.

"In defense of Señor Cespedes, he was dedicated and strict and you didn't get the sense that he resented working in the campo. Some teachers do."

He let that idea hang in the air.

Cori wanted to demur, to defend herself, but sensed she was expected to listen.

"Some of the young people were very taken by him, believed him to be intellectual and adventurous, and some of the señoritas saw him as dashing. This caused certain jealousies. Then he started to defend the actions of the rebels over near Ayacucho. Once, a teacher in a village not far from here came back from the weekend late on Monday morning to find his pupils assembled in the schoolyard listening to speeches from the rebels. The guerrillas demanded that the students tell them what the teacher did to them when they were tardy and some said he whipped them. So the guerrillas tied the teacher to a post, took down his pants and beat him severely with a switch. Our teacher here, our Señor Cespedes," Señor Huanta said, speaking the name with some spite, "said he deserved it. That the party—these communists—would impose the discipline needed to bring about a new order."

He stopped talking, as if waiting for Cori to consider his story.

"Police started patrolling the area," he continued, "and there were confrontations in some of the districts around Ayacucho. The government sent in soldiers. People disappeared in some villages, suspected guerrilla sympathizers. Here one day. Gone the next. So, when Señor Cespedes didn't return one weekend, people suspected the military grabbed him. We have never heard otherwise."

He sat back and settled his hands on his knees.

The ministry had told Cori none of this. Her instructions were simply to show up and teach. Even in the Ayacucho office, where this had to be known, they had acted as though everything was normal. The woman she had dealt with didn't even know how to get to Urpimarca.

"Could he have quit without telling anyone?" Cori asked. "People do it all the time. Maybe he was scared."

"Or maybe he joined the guerrillas, or perhaps he ran off with a woman," he smiled. "People have different theories. He didn't bring much with him and left little behind, a few articles of clothing and some books. He was very orderly. If he planned to leave, why not take what little he had? Or maybe he didn't need those things where he was going.

"I informed the Education Ministry in Ayacucho of his disappearance. They said it was news to them. We heard nothing more about it until a man from the ministry came out last year and said they were still trying to find a teacher. This man said he knew nothing about what happened to Señor Cespedes. And no one else ever came. We complained many times that we needed a teacher and they said it was difficult to find teachers for the smallest communities. That is as far as it went."

"What about...what about the police or the military?" Cori asked. "Don't they know anything about it?"

"To ask them might be taken as an accusation," he said. "That's why I informed the Education Ministry. They should have been concerned, but they told us nothing. If anyone here knows what happened to him, they aren't saying. No one has ever come to inquire about his disappearance. He wasn't from the sierra, maybe from Lima. He never said. Who knows where he came from or where he went? He's gone. That's all I know. That's all anybody knows. Now you know."

Cori felt the enthusiasm she had managed to muster to come to Urpimarca slip away. What in God's name was she doing here? She longed to step back to the days at university, time spent with Wachi after classes and on weekends. She had never even told her parents about him. Her mother didn't believe a man could love her. Cori wondered if things might have been different had she been more open with them about Wachi. Now she wished she had explained why she really needed to take this job—over their objections. She had left so quickly. It must be hard on them. Now what could she do? She was certain she couldn't walk away from this job before starting. How unfair that would be to these children. And it would be the end of her career, stillborn before she could even prove herself. She couldn't do that.

"I don't mean to scare you," Señor Huanta said, pulling her back to the conversation. The room was growing darker as evening fell. "I'm sure you'll do fine and I'm very happy we now have a teacher. But these are things you needed to know."

"Yes. I needed to know."

She could feel the mayor's genuine concern. Maybe she should reassure him. But what could she say? That she was happy to be here? She wasn't sure anymore. She was no longer so sure everything would turn out as she had dreamed. Fatigue overwhelmed her and the one good idea she had now was to go back to the school and sleep. She stood.

"It has been a long day. A bus ride from Ayacucho, a rough taxi ride on the road from Huamanguilla, and a long walk for me."

"Yes," he said, stealing a glance at her leg, askew as always, even in her loose black slacks. "It's not an easy trip for anyone. And the altitude will make you tired for a few days."

"I'd better get some rest."

Señor Huanta accompanied her out the door, pulling the rope to shut it behind them. They walked without talking in the fading light. At the plaza she thanked him for dinner, mustering enough Quechua for the short sentence.

He merely nodded. As he turned to go home he looked back at her again.

"I'm sure you will be fine," he said, and paused before adding, "but lock the door."

7

Father Steven's new quarters were in an old colonial monastery attached to one of Ayacucho's thirty-seven churches. Small by the standards of the big abbeys that once housed thousands of priests and brothers at the church's zenith in the Andes highlands, the monastery's architecture was typical New World Spanish, with a central courtyard enclosed by four colonnades. The dining room looked out on one side, and common rooms another, while dormitories lined the other two. Several rooms were taken by Peruvian priests who tended to the church itself and said Mass there. Steven's host, the semi-retired Father Jaime Driscoll, an American missionary who had come to Peru in his youth and spent most of his life in the sierra, lived in another. Twice as many rooms around the grassy courtyard were empty, housing nothing more than dust and cobwebs.

For his first few days there, Steven found welcome refuge in the monastery. The quiet was a relief after the pulsing mass that was Lima, with its teeming shantytowns, its decrepit buses and taxis, and its pushing and jabbing markets. He didn't miss the clatter of the city or the blare of discordant music coming from all sides—salsa and merengue dueling with the piping of highland zampoñas and the flutter of criollo guitars. While he was happy with his progress in Spanish, he felt fatigued from trying to decipher the machine-gun chatter of urban speakers. Steven had come to Ayacucho to find a slower, more authentic place to do mission. Instead, he found himself shell-shocked from the robbery on the bus. Losing a few hundred dollars hadn't bothered him as much as the fear that descended upon him soon afterward. He realized only in retrospect how foolhardy the trip had been, and he was unnerved thinking of what would have happened had the Shining Path halted the bus.

Finally, when he arrived at Ayacucho, the effects of the altitude in the mountains hit him. He was breathing slowly and his movements were weak. Father Jaime told him to take his time and rest.

"You need to acclimate," he admonished Steven. "You are a fish out of water. Let your body get used to this thin air for a few days without worrying about what you are supposed to be doing here."

"I just didn't expect to feel so tired."

"Don't push yourself too soon. You will adjust. Get used to the air. Get used to the language. Get to know the staff and people around the church. Find your bearings."

After sleeping late one morning, Steven sat alone at the dining room table, a heavy plank affair whose ebony tones blended with the dark wooden floor. Light spilling in from the vaulted veranda outside brightened the cream-colored walls.

Eugenia, the cook, brought a cup of coffee unbidden and took his order for breakfast. Steven retrieved several newspapers from a cart near the door.

The local daily headlined the killing of a radio station reporter a block from the main plaza in Ayacucho the day before. The man had stopped for a shoeshine after lunch and was walking back to work. A car pulled to the curb. A man wearing a ski mask stepped out, shot the reporter four times, got back in the car, and sped away.

The police said the killing was most likely the work of the Shining Path. The radio station's manager demurred, saying the reporter had been investigating allegations of the military's involvement in the disappearance of local peasants. The local army commander agreed with the police, saying the Shining Path most likely killed the reporter, but added that for all they knew it might have been the vengeance of a jealous husband.

In the Lima papers, Steven read of a labor strike paralyzing transportation in the capital. Other unions, mainly the teachers and construction workers, planned to join in. All were upset with higher prices. Inflation was reported to have run at a rate of thirty-four percent the past month.

As he closed a big broadsheet from Lima, he noticed another story, not on page one. The guerrillas had attacked a police station in a small town outside of Huancayo, a city northwest of Ayacucho that is the main market town in central Peru, where the mountain road turned west to descend to Lima. Four police officers who resisted the assault surrendered after running out of ammunition. They were slaughtered anyway and the cement-block post leveled with dynamite, their bodies still inside it.

Steven piled the papers together and tossed them onto a chair out of sight. Eugenia brought a plate of fried eggs, toast, and crisp potatoes and refreshed his coffee, and he ate in silence. In the sunny courtyard, Father Jaime walked, immersed in his breviary. At the far end of the yard, a gardener planted flowers along the border of the colonnade. Steven sipped his black coffee.

Two things were roiling within him. He was drawn to this society, to the extraordinary traditional culture of the Quechua, but at the same time he was repulsed by the baffling violence erupting all around him. He wanted so much to move deeper into the campesinos' world, to leave this oasis of a monastery and live among the people. He wanted to move into the campo, not to retreat into this cloister at the end of the day. Yet he was afraid he might have arrived too late.

Steven had never seen himself as an apostle sailing to the edge of the known world to be skewered and roasted in God's name. His was not an ordination to martyrdom. If refusing to renounce his faith meant being tossed to the lions, he had no doubt he could face even death, though not perhaps with the courage of a martyr of the early church. A life of service in the name of Christ offered abundant opportunities to alleviate suffering in many other places. Safe places. The poor and needy—physically and spiritually—were everywhere in the world, and would always be with us, as Jesus had said. He couldn't delude himself into thinking his call to Latin America was the only way he could serve God and his people. Besides, he had come to realize that it had also been an exciting, convenient, and in some ways even trendy way of leaving his former life.

Escaping might have been a better word. She had been a parishioner at the church outside of Hartford where he served as assistant pastor. Young, lively, and increasingly present as he went about his work, she was always willing to volunteer and seemed to have slipped effortlessly into his life. Had he felt he loved her, it might have been different. Rather, he had found himself wrestling with desire that he would be powerless to resist if he proceeded heedlessly. Fantasy and reality were so tantalizingly close he could think of no alternative but to run.

Father Jaime stopped his amble beside the eighteenth-century stone fountain in the center of the courtyard. It had been dried up for as long as anyone at the monastery could remember. He noticed Steven looking out the window of the refectory, raised his hand in greeting, shut his book, and came in to join him.

The old priest still stood a head taller than most natives of Peru, and as Jaime entered the dining room Steven imagined his colleague must have seemed a giant to the campesinos in his younger days, before being stooped by age. Jaime still struck an impressive figure with his thin white hair under a fine straw Panama that kept the sun off his milky skin and out of his blue eyes. He was one of an older generation of priests who always wore a Roman collar. Steven wore one only when required, or when prudent or advantageous, such as, he was a little embarrassed to admit, when he flew. It seemed to help move him quickly though the airport. The snow-white square at Father Jaime's neck shone against his black shirt and trousers. Clerical garb was as natural for him as a suit was for other men of his generation.

Steven's father, who had been a sales representative for stationery and office supply companies, had been like that. He wore suits. That's all. They had been as casual a part of him as the cigarettes he smoked with the unapologetic ease of that bygone era. For men of his generation, to wear anything more casual was to be underdressed. It took little imagination for Steven to see the two men together. The aplomb was the same. Only Father Jaime didn't smoke.

"Steven. Good morning. I missed you at breakfast," Jaime said.

"I got a bit of a lazy start."

"Nothing wrong with that," Jaime said, pulling out a chair and sitting down with a wince.

"Are you all right?"

"Too many years traipsing up and down those hills on horseback," he said. "Even where you can drive now, all that rattling around on unpaved roads is still brutal on the spine. Stay here long enough and you'll carry a memory of these mountains around in your bones like I do."

"I can believe it. Can I do anything for you?"

"No, no, you can't do anything about age and the toll the years take. But, mind you, there are still a lot of places here you can't get to except on foot or beast," Jaime said.

He would know. If Steven needed a model of the intrepid

missionary, he needn't look to the Franciscan missions of Old Mexico or even the seafaring disciples who preached Jesus' message of universal inclusion to the Gentiles. Jaime was a monument en vivo. Yet the old man had always done mission from Ayacucho, making his forays into the campo from his base in town. Steven wondered if Jaime had ever questioned doing ministry that way. Somehow he didn't think so.

Eugenia came out of the kitchen.

"Can I bring you anything, Padre?"

"No thank you, dear, I'm going to go rest." He turned back to Steven. "I know what you want most is to get out into the campo, so I won't try to dissuade you. I felt the same way as a young missionary. Just be aware, it's getting dangerous in ways I never had to worry about. These Shining Path communists—these Maoists—scare the devil out of me. Not for myself. I don't get up where they operate much anymore. But for the people in these villages, people I know, they are a very real threat. I'm going to put you in touch with a young catechist who will help you. He's quite dynamic, a very unusual fellow. He's well educated, but has gone back home to his village. He has a wife and children there. He'll watch out for you, and he'll do a better job of orienting you to the culture than any of these young Peruvian priests around here. They love the Catholic Church, but are too quick to disparage local traditions. They're more Catholic than the pope."

Steven laughed, having already experienced the conventionalism of his native colleagues at the monastery.

"That would be great, Father. I'd love to meet him," he said.

"This young man's name is Angel Yupanqui, and he comes from a charming village on the mountainside called Urpimarca."

"I've heard of it. I met a woman on the bus ride up here who will be teaching there."

"Angel helps with catechism all around there. He will open a lot of doors for you. I haven't been to Urpimarca in some years

84

now, but it was always one of my favorite places. Even in the days of the hacienda, it was something special. The view alone is worth the visit. And then there's Our Lord of the Hacienda."

"What's that?"

"There's a painting up there that the locals believe possesses miraculous qualities. It has hung for decades, maybe centuries, in the chapel out by the manor house, a depiction of the cruci-fied Christ known as Our Lord of the Hacienda. The owners of the manor were apparently powerless to discourage the belief once it got started. The bishops, of course, neither endorsed nor disavowed it. What harm is there in the adoration of an image of our Savior?"

"None," Steven interjected. "But it isn't what the Gospel message is all about."

"True," Jaime agreed. "But as a local bishop once told me, 'Better Christ crucified than some mountain apu.' Those are the mountain spirits that, like it or not, most of these people still believe in and pay homage to, right alongside Jesus, Mary, and all the saints. You might say they hedge their bets."

"I guess that's one way of looking at it," Steven said, chuck-ling and shaking his head.

"Anyway, over time the painting gained a local following. We have plenty of miraculous devotions in Peru already, like the Lord of Miracles in Lima. Elaborate processions are part and parcel of Catholicism here in a way you just don't find back home, like the Corpus Christi procession in Cuzco and Holy Week right here in Ayacucho. You'll see soon enough. It doesn't bother the church when people swarm to Urpimarca for the feast day of Our Lord of the Hacienda.

"That painting hung on the wall behind the altar in the ha-cienda chapel since beyond living memory without much notice. Then, one day in the 1940s, an Indian girl setting flowers on the altar in preparation for the arrival of the priest later in the morning noticed tears trickling down the face of Jesus. She remained transfixed until hours later when the priest and others found her there. They too saw streaks on the cheeks of the weeping Christ. As word of the occurrence spread, that little chapel filled with worshipers. Sometime later, the family of a dying campesino carried him to the chapel to pray before the Christ. Their prayers were answered. They say he walked out with his strength restored. Others began to claim to have benefited from its miraculous powers. People started petitioning Our Lord of the Hacienda for help in their time of need, making pledges of devotion or good deeds in exchange for favors granted.

"The local pastor at the time was a pretty shrewd Peruvian who was frustrated with the resurgence of traditional Andean beliefs and blamed them for the decline in religious vocations. He was more than happy to find a Christian focus for campesino worship. The bishop wouldn't grant official permission for veneration of the image, but the pastor made a point of encouraging it himself, keeping everything low-keyed to avoid crossing the church hierarchy. When the leftist military government began breaking up the haciendas in the 1970s, the villagers took up regular processional devotions to the image, probably to discourage the hacendado from taking it with him when he lost the land. The annual day for the celebration settled logically on the Feast of Corpus Christi, since it is an image of Jesus."

"Anything ever happen that could be called complete, spontaneous, and lasting? Anything defying scientific explanation?" Steven asked, unable to keep a bit of skepticism out of his voice.

The old priest smiled at the well-known and oft-ignored church rules for a real miracle. He patted Steven's hand.

"You know very well, Steven, that God shows us miracles every day. If you believe, you see them, and if you don't, no one can ever show them to you, no matter how hard they try."

8

Cori awoke at mid-morning. The closed room felt stuffy. An even light suffused through a wide set of iron-framed windows on the wall opposite her bed. A layer of dust inside and a film of grime outside provided her as much privacy as a curtain.

Wrapped in a blanket on the bare tick mattress, her sweater for a pillow, she saw her main task for the next few days: cleaning. The dust, which she had noted cursorily the day before, appeared from this low angle like gauze draped over every surface. Cobwebs she hadn't noticed yesterday ran like lace trellises from every corner of the ceiling. A faint path on the floor traced where she and Señor Huanta had trodden the day before.

She stretched her legs out from the fetal curl in which she had slept. She ached. The bottoms of her feet were tender. Her calves were tight. Her good hip throbbed. She eased herself out of the depression her weight made in the thin mattress and stood, balancing lightly on the balls of her feet before settling her weight on her bones and joints. She would be hobbling worse than normal today. She put on a dark-blue sweater against the morning chill, leaving it unbuttoned, slipped into her shoes, made her way across the gritty concrete floor, and unlocked and opened the patio door.

The flagstone courtyard was shaded by the school building on two sides and by thin trees on a third. It would stay cool back here until the afternoon sun struck the patio slabs. Walking toward the open end, where the courtyard gave way to flowers and shrubs, she began to completely awaken.

A path led into wild brush and over a berm to a field. She searched the border between grass and bushes until she found a sheltered spot for a makeshift toilet. She had not found one at the school. Undoubtedly, with a little more effort, she would come across an outhouse. A hole in the ground with planks thrown across it was not her idea of a bathroom. Cori had reasonably expected that a government-built school would have an indoor lavatory, just like in Lima.

Returning to the school, she found the stove, but no kerosene. She washed her hands and face in cold water over the kitchen sink, apparently the only running water in the building, and let them air dry as she went back to her room, carefully closing both doors behind her. She pulled a handful of lemon drops from a bag in her pack, opened one, put it into her mouth, and stuffed the others into her sweater pocket. Cori went through the classroom and out to the plaza, making sure the door was locked.

Perhaps someone in the village would sell her a hot cup of coffee or tea or, more likely, emoliente, an herbal tonic thickened with barley and boiled flaxseed and served piping hot in tall tumblers. On most misty mornings in Lima, a half dozen people would join her near a pushcart where she liked to stop, warming their hands around the hot glasses while sipping the steaming infusion. Now, near the end of summer, the air was already warming. She had no idea what campesinos drank for breakfast, and by now it was getting closer to lunchtime. Even a glass of water would be welcome, if she could be sure it was safe. She was afraid to drink the water from the school's faucet.

The street was becoming familiar to her, not so much the houses along it as the dusty roadway itself. This was the fourth time she had walked its tilted and rocky surface, broken with patches of grass and muddy puddles. She chose each step carefully, especially with her feet so sore, stopping to check each house she passed for signs of life. No one seemed to be about at the homes nearest the square. Here and there a chicken pecked beside the road. Clucking and quacking rose from behind rough wooden fences in a few of the yards. Somewhere a donkey brayed. A few dogs barked.

One door stood open in a house midway down the street. Over the doorway a wooden pole stuck out at an angle, a red rag wrapped around the tip. The edges of the adobe walls were rounded and smooth. Pebbles bulged in relief from the earthen blocks, the softer dirt that had encased them dissolved by rain and worn away by wind. The roof was half moldy thatch and half corrugated metal. The door was set to one side, rather than in the middle of the cottage. A poorly fashioned repair and old stone lintel betrayed where the entrance had once been, in the center of the front wall. Cori recognized the stick and cloth as an Andean shop sign and went to the doorway where she stood tentatively, leaning to look inside. The room was dark and the earthen floor was a steep step down. With the light of day behind her, she could just discern a woman standing at a table deep in shadow, her back to the door.

"Good morning, señora. Is there coffee?" Cori asked.

"Chicha," replied the woman, without turning to acknowledge Cori.

For breakfast? She was thirsty though.

"No coffee? Tea? Cola?"

"Manan kanchu," the woman said in emphatic denial, waving one hand as if in irritation. "Chicha," she repeated.

"Okay. Chicha."

The woman nodded to a ledge along the wall just inside the door. Cori sat. The simple adobe bench was level with the ground outside and ringed the single room of the hut. The excavated floor was cool and damp. The walls grew darker toward the ceiling, and they were black with pitch near the roof. Thin patches of plaster an eighth of an inch thick had fallen away from every wall. Against one wall was a double bed, the white paint of its baroque headboard worn to bare metal over much of its surface. A few brown-and-white-spotted guinea pigs chewed on freshly cut grass strewn under the bed. The woman worked in silence at a heavy wooden table against the far wall.

She ladled a foamy, cream-colored beverage into a large glass from a huge porcelain bowl, its white enamel chipped in black circles. She carried the drink to Cori, who took it with both hands. The woman turned around without saying a word and went back to her table, heaped with corn and other grains. Her dark hair hung over a pink blouse in a single, thick braid to her waist, where she wore a dark, knee-length pollera.

The chicha was cool, the temperature of the room, and was rich and tasty, slightly sweet and bitter at the same time. Cori wondered if such a big glass would make her tipsy. The drink was filling, made from fermented corn, and might not make all that bad a breakfast if she didn't overdo it. All she needed was to be seen staggering around the village. She sighed. Maybe they would judge her harshly anyway. She settled back against the wall, sipped from the glass and marveled at this place where she had finally arrived.

She was sitting in a Quechua home deep in the heart of the Andes for the second time in two days, in this old hut hundreds of miles from Lima's shopping centers and glass and steel office buildings. Yet she felt more distant from Lima than mere miles suggested. Cori was removed in time. How many generations of Quechua women had lived here, worked here, slept here, made love, laughed, cried, and raised families here? And how many outsiders had crossed that threshold, the current proprietor's indifference notwithstanding? She was centuries away from Lima.

Cori finished her chicha and held out a fifty-centimo coin from her purse.

"Manan kanchu wilto," the woman said, shaking her head.

"Está bien," Cori said, closing her purse as she realized the woman was saying she had no change. Cori pressed the coin into her hand and nodded. "Okay."

Cori ascended into the blinding light outside. Squinting, she stepped back down the road, stumbled, and then caught her balance. Bending her head down and shading her eyes with one forearm, as if fending off the sun, she picked her way back down the lane.

Past Señor Huanta's house the main road branched left. That route followed the steep ravine that defined the north side of the village. Cori had come in that way yesterday. She looked to the right fork and walked up its incline toward a cluster of houses.

At one of the houses, a woman sat on the ground arranging piles of potatoes, each mound a different variety. Several of the adobe-colored heaps were potatoes Cori knew well in Lima, while another contained the knobby huayro potatoes rarely seen on the coast. Those on yet another pyramid were black-skinned and shiny. On a flattened burlap sack were finger-shaped ollucos, sweet, delicate little tubers in bright yellow skin splotched with red and orange. Along with the potatoes were purple-skinned onions, fava beans in their lumpy green pods, and choclo, fat corn with kernels the size of a thumbnail.

A boy and a girl played in the dirt nearby. The boy, about three years old, wore only a T-shirt. The girl, six or seven, mirrored her mother's clothing, a blouse and pollera.

Cori greeted the woman and attempted a textbook exchange of pleasantries in Quechua. Her presence did not appear to

surprise the woman. She inspected Cori with apparent disap-
proval. From her hatless head of shoulder-length hair to her
white T-shirt and open sweater to her black slacks and shoes,
everything about Cori marked her as an outsider. She could do
nothing about that. It would have been unthinkable to dress like
a campesina. She would feel as if she were in costume. Worse
yet, she might offend the village women, appear to mock them,
parading around in parody of their culture. She feared that even
in her most sincere attempt to conform she might blunder. She
didn't know whether the color or style of the skirts signified
something, whether a subtle variation might denote social class
or marital status, one type of pollera for señoritas and another
for señoras. Did wearing one braid signify one thing and two
another? Were the mantas they wore around their shoulders,
and in which they carried everything from groceries to children,
coded in some way, the exquisite embroidery a private alphabet
indecipherable to outsiders like her?

The woman's hair was capped with a manta folded in a
square and balanced on top of her head to keep off the sun. Her
hair disappeared behind her, and Cori couldn't see how it was
braided. The woman's skin was dark copper, with a burnished
glow in her cheekbones. In Lima, Cori felt dark-skinned herself,
the indigenous genes in her mestizo lineage trumping the criollo
blood of past generations, especially compared to the Castilians
who taught in the universities, who ran the better businesses,
who worked in the banks. Beside this señora de campo, however,
Cori looked pale and white.

The children stopped their play and stood watching her. Cori
wanted to talk to them, play with them, engage them in some way.
She was anxious to get to know the village children. But she re-
strained herself for now. She was a stranger. Superstition abound-
ed among campesinos, and their mother might suspect Cori was
casting an evil eye on them. She didn't like thinking so defensively.

After all, she would be the children's teacher soon enough. She thrived among children, had the gift to see the world as they saw it. As life opened up to the young ones, it opened up once more to her as well. Go easy, she reminded herself. Good things will come in time. Today is for introductions and orientation.

"Señora," she asked, "Would you sell me some potatoes and onions?"

"No. There are none to sell." the woman replied sharply in Quechua. Then, in careful Spanish, she added, "You should know someone better before you ask to buy their things."

Cori's budding optimism burst in the rebuke. Embarrassed, both for herself and for the woman's rudeness, Cori could only think now that the woman might have little to spare, though a fair crop seemed to be sunning on the hard-packed earth.

"I'm sorry. I'm the new teacher and—"

"Yes, we all know who you are. You'll just bring terrucos or soldiers to Urpimarca. You'll be trouble just like the other."

"Señora!" Cori exclaimed, stunned by the attack. "I'm here for the children, not for politics."

"Either way, we'll suffer."

"Why do you say that? I am only here to help."

The woman studied Cori again, seemed to find her wanting, and looked away without speaking further. Cori had been dismissed. More precisely, she had been made to disappear. Was this an indication of what was to follow, or the groundless whining of one peckish woman? Cori said goodbye as formally as she could, hoping to recapture a sense of cordiality. But she remained invisible as she began to make her way back toward the main street.

She now knew her acceptance into this village would be difficult. Had she worked with another teacher already here, or been received by an outgoing teacher, her introduction might have been smoother. Instead, she found herself dropped into a badly broken situation. Though it had never been directly articulated, she was expected to fix it. A good teacher in the campo was the thread that tied young lives to the greater fabric of the nation. Here the fibers had snapped. She would need, with minutest care, to knit the frayed ends together once again.

For now, Cori decided, she would fend for herself. If she could find enough kindling to make a fire she would boil water to drink and prepare a package of soup. Later in the day she would press Señor Huanta for help in securing supplies.

As she passed the next house heading downhill, a small figure darted from the brush and the little girl from the potato yard stood smiling at her. Cori, who saw in the child's face her first true welcome, smiled back through rising tears. She stepped closer and squatted down to the child's eye level.

"Hello," Cori said in Spanish. "How are you?"

The girl held out her hands, each bearing a potato.

"Oh, thank you," said Cori. "But I can't take these from you."

"Miski," the girl said. "Miski." She balanced both potatoes in one hand and stuck out her empty palm and waited.

"Candy! You want candy?" said Cori, laughing. She dug into her sweater pocket and pulled out four lemon drops. Placing them into the outstretched palm, Cori caressed the little hand with both of her own.

"Share them with your little brother," she said as the girl's face brightened and the smile doubled in size.

"Gracias, Señora."

"Señorita," Cori corrected, taking the potatoes.

"Señorita," said the girl, who turned and skipped around to the back of the house.

By the time Cori got back to the school, it was early afternoon. At the door she felt in the pocket of her slacks for the key. But as she touched the key tip to the lock, the door slid ajar.

She had locked it. She was positive. She listened. All was

quiet inside. With one finger she pushed the door open as quietly as possible and stuck her head inside. She saw no one.

"Hello?" she called, not too loudly.

She entered the school and looked around. The door to her private room was also open. "Hello?" she said again. Nothing. She went to the door of her room and looked in. The door to the patio was open.

Nothing looked amiss in her room. Her bags were where she had left them and the armoire was closed. Señor Huanta was probably in his fields. Who else had a key? Could she have missed Señor Huanta if he had come to the school while she was out? Why would he leave the doors unlocked? Who else had business at the school? She stepped softly to the patio door to close it. Across the courtyard, the kitchen door stood open. She remembered closing it as well.

She tiptoed outside toward the kitchen. Halfway across the patio she stopped. Just beyond the threshold she saw two feet on the floor. Metal clicked against metal. She held her breath.

The feet were stuck in sandals fashioned from tire tread. The soles, showing the bare tread, were turned toward her. Above them protruded ragged and blackened toenails. Cori looked a little closer. Whoever it was lay supine on the kitchen floor.

"Hello?" she said.

The feet slid out of sight, and after some shuffling a tall man appeared in the doorway, holding a wrench.

"Good morning, Señorita Cori," he said.

Above his ojotas, as the campesinos called tire sandals, the man's dusty black pants stopped before his ankles. His belt went too far around and was marred by ill-punched holes to make it fit. The long sleeves of his beige, sweat-stained dress shirt didn't reach his wrists. His facial features were sharp and his black hair tousled. What Cori noted most was his skin, closer in color to hers than that of the campesinos she had met here, and his

95

height, which at about six foot, set him well apart from most sierrans.

"I'm Juan. I got the stove working," he said. "Don Javier told me you were here. He let everyone know."

"They don't seem to care."

"Sí, señorita. They care. They want their children to learn. And I'm going to help you get the school ready. I guarded it all year, even with no students."

"You're the custodian, then?"

He grinned. "I kept thieves from stealing the kerosene." He put the wrench down on the stovetop. "When the teacher needs work done—furniture moved, a door fixed, something carried, painting, anything—Juan does it. When something breaks, Juan fixes it. Nobody pays me. But if you need anything, I will help you."

"Well, thank you. Is the water potable? I could use a little of that."

"It comes from a spring right into the kitchen most of the time. In the dry season it comes from a cistern. But you have to pump it by hand behind this building."

"Do people here boil their water?" she asked.

"Nobody here boils it. We don't get sick on water. But maybe it's not good for a gringa. You can boil your water if you want."

Cori refrained from correcting him. She had never been called a gringa before. In Lima it would have been ludicrous. Here she understood it. For the Quechua, the word for foreigner applied as easily to her as to the blondest, most blue-eyed tourist from the United States, or Gringolandia, as some of her friends liked to call it. The worldview of the campesinos never much advanced beyond the four suyos, the four quarters that defined the Inca empire.

"We gringas in Lima boil it all the time," Cori laughed. "So better safe than sorry, if there is enough kerosene."

"Only because Juan protected it," he said.

"I'm in your debt. Thank you very much. I'm glad I have one protector around here."

"Don't worry. I'll watch out for you."

Cori wasn't sure how she felt about that. Juan seemed harmless enough, but he had just wandered through her bedroom while she wasn't here. Setting some limits soon, and getting some padlocks, might not be a bad idea.

Juan lit the stove and showed her how to work the burners. While he washed his hands in the cold water without soap, Cori dug up a blackened and dented pan. She diced her two potatoes and cooked them with the two packets of soup for their lunch. They sat to eat at the small table in the kitchen. Just as Cori was about to sip her soup to see how hot it was, Juan bowed his head and muttered grace. She set the spoon back into her bowl, folded her hands and let him finish, then crossed herself and added, "Amen."

"Tell me about the last teacher, Juan," Cori said.

"Maldito!" Juan spat. Cori was surprised by the vehemence of his response.

"Why is that question upsetting?" He didn't answer and she had to repeat her question with a light tone of reprimand, as she might a student who didn't want to tell why he hadn't done his homework. "Tell me. Why?"

"He was a communist. What he taught the students was bad. It would only bring trouble here."

"I guess you didn't help him like you are helping me?"

"At first I did, but he thought he knew everything about everything and told me to stay away from the school."

"You've no idea what happened to him?"

He shook his head. "No. Maybe the soldiers took him. It would serve him right."

"That's terrible, Juan," she scolded.

He hung his head and stirred his soup. "Maybe you don't know very well what terrible is," he mumbled.

The school's bathroom did turn out to be a latrine—in a small shed, roofed with the flattened tin of cooking oil cans, in a thicket behind the school. Juan pointed it out to her, and she inspected it while he was off getting rags for dusting. Though the platform seemed solid enough, and was probably better than what many students had at home, Cori shuddered at the idea of using it.

Juan's responsibilities toward the school didn't extend to routine cleaning, so he absented himself when she began to wipe away the last year's worth of neglect. What she would have liked was a fan to expel the dust she was stirring up. The open windows and a slight breeze would have to suffice. Even if she had a fan to assist her, Urpimarca had no electricity. The ministry had somehow neglected to mention that.

Juan returned late that afternoon. He brought a plastic bag with half a dozen potatoes, a couple of onions, a piece of orange squash, fresh cilantro, some dried lentils, and a small, half-empty bottle of cooking oil. When Cori offered to pay him, he refused to take anything.

"I'll find out who has food to sell and get you plenty for the week ahead. I'll go into Ayacucho next week. You can make a list of what you need. Like cooking oil, soap..."

Cori reasoned that when she started getting paid she would have money to buy in greater quantities. She would send a letter into Ayacucho with Juan addressed to the Education Ministry to inquire about supplies for the school year.

"I have to go now," Juan said, "but I will come back tomorrow to check the cistern. The kids would bathe in it if I didn't lock it. These brats always get into things. This place used to be a lot nicer—until everybody ruined everything."

She would have liked to ask what he meant, but didn't want

to keep him. She suspected she'd hear more eventually.

When Juan had gone she made a dinner of lentils with a bit of onion, squash, and cilantro and by the time it was ready night was falling. Cori ate on the patio alone, sitting on a settee. The sun-bleached finish and rain-swollen grain of the bench belied the workmanship in the curve of the armrests and the taper of the legs. Through the open side of the courtyard, the sun's afterglow spread across the sky, and the shadow over the land and the failing penumbral light seemed to stretch before her like a tunnel back to the city.

Could she have wandered down that moonless shaft to Ayacucho, she would not have done so at that moment. She stretched her legs out like a mountain climber who stops for a night's rest along the high slope and considers with a dispassion born of weariness the difficult ascent ahead.

For the next month, she and Juan readied the school, and bit by bit she grew to know the villagers. Some she simply happened upon in the plaza. She made a point of going there as often as possible to meet people. A certain formality prevailed when she saw anyone. Obviously, and appropriately, the women mingled with her much more than the men. Neither the señoras nor señoritas offered real camaraderie. Not all were standoffish, however, and Cori began to note a softening in the demeanor of many that gave her hope.

Occasionally a few women would mill about the wall dividing the plaza, taking in the sun while knitting. Their handiwork was one of two things: baby clothing or sweaters with Andean motifs, mostly llamas, condors, or tumis. When she joined them, some offered nothing more than polite greetings, while others asked about her background and her perception of the village and their way of life. Her readiness to share details of her life went unreciprocated.

"My father was a teacher too," she told one woman who asked about her family. "My mother too, but not for long. She needed to stay home to care for her own children."

"You went to some college?" the woman asked.

"Yes," Cori said. "In Lima."

She knew that none of these women had gone beyond fifth grade. The older they were, the less likely it was that they had any education at all. Her conversations became rote, a pattern repeated with different women at different times, though what information she did succeed in coaxing out of them was about their children, usually no more than she really needed to know.

Of Señor Cespedes, her predecessor, Cori learned little more than what Juan and Señor Huanta had already told her. Some whispered that the soldiers had grabbed him, others that he had joined the rebels, and still others that he was a womanizer and had probably taken off with someone's wife, though no one had any inkling who his paramour might have been. What she did learn she mainly intuited from their tone. They spoke not as gossips or tattletales, but in hushed voices, bearers of secrets, who knew the story no one dared speak aloud. Whatever their opinions of Señor Cespedes, they seemed more afraid of him than worried about him.

The children, on the other hand, found their way to her quite easily. By ones and twos and sometimes threes they would appear at the classroom door watching her or come to the edge of the patio or approach her as she walked around the village. They frequently greeted her with cries of "miski," particularly when she was away from the school. Her supply of lemon drops dwindled. She tried not to give the treat to the same child twice and never gave candy out at the school. After the first week, names began to match little faces. They soon realized repeated appeals for sweets fell on deaf ears. They began to smile and wave with no more expectation than a smile back. They bantered with Cori about the sheep or llamas or alpacas they tended and discussed with gusto the unfolding events of their young lives.

Señor Huanta—everyone in the village called him Don Javier—came only once before school opened, inquiring whether everything was ready. Cori thanked him for sending Juan to help her.

"You owe no gratitude to me for that. He has his own reasons for helping," he said.

"Which are?"

"When you know us better, you'll understand that some things are not so easily explained."

Cori didn't appreciate all the mystery, but she was growing used to it. Life in Urpimarca was a dance in which one learned the moves first without comprehending their meaning. As a teacher, she understood that sometimes form must come before function.

Juan, so much more than Señor Huanta, became her emissary with the village, her mentor and goodwill ambassador, paving her way into the community by his willingness to accept and assist her. At least, so it seemed.

He might appear without warning at any hour of the day, asking what she needed him to do, and was often prescient in his timing. She might stumble upon him tackling a task she hadn't known was required. One morning she woke to find him perched on the roof like a condor, replacing a few broken tiles. He was almost obsequious when approaching her, and he would do forthrightly whatever she asked and then be gone.

A couple days before school was scheduled to open, Cori joined a few women gathered near the wall. Her greeting was answered amiably and they shifted to make room for her, turning in a way that made a half circle of four rather than a knot of three.

"All is set for school?" asked a heavy woman named Silda, who had three school-age children.

"As much as can be expected. We're very short of supplies—paper, notebooks, and pencils." Cori knew as she spoke that it was a complaint any public school teacher in the country could make.

"It's always that way," affirmed a thinner woman whose name Cori couldn't remember. Her companions nodded.

"Juan brought a mule-load of food from the ministry the other day, so the children will have something to eat at school," Cori told the mothers. "He has been a great help in getting the school ready."

The señoras snickered.

"Sí. Juan is always a big help. Always taking care of things," Silda said, as the others giggled a little more.

"El hacendadito," the third señora said, making them all laugh loudly and shake their heads in agreement.

Cori couldn't help but laugh a little too, by infection as much as anything else. The little hacendado? The little lord of the manor?

"Why do you call him that?" she asked, keeping up a merry tone, honestly wanting in on the joke as much as to understand what they meant about Juan.

"Ah, he's always taking care of things, as if it all were still part of the hacienda," Silda said.

"He's waiting for the return of the old days," said the thin one, provoking a new round of mirth. The señoras still tittered as they got up to return to their homes. Cori stayed for a little while on the plaza, alone.

"The little lord," she said to herself, remembering again the pale complexion that had surprised her at their first meeting when he frightened her at the school, arriving unannounced, acting very much as if he owned the place.

9

S teven watched as Angel Yupanqui strode across the main square of Ayacucho, the Plaza de Huamanga. Shoeshine boys, who dressed in torn T-shirts and tire-sole sandals and prowled the city center in little packs looking for mischief, gave ground around him. A young couple sitting on a bench glanced his way and did a double take. Two soldiers on the corner in black turtleneck sweaters, green fatigues, and high-laced boots repositioned the straps of the assault rifles hanging over their shoulders as he passed. Tall and thin, wearing a dark, brimmed hat over shoulder-length hair, Angel marched from the basilica, along the sidewalk that cut the square into triangles of grass and shrubbery and across the stone-paved street to the archway shading the priest from the morning sun.

"Hola, Padre!" he exclaimed, a wide smile spreading below his high-ridged nose and dark brown eyes. He gripped Steven's hand firmly for a second before embracing him in a hard hug, patting the back of Steven's tan flannel shirt with both his hands.

"How are you, Angel?" Steven asked, stepping back out of the enveloping arms.

"I am wonderful. How else would I be?" Angel said, spreading his hands out, palms up, and shrugging his shoulders. "The Creator has given us this very beautiful day and we are going out to be with the people—my people. You cannot ask for more than that to be happy,"

"Maybe something to eat before we start out?" Steven suggested.

"Nah. Let's go," Angel said. "We can get something in Huamanguilla."

Father Jaime had put Steven in touch with Angel, as promised, and the two hit it off immediately. During the seven weeks Steven had spent in Ayacucho getting acclimated and practicing his Spanish, he had met several times with Angel, a man with boundless reserves of energy that kept him bouncing between the city and the countryside.

The two men walked under the vaulted colonnade to the corner, stepped out into the open street and turned up Jirón Callao. The red Volkswagen bug that Steven had bought the week before was parked half a block up. They squeezed in and Steven drove to the corner, negotiated a right turn onto Jirón Garcilazo de la Vega, went two blocks and turned right again onto Avenida Mariscal Cáceres. They drove through the city, past the Temple of Magdalena to the little plaza and the wide street where the buses laid over for the trip north to Huancayo and from there on to Lima.

"This is where we would take a minibus to go out to the communities if we did not have your car," Angel said. "Then we would have to walk much of the way to Urpimarca."

"We may be walking yet if those miserable llama trails you call roads finally destroy this poor old thing. I can't believe it still runs," Steven said.

"Don't worry. People keep things running here. They have no choice. They can't buy anything new. They are so, so, so poor. Padre, we are riding like kings. Still, we will make an offering to the apus so the roads are nice to your little car."

"Angel, I'm a Catholic priest. I'm not supposed to be making offerings to the spirits of these hills. A catechist like you shouldn't be performing pagan rituals either."

"Ayiiiii," whined Angel. "What have you done? Now you have offended the apus! You are going to have to buy a lot of food and chicha for the offering. You want a landslide to knock this little car off the side of a mountain? Then I will have to carry your body back up the ravine to the road so you can have a Christian burial."

"And you?" Steven said. "You would survive being tossed into the abyss?"

"Of course!" Angel leered smugly into Steven's face. "I'm not the one showing disrespect."

"So I get to choose whether to die a Christian martyr, slain by an angry animist spirit, or to be defrocked for idolatry."

"Now you are beginning to understand this place," Angel said, settling back into his seat. "But don't worry. God never changes his mind. You are a priest forever."

"You are too much, Angel."

"Ya, sure. Don't worry though. I will make the offering on your behalf, Padre. You're not ready yet. You're still green."

You really are too much, Steven thought. He enjoyed the banter with his new friend and was awed by the insight he provided into the Quechua culture. What perplexed Steven was the fuzziness of the people's beliefs, the paradoxical embrace of both Christianity's bright message of hope and the ancient superstitions of such mountain haunts, of vengeful, covetous, and capricious deities of old Peru. He joked about it with Angel, but felt conflicted. That the common people might cling to traditional beliefs, especially where priests were few, was one thing. That his catechist, a trusted instructor of the faithful, embraced both worlds was another. He was unprepared for this in coming to what he naively thought of as a Catholic country.

It had certainly looked Catholic enough during Holy Week processions the week before, from Jesus riding a donkey through throngs of admirers on Palm Sunday to the dawn Resurrection

105

on Easter morning. Father Jaime had been right. Steven had never seen such a display of religious pageantry or such passion, nor had he ever seen such a shocking enactment of the scourging of Jesus, and only the New Year's apagón, the blackout in Lima with the blazing torsos of dummies, had compared to Good Friday night in Ayacucho. This city went black voluntarily, except for the light of thousands of candles, a vigil for the executed Savior and his heartbroken mother. The weeping, though, the real honest-to-goodness sobbing of the women, and some men, campesino and city folk alike, for the two-thousand-year-old death of Jesus, is what had moved him most.

"Angel, last week, all those people crying real tears, as if Jesus actually just died," Steven said. "That kind of Christian devotion doesn't square with all this apu stuff."

Twisting in his seat, Angel stared at the priest for so long that Steven tossed several glances at his passenger, awaiting a reply before one came.

"Green. So green," Angel said, shaking his head side to side ever so slightly. "To them—to us—he did just die. And he did just rise again. That's as simple as the Eucharist at Sunday Mass. Am I going to have to teach you everything?"

For the next hour they drove on a road that was sometimes asphalt, sometimes packed dirt and gravel. They passed through a rocky terrain with fields of prickly pear cactus and around a treeless hill where Angel said there was a cave that had been inhabited by people more than 10,000 years ago.

"We have been here a long, long time, my friend," Angel said. "I will show it to you one day."

"I'd like that. Though I suspect you'll claim Adam and Eve among those cavemen."

"Maybe. Who knows? Wouldn't that upset your Eurocentric theology?"

"Maybe. But Jesus was born in Bethlehem in Judea—on the other side of the world."

"Yes, but some people believe Jesus also visited the Native Americans." Another big smile crossed Angel's face. "This is part of America and I am Indian. So maybe he got here before you missionaries, and everything just got interpreted differently in the Andes."

Steven pondered that for a bit.

"I think I'm going to end up giving catechism classes out here myself," he said, more to himself than to Angel.

At the market town of Huamanguilla, they parked in front of a white-washed building along the central plaza. "Desayuno," Spanish for breakfast, was written in white chalk on a black-board hung on a nail outside the open door. Steven and Angel went in and sat down on metal chairs with vinyl seats at a square Formica table.

When the señora running the restaurant came over, she and Angel exchanged greetings. He held up two fingers. "Dos desa-yunos, por favor," he said. Turning to Steven, he added, "I hope you're hungry."

"I've only had a cup of coffee."

As they waited, three adolescent girls entered, dressed in matching gray skirts and sweaters with white blouses under-neath. They bought candy from a wooden display case at the counter and dallied outside the door with school books cradled in their arms and unwrapped the sweets.

The señora brought platters of fried eggs and potatoes, rice, fresh bread, and a hot drink of cocoa thickened with oatmeal. A truck with a long, empty bed pulled into the plaza. Two men got out of the truck, stretched, and came in, nodding affably to Steven and Angel as they sat down at another table. They wore work boots and caps with logos for two different companies. They were heavy men with broad shoulders and pronounced paunches. The woman held up one forefinger without asking what they wanted and went back into the kitchen. A short time later she brought them plates with the same breakfast Angel had ordered.

While they attacked their meals, the truckers chatted with the señora. They told her they were headed down the mountains, into the jungle to pick up lumber. From their conversation Steven learned they would haul potatoes during the harvest in a few weeks.

"Might be a small crop," one said.

"It was very wet," the señora agreed.

"That isn't the worst of the problems," the other trucker added. "The bigger growers are getting scared of the guerrillas. They have been warned not to produce for sale. Not to be tools of the forces of oppression," he said.

"Yeah, for big capitalistas like me," the señora scoffed. "How am I going to get potatoes to make good breakfasts for big guys like you?"

"Good question," one said. "They haven't been bothering campesinos who sell off only a few quintals of potatoes, but I can't drive my truck all over hell picking up a few sacks here and a few there. But now, some of them have been told to harvest just what they can eat themselves this year. The rest, let it rot in the ground."

"They haven't bothered the lumbermen yet," the other trucker said, "but I heard they're warning the coca growers that the drug men have to start paying a tax to support the people's war."

The señora returned to the kitchen shaking her head and wringing her hands, uttering "acha chau," an interjection Steven had heard the locals mutter when worried.

"What are they trying to do? Starve the cities?" Steven asked Angel in a low voice.

"I think so. They are communists. They want to stop the

capitalist commercialization of the fruits of the workers' labor, no? I'm not concerned. I have enough for my family."

"This isn't an issue for you?" Steven asked, nonplussed by Angel's apparent lack of empathy for those who might go hungry.

"All this is not a problem for me, because I don't commercialize what Pachamama gives to me," Angel said. "Yes, I have some extra and I trade it or sell for a few other things we need. But you are thinking like a gringo, Padre. Your goal is always to produce more than is sufficient. I prefer to stay in harmony with this world, with my pacha. I don't know how I would do that if I coveted big fields to grow hectares of potatoes for those men over there to come and haul to people I don't know in the cities."

While most campesinos were subsistence farmers like Angel, many brought produce into the markets to sell. Steven was sure, too, that those with extra fields would grow crops just for sale. How else were they going to get any money at all? The days of total self-sufficiency were pretty much past, even in the Andes. He had heard of villages high in the mountains where people's food came strictly from the crops they grew and the animals they raised, and they even spun wool and made their own clothing. Yet, it was only a matter of time before life in those harsh places changed too.

"Angel, are you saying you think it's wrong for people to use the land to produce for market, to grow plants and raise livestock for food, fibers, and leather? I mean, people in the cities depend on the campo for what no one can produce in the cities."

"Of course, those in the city need what people in the countryside produce," Angel said. "But the campesinos don't really need anything from the city. Not really. They have been here without these cities for thousands of years, like I told you. They are part of the cycle of nature. Yes, as a practical matter the campo feeds the cities. But for me, for my own spirit, I choose as much as possible not to buy into that."

When the truckers had finished their breakfasts, one took some money to the counter and the señora came out of the kitchen and counted it out.

"Ya, ya, gracias," she said. "Bring me back some fruit from the jungle."

"Before you run out of potatoes?" the man who paid asked, laughing. "See you in a few days, señora capitalista."

Passing Steven and Angel, he stopped. "Excuse me," he said, looking at Steven, "but if I were a foreigner, I would be very careful around here. Those Marxists bastards are crazy."

Not until they had left Huamanguilla and had driven for half an hour on the dirt road to Urpimarca did Steven, ruminating over what the trucker had said to him, ask Angel about it.

"How dangerous is it getting out here?"

Angel let out a long whistled breath before speaking.

"I don't know. For you it's more dangerous than for me. The last teacher in Urpimarca was criollo. He disappeared. The police and army said maybe he ran off to join the guerrillas. He talked a lot about injustice and of the discrepancy between rich and poor in my country. Though, maybe he was more a communist to the army than in the eyes of the guerrillas themselves."

"You think the army disappeared him?"

"Maybe. It happens. Maybe he just ran away. He left one weekend and didn't return. Everyone said they knew nothing. The Education Ministry says he just abandoned his job. He wasn't from the sierra. Probably they didn't even know where to look for him. Still, I don't think he just ran off."

They rode again in silence as Steven pondered this mystery. He wasn't worried for his own safety, not yet anyway. But disappearances were a terrifying tactic, if that's what this was.

And what else would it be?

As they crested a slight hill, they found themselves approaching a roadblock in front of a small adobe house. Standing in the middle of the road was a soldier with one hand raised. Several others were pointing rifles in their direction.

"An army patrol," Angel said. "We'll need to show our documents."

Stopping the car, Steven rolled down his window.

"Documents," the solder said, gesturing with his hand for them to be given to him. Steven and Angel complied.

"I'm a priest," Steven said.

A lieutenant, embroidered bars sewn to the epaulets of his black sweater, came up behind the soldier, took the documents, studied them, and stepped to the window.

"Good morning, Padre." He looked into the car, frowned over his thick mustache, and nodded officiously at Angel, who returned the greeting.

"Where are you going?" the lieutenant demanded.

"We're going to Urpimarca," Steven said.

"To say a Mass or something?"

"Yes."

"And him?" the lieutenant asked, motioning toward Angel with his chin.

"He is my catechist, Lieutenant. My guide. My interpreter with the Quechua."

"This area is under military control, Padre, so anyone who comes in here is my business."

"I understand," said Steven. His attention was drawn to the side of the house, where an old campesino couple appeared to be arguing with the soldiers, one of whom was holding a young man by the shirt collar. The lieutenant followed Steven's eyes.

"What's going on there?" Steven asked.

"A military matter, Padre," he said, handing back their documents. "You two can proceed." He waved them on with a sweep of his hand, like a transit cop directing traffic.

Angel exchanged words with a soldier who had come up on his side of the car, all spoken too quickly for Steven to catch.

As the lieutenant headed back toward the campesinos, Steven set the VW into neutral and pulled the handbrake. He opened the door and stepped out, placing one foot on the ground, the other on the running board, and called over the hood to the officer.

"Perhaps we can be of some help," Steven offered.

The lieutenant spun around and put up his open palm. "Please, do not get out of the vehicle! Move on. This is not a religious matter."

Angel got out of his side of the car. "Lieutenant, this couple is old—"

"Get back in the car!" the officer yelled, stepping forward and resting one hand on his pistol stock. Several soldiers aimed their rifles at Angel.

Steven and Angel ducked back into the car. "Vamos," Angel said. "We had better move. They might detain us. They don't need a reason. They do whatever they want."

"What is going on?"

"In a minute. Drive. Vámonos!"

Three or four soldiers stepped aside for the car as it rolled by under the gaze of the officer. Past the soldiers Steven got a clear view of an adobe wall forming the side of a corral.

Viva Presidente Gonzalo! Steven read to himself. *Viva El Maoismo! PCP.*

Steven recognized the nom de guerre of the Shining Path's founder, who had once taught at the university in Ayacucho. He remembered that PCP stood for the terrorist group's official name, el Partido Comunista del Perú.

When the soldiers were behind them, Angel slapped his leg in anger.

"I know these folks. Humberto and Dosia Pachari. The young man is their son, Manuel. The soldiers say he is not registered for military service."

"What will they do?"

"Maybe take him to the barracks and induct him. That is how it is done here. But it might be worse for him because of the slogans on the wall. They say maybe he is a terrorist, and maybe they should just shoot him and be done with it."

"Why would a terrorist put graffiti on his own house?"

"He wouldn't. They know that. They are harassing the old couple. The soldiers are threatening the son to find out who's painting slogans. These people are way too old to work the land themselves. They need their son. Either way things turn out, they lose. They can remain silent and starve. Or, if they know anything and betray the guerrillas, they'll be killed anyway."

10

Juan appeared at the school early as Cori was on the patio boiling water for coffee. He carried a sack of ollucos, explaining that Señora Yupanqui, who often helped with school lunch, had sent them and would make olluquito con charqui, a dish in which the little tubers were shredded and cooked with tiny pieces of dried lamb or alpaca meat. Cori's mother used to make it in Lima when ollucos were in season.

Cori considered how much she already had grown to count on Juan. He made regular trips to Ayacucho and brought back whatever she needed. Since hearing the señoras' insinuation that Juan was the son of someone from the hacienda—and seeing how they snickered about him—Cori had taken pity on him. It was as if he were one of her eager older students. She felt a level of comfort around him that she did not feel with others in the village. By rights such a relationship should have developed with the women who helped her with lunch at school. Yet as much more cordial as these women had become, there remained a reticence on their part, an absence of openness about their lives that stifled any impulse toward intimacy Cori might have felt. Yet she and Juan hadn't ever really conversed. They merely chatted about what she needed him to do or the things she needed him to fetch. She never asked how much education he had, but she suspected it wasn't much.

Juan dumped the bag of ollucos onto a bright spot on the

edge of the patio, where they would sweeten in the sun. He laid the burlap on the ground and arranged the ollucos evenly across the sack.

"Would you like some coffee?" Cori asked.

"Yes, please," he said, accepting the invitation eagerly.

She poured a cup for each of them. Juan accepted his cup and settled on his haunches near the ollucos. Cori pulled a little stool out of the kitchen and set it across from him, so that her face warmed in the sun along with the tubers.

"Juan, I know next to nothing about you," she said. "Do you have any children?"

"No children, señorita. I never married."

"Do you live with family?"

"Sí, with my mother and her husband and some of their children, but I have a room apart from them. And you, Profesora?"

"No, me neither. I was going to marry someone, but I broke it off before I came here. I wasn't ready."

"Is it true what they say, that in Lima they don't allow trial marriage, servinakuy?"

"Oh, no, not in Lima. Most parents would be scandalized if their children did that. I guess it's not like that here."

"It's always been our way."

"But never yours?"

Juan looked directly at her, something he rarely did.

"I would not marry someone from this village. I could not. I wouldn't want any of them."

"Seriously? Juan, that's—"

"I'm not interested in any of them, and none have been respectful to me. You know what they call me? 'Hacendadito.'" He said it mockingly, enunciating each syllable separately. "You've heard that?"

Cori nodded.

"When I was little, I knew nothing about that. I was close

115

to my mother and her mother but not to my father. He was very distant, and when he was in the house my mother would push me away from her and pay more attention to her husband and my little brothers and sisters. I would cry to my grandmother, and she would say all the children must have their turn. My father's parents paid very little attention to me. Also, since I am the oldest, I had lots of chores and little time for school. My mother would argue with my father that I should go to school and sometimes I did, but then my father—or the man I thought was my father—insisted that he needed help at home. I was big and strong and I liked to work and be outdoors and with the animals. My father was often impatient with me, but I wanted to be there, working with him anyway."

"Was he mean?" Cori asked.

"I don't know. He didn't hit me or yell, but sometimes it was like I was hired labor, an empleado, not a son. That's how I felt, but I didn't think those things then. That was just how it was."

"So, if you didn't go to school very much, how did you learn Spanish? Most of the children here don't understand it very well. That's why I'm working so much on my Quechua."

"My mother taught us," Juan said. "She had worked in the manor when she was young, cooking and cleaning, and she lived in Ayacucho for a while after I was born. She would speak to us in Spanish, but only when her husband wasn't around, because he didn't understand it very well. She said we would always be ignorant if we couldn't speak Spanish. My mistake was thinking that was enough. I could do all the work on the land, could count and read a little, and could speak Spanish. I thought I knew all I needed. But I only knew all I needed to be a farmer."

"You can always learn more, Juan. I can help you."

Juan stared down at the ollucos and didn't answer. Cori waited, but decided not to press when she got no further response. She finished her coffee and started to get up when he spoke again.

116

"Do you know why the big house is still there? Why no one is allowed to live in it or use it for the school or a clinic?"

"No. No one talks of it."

"It's because one of the generals, or I think maybe he was only a colonel, said he loved that house and wanted to come back and live in it someday. He told the villagers the land was theirs but not to ruin the house or take it apart for their own houses. For a while, they say, he would come and check on it and even stayed there for a few days now and then. But then there was the second coup, and I think this colonel maybe wasn't on the winning side. He never came back.

"After that, the house was abandoned. Some of us children began to explore the building. That's how I learned who my real father was. Some of us got into the house. It still had a few of the old furnishings. We were playing, and since I was the tallest I thought I should be the hacendado. But not everyone agreed, and we began to argue. Some of the men heard us and came to find out what we were doing and scolded us for being there. One of the other boys complained that I was insisting on being the lord of the manor and that it wasn't fair.

"The men laughed and one of them sneered at me, 'You little bastard, you think because you were sired by the hacendado you have some special claim? He never even recognized you. You're lucky to have a stepfather who doesn't put you out in the streets like a mongrel.'"

Juan sat up straight and breathed in deeply, still keeping his gaze down. Had she been sitting closer to him, Cori might have reached out to touch his arm to comfort him.

"One of the others told the man to shut up and then told us all to go home. None of the boys said anything just then. They were as surprised as I was. I ran home and confronted my mother. She cried and admitted it was true. She wouldn't tell me much more, except to say she had been very young and I should just forget it because my true family was the one that raised me and my father—her husband—loved me like his own son.

"But you can't forget something like that. The other boys didn't forget either. That's when the kids started calling me 'Hacendadito.' After that I didn't play with the others anymore. Instead, when no one was looking, I would sneak back into the big house and wander the rooms. I would look for things that belonged to the hacendado. I wanted to find a picture, or an address of where my real father lived. I never did."

"How old were you when all this happened?"

"Maybe eleven. People in the village had always known. Then everything became clear to me. The way I was always treated. And I could see I wasn't wanted by anyone but my mother and grandmother—just tolerated by my stepfather and his own children.

"I'm not embarrassed about who my true father is," Juan continued, looking at her directly again. "That's what I learned. That was my education. That is who I am. Unfortunately for me, the generals drove my father off before he had a chance to recognize me as his own. But someday he will. I believe that. I know it."

Children's voices interrupted them as a group of young students came running around the corner and called out to Cori.

"We'll talk again, Juan. Okay?"

Juan's gaze fell as he muttered, "Fine."

He slipped away as the children surrounded Cori, greeting her with brief hugs.

"Vamos," she said to them. "Let's go ring the bell."

11

At the head of a ravine the land opened up, and stretching before Steven and Angel lay a gently rising slope of green pastures, beyond which the hills rose purple in the distance. The road they had walked doubled around to the right and wound past earth-brown houses before ending at a plaza. To the men's left Angel pointed out a cluster of buildings farther up the hill.

"I'm up there. Just over this hill," he said.

The men cut through the fields to Angel's house, which was tucked into a grove of small trees. Angel hailed the house but no one answered.

"The children will be in school," he said. "Their mama might be there as well. Sometimes she helps to make lunch. Or she might be giving the neighbor a hand with chores."

He unlocked a padlock, flung the hasp and opened a wooden door into the kitchen. In one corner of the dirt-floored room a mud fireplace glowed with embers still warm in the grate. Angel stirred the coals and added wood.

"Some coffee?"

"Sure," Steven said, watching from the doorway as Angel tended the fire. When the wood was blazing Steven went back to the yard and sat on an upright log cut for a stool.

Angel brought two coffees in thin enameled cups, one white and the other dark blue with white specks. Both were hot and he carried Steven's carefully by the rim so he could offer him the cool handle.

"The chapel is behind the manor house, on the other side of the village. In the old days the priest would say Mass in that little chapel," Angel said. He took a seat on a log stool matching the one Steven sat on and sipped from his steaming cup. "The hacendado and his family would sit inside. We peons gathered around outside to listen. On the rare day that a priest comes now, Mass is celebrated on the plaza, or in the school if it is raining.

"Padre Jaime used to visit a lot when I was little. He would come on horseback, maybe once a month, and it was worth his effort, because the hacendado took good care of him. Afterward, he still came for a few years, but it got harder on him as he got older. When he stopped coming it made some people angry. Not the older ones, though. They were sad but they understood. I was a young man and angry because I thought I had a vocation to be a priest."

Steven recalled Father Jaime's nostalgia for the rigors of his early mountain ministry, for a way of life reaching seamlessly back to the days of the Spanish colonies. Unjust though it may have been, it was a time when to be a priest was simpler and the established order was rarely questioned. Some priests preferred the campo and some the cathedral. It didn't matter. All was God's work. No one measured how much time one spent with either the rich or the poor. The radicalism of Jesus was understood to have been directed against the Pharisees and the Roman legions. He was a threat to that imperial hierarchy, not to any social injustice of the present day. There had been none of these ideas about social gospel.

Father Jaime might never have expressed it quite like that, but Steven often sensed in their conversations a longing for those simpler times. The older missionaries in Peru had lived through a social revolution, an upheaval perhaps much akin to the Reconstruction of the American South after the Civil War, and Steven found himself musing at times about what the country must have been like before the coups, a time so vastly different, but so recently past that its footprints remained everywhere one looked.

Steven felt the older priests and their view of the world mirrored his own understanding as a young man contemplating the priesthood, coming from a family that had bristled at the sheer audacity of saying Mass in the vernacular, replacing the Latin that had served so well for so long. His father grumbled every Sunday about the Mass being in English, especially the Consecration: *Hoc est enim corpus meum*. It was a magical incantation, invoking a miraculous transformation wrought by the priest through the power of God. It belonged in the sacred ancient tongue, his father believed.

Steven saw more than a little of his father in the old priest, who knew Quechua and brought the church, and his vision of it, to the campo, to this conservative, traditional people who, he said, did not need to have the notion of mystery explained. They knew instinctively that the form of something is not its essence, that manifestations are mere mantles covering, even cloaking, an unalterable core.

"You say you always knew you wanted be a priest," Angel said. "You must have decided when you were still just a little boy. But now you are a grown man. A man's desires are not those of a little boy."

"That's true. I had a girlfriend as a teenager. And a lot of my friends left the seminary because their vocation to be husbands and fathers was greater than their calling to the priesthood. I know it sounds simplistic, and really it's much more difficult personally, but in the end that's what it amounts to. You choose. You get used to being celibate. Your community is your family. It's not just about refraining from sex."

"Sometimes it is not about refraining from sex at all, Padre," Angel laughed. "Priests here have their amigas, their lady friends. At least some do. I don't recall that the old priest had anyone, but who knows, perhaps when he was younger. Or maybe he kept his chica tucked away in some other village."

"The alleged dalliances of priests have always been greatly exaggerated," Steven said. "But it wouldn't be unheard of. Not everyone can live up to the rigors of this vocation. It's a difficult problem."

"Yes," Angel said more seriously. "It's always a problem if someone cannot live up to his responsibility. You know Cesar Vallejo, the poet? His grandfathers on both sides were priests. Amazing, no? Or maybe not amazing at all. Maybe the children of priests get special blessings."

"I don't know. I can't speak for those Peruvian priests—"

"Foreign priests, too, Padre. Those Spaniards, ayiii!"

"Okay. I can't speak for other priests. Just for myself. I didn't come to Peru looking for a woman. I came to serve my church, to be a missionary and minister to people like the ones in this village who haven't seen a priest in a long time. No more."

Angel nodded. "And that should be enough. These folks will be happy to see you. Some go all the way to Huamanguilla, even Ayacucho, to have their children baptized."

A bell rang in the village. Steven looked in that direction. He could see nothing of the village for the hill behind them and the trees sheltering Angel's house.

"The school bell," Angel said. "Probably they will be having lunch or have just finished. Vamos. I will show you the village."

Urpimarca was the most isolated village Steven had visited. Others had been more distant from Ayacucho but could at least be reached by car. Topography, Angel explained, dictated a round-about approach to Urpimarca. A traveler taking a direct line from Ayacucho would have to cross two swift rivers and scale cliffs fit only for condors. The road ending at the village had never been more than a narrow access to the hacienda. Urpimarca was knit into the fabric of the countryside like thousands of villages across the campo.

As they walked, Angel acted as tour guide. He pointed out a stone hut, the ruins of an Inca granary, now used as a home by a neighbor too lazy to build a warmer, drier adobe house. The mayor's house was the village's newest and nicest. A little farther on, a low hut, pushed into the ground, with a rock lintel in the middle of a solid wall, was the first structure of the old hacienda, dating to colonial times.

"The school," he said, pointing from the outside, since class was in session, "was built by the military when they drove off the hacendado. It replaced the stable, which had lots of fine horses. The corral became the plaza. There were steps here," he said, indicating a rise at the end of the plaza, past the school. "The hacienda house is beyond those trees, right at the top of the knoll. Before it got so overgrown it used to stand out above pasture and cropland."

He jerked his head toward the knoll. "Now we must introduce you to Our Lord of the Hacienda."

They skirted the school and crossed the hillside, coming out into an open pasture. The vista that now unfolded before him justified the whole journey for Steven.

"That is Ayacucho," Angel said. He pointed to a mere blur in the distance.

They turned and walked toward the chapel, just up the hillside behind them. It was no larger than the poorer houses in the village. The interior was simple, with plaster walls and just four rows of benches before a plain altar. It was cool and damp and dark, with most light coming from the open door at their backs and two small windows. Above the altar hung an unremarkable painting from the Cuzco School of colonial art, a crucified Christ with unmistakable mestizo features, painted in the somber tones of that style.

"The people here are very devoted to this image: Our Lord of the Hacienda," Angel said as he extended his hand toward the painting.

Steven had expected something grander. The painting measured only about three by four feet, in a cheap-looking gilded frame, probably just gold paint on plaster.

"You are disappointed," Angel said.

"Not really. What could be more appropriate in this place than a simple Jesus in a humble frame?"

"Exactly."

"Has anyone claimed any miracles here lately?" Steven asked.

Angel stepped back and looked appraisingly at the priest without answering at first.

"Padre," Angel said, "for a man of God you seem to believe in very little."

"Wait a minute, Angel. Even the bishops, the church, would want to make sure something was real before sanctioning it as worthy of devotion. I'm just asking."

"What church, Padre? This chapel is the only church in Urpimarca. There is no other. You don't need to judge. You need to listen and receive."

Angel turned and left the chapel. Steven followed.

"So we can expect you back here in June for Corpus Christi?" Angel asked outside.

"Of course you can," Steven replied, relieved. "If I do nothing else while I'm here, I'll join your procession."

They headed down a long path beside the chapel that narrowed into trees and brush. It merged with another path that ran along the side of a ravine, and Angel led Steven to the right for a bit. Then he tapped the priest's arm and pointed.

"La casona," he said.

There, through a break in the trees, was the decaying mansion, its façade a faded gray that might once have been white, its roof tiles as blackened as those on any hovel in the surrounding hills. Except for the distinctly Spanish style of the architecture, the building reminded Steven of a haunted house.

"Abandoned?"

"Almost. The bastard keeps it from falling down."

"Who?" Steven said, stopping in his tracks.

"The illegitimate son of the old hacendado. Unrecognized. Except by the gossips in the village," Angel scoffed.

"Ah," Steven said, looking over the building. "So an unrecognized son lives in the old house and harbors pretensions to his father's throne."

"Oh, no," Angel laughed. "He doesn't dare to live there. The people would never allow it. They would burn this house to the ground first."

"But they let him maintain it, such as it is?"

"If he wants to waste his time, that's his problem, they figure. He does no harm."

They took a few steps forward for a better view.

"When the generals broke up the haciendas," Angel explained, "some landowners supported them and kept a little of their property. Others, who called the generals communists or sent their wealth out of the country or had been very abusive to the campesinos, lost it all. Don Sebastian was not mean. The campesinos liked him and he liked them. He worked hard and was not afraid to dirty his hands. But in politics he was a rightist. They say his wife's family had a home in Lima and that he now owns a hardware store somewhere in that city. He sells nails."

"And the son?"

"The hacendado and his wife took their children with them. The señorita who bore his illegitimate son was young and worked in the big house. The hacendado refused to admit he was the father, probably because of his wife. She disapproved of his friendliness with us cholos. Acknowledging the son would have caused a scandal. The girl and the baby went to Ayacucho, and she washed laundry. After the reforms she came back. Her father was sick and needed her. She married a campesino from the village. Now this son of the hacendado is a peon who dreams of someday dining by candlelight in the mansion. His pretensions annoy people. They think he is a fool."

"And his mother?"

"She's a good woman, a little embarrassed by her son's delusions. She taught her children Spanish and Quechua, and she and the campesino worked to make sure their boys studied. She sent them to secondary school in Huamanguilla. One even went to the University of Huamanga in Ayacucho."

"The hacendado's son?"

"No, no, no. He is a dreamer. A pretender. The educated son sees no shame in being a campesino. He's proud of it. He aspires to a higher calling than hacendado. You have been to his house, and he is telling you this story."

Children were playing in the plaza when Angel and Steven returned. Steven spotted Cori immediately, wearing blue jeans and sitting on the concrete wall watching the students and talking with a couple of the smaller ones milling around her. Angel suddenly clasped his arm around Steven's shoulder and pulled him near.

"There is the teacher you have been dying to see again," he said in a conspiratorial voice.

Steven shook himself free, showing his annoyance. Cori might hear them.

"Hola, teacher," Angel called.

Cori looked up. "Hola," she said, standing up to greet him. "Angel, no?"

"Sí, and I bring you your old friend, Padre Esteban," Angel said.

As Steven approached Cori, he debated how to greet her. Peruvians generally exchanged a kiss on the cheek, even among casual acquaintances. He was preparing himself for that when she extended her hand.

"Hola, Padre," she said with a bit of surprise in her voice. "I never really believed I would see you here."

"I told you I would remember Urpimarca. Then I met Angel. He is my connection."

"Ah, sí?" She looked at Angel in mock suspicion, tilting her head to one side, a gesture Steven would remember later.

"Sí!" Angel said. "And this priest is a doubter of miracles. But see, Padre. God is already working his little miracles."

"Granted," Steven said. "I wouldn't be a priest if I didn't see God's hand behind coincidence."

"Well, welcome to Urpimarca, Padre," Cori said.

"Padrecito, Padrecito," called a small woman, using the diminutive for "Father" in Spanish. She wore a brown hat with an upturned brim, two long slender braids, and a wide blue skirt. She took Steven's hand and shook it in both of hers. Smiling, she said something to him in Quechua.

Steven glanced to Angel, who translated.

"She is inviting you to lunch. She just heard you were here and is concerned I'm not taking very good care of you."

"That's very nice. But just me?"

Angel spoke to the woman, who grabbed the priest's arm and turned from the plaza with him in tow.

"She says we all should come," Angel said.

"Oh, no," Cori said, waving her index finger. "You'll have to excuse me. I have had lunch and now have class."

"We'll talk later," Steven said as he and Angel followed the señora.

"Please," Cori said. "Provecho."

Assured that Steven would come to lunch, the woman dropped his arm and hurried a little ahead, muttering and shooing children out of her way as she went.

"Señora Eulalia is one of my colleagues," Angel said. "She helps manage whatever ceremonies are connected with our little chapel, which might as well be a cathedral in her eyes. I think she is bothered that I didn't take you straight to her. If you are not careful she'll overwhelm you."

"I know her well."

"Really? How?"

"I mean I have met señoras like her before. Like God's grace, they are everywhere, even back in the States. We call them the ladies of the altar guild. And we never stand between them and where they are going."

"You do know her well."

Steven and Angel sat at a small table in the rear yard of one of the houses near the plaza as Señora Eulalia ordered about a younger woman helping her cook. A boy came into the yard carrying a plastic pitcher, from which the señora poured two large glasses of chicha. As he sipped the chicha, Steven became aware of other people near the house, and occasionally would catch a glimpse of a woman or child peeking around the building to watch them.

"This is puka picante," Angel said when the señora placed a plate of something bright red in front of them. "It's potatoes in a sauce made from beets. That meat on the side you know is cuy."

Cuy was the Andean word for guinea pig, which they also called "Indian rabbit." Steven had never eaten rabbit, so he couldn't compare the two. Still, he was beginning to get the knack of picking out the tiny morsels of meat. Being served cuy was considered an honor, which he presumed was intended for him, not Angel.

Steven thanked Señora Eulalia elaborately in Spanish, while Angel echoed his words in Quechua. She apparently understood Steven's intentions if not his words, because she began responding to him before the catechist finished translating. Steven likewise understood the woman without an interpreter, intuiting what she was saying, so Angel stopped. With her beaming face and the gesture of her hand, she was obviously saying, "Fine. Fine. Now eat."

"So if puka means red in your language, we are eating red hot or spicy red," Steven said.

"Yes. You are learning," Angel said.

"I'm gaining a lot of confidence in my Spanish, but I'm still struggling with Quechua. I'd love to learn it eventually, though I don't see how it would serve me back in the States."

"So don't go back to the States. Stay here. We need you more."

"But I would always remain an outsider here in some ways."

"The old priests didn't think so. They came here. They made lives here. They died here."

Just the thought of never moving back home made Steven anxious. A feeling of loneliness swept over him as he imagined what it would be like to live the rest of his life in a culture so foreign to him. He already had a taste of living in a strange place with no one he could truly relate to. He sorely missed shared histories, unspoken understandings, common values, just being around people without worrying whether an ignorant slip in his Spanish might give offense.

"What are you thinking?" Angel asked.

"Making a new life means letting go of an old one. That's what immigrants have always done, gone someplace new, lived and died there. Like my grandfather did when he left Ireland. He went to the United States to keep from starving. There was never enough money to go back. It was like he died to those he left behind, and they to him."

"Like Peruvians who go to your country now."

"My grandfather once told me that when his generation left Ireland years ago, their goodbye party was even called a wake. That's how final it was."

A silence passed between them. Steven imagined sad farewells, the parting embrace between a son and his mother in a humble doorway in County Clare. He could not help thinking of the way a priest is asked to leave behind family, friends, even parishioners, and he felt a familiar twinge of fear at being set adrift himself.

"You told me earlier," he said, "that I was here to listen and to receive. Now you are saying I should stay because people need me. Which is it?"

"There is no contradiction. It's like a great love that needs a lover to receive it. The spirit here needs a receiver. The people here need real ministry, not just some gringo coming here to deliver the sacraments like so much cargo. We've had enough of ecclesiastical imperialism. If you are going to minister here, you have to listen first. Pachamama and the apus might have some things to teach you, too, Padre."

"In the seminary they called that kind of thinking syncretism—the mingling of aboriginal beliefs with biblical truth. The folklore here is fascinating, don't get me wrong, but when you try to blend it with church teachings I'm not sure you get anything coherent."

"No? Maybe you get somehow that much closer to touching the face of God."

"I wouldn't go that far, Angel. Some call it the syncretistic heresy."

"You haven't been here long enough to understand, Padre." Angel slammed the table with the palm of his hand, startling

130

Steven. "God and the devil dwelt here long before any priest of Rome. And that's why you need to stay here. We'll make a campesino out of you yet. We'll also find you a lovely señorita with the deepest brown eyes and cascading dark hair so you forget the death of your old life and finally find God where he is lurking. And maybe the devil too."

Angel laughed and Steven once more shook his head in exasperation at the puckish lecture of his new friend, this farmer turned universalist. The commotion brought the señora running. Steven wolfed down a few forkfuls of food to reassure her.

For the rest of the afternoon Steven was swept up in doing what a good priest does: meeting villagers, visiting the sick, ministering to children who would have been better served by a doctor than a priest. Angel took him on a tour through fields of potatoes and quinoa, past pens squirming with cuys. They snacked on raw honey, broken from combs hanging from rude sticks in hives fashioned from wooden crates, the sweet liquor running to their elbows as fat bees thrummed in ambling flight all around them.

Early evening found them closer to Angel's house than to the plaza. Steven had not made it back to the school as he had hoped. He had thought of the teacher often that afternoon. He still wanted to speak with her. To hear one voice unfiltered by Angel's translation of Quechua. Now it was late, and Angel's wife, Dolores, was preparing dinner. He would make time tomorrow for the teacher, even if he had to extend his stay in Urpimarca.

This time Steven sat in the kitchen on a low dirt wall opposite the fireplace. The wall divided the kitchen from three pens, each about a yard wide and twice as long, with cuys running around inside them. Overhead, pans hung on a tangle of branches embedded in the mud ceiling. There was no passage between the kitchen and the house. One had to go outside again to get into the main building. Steven had not been invited there.

Sitting with Steven were Angel's three children, the oldest a girl about ten, a boy a couple of years younger, and another girl about five. The boy sat to his left, the youngest to his right, and the oldest beyond her. As they ate the soup Señora Dolores had prepared, Angel spoke to the children, occasionally translating for Steven, but mostly directing his attention to the youngsters. Sometimes they would direct a remark in Spanish to the priest or even their father.

"They speak Spanish and Quechua," Steven observed.

"We speak Quechua at home. Dolores knows very little Spanish. But outside the house I speak to them mostly in Spanish."

When they were finished eating and it was growing darker outside the kitchen than within, the children clamored for a story. Angel agreed and proceeded in Spanish.

"Once upon a time on a hacienda in the district of Huamanguilla not so far from here lived three brothers, whose parents labored for the hacendado. One day while playing, the boys grew tired of being soldiers with stick muskets and fell to the ground to rest under a tree. The oldest brother said he had heard of some Inca ruins where some mummies were hidden. He suggested they go to the ruins and uncover the mummies and take the gold that was surely buried with them. The idea excited the two older boys, but the youngest began to cry, saying he was afraid of the dead.

"The second brother told him not to worry. 'Old leathered skin and dry bones cannot hurt you. We will be rich and our parents will be happy not to have to work anymore!'

"With much reassuring and cajoling they convinced the younger boy, but as the hour was getting late, they decided to go the next day. They set out early for the ruins, which lay on a hill far from the village. By midday they had arrived at the ruins and quickly discovered a half-dozen mummies in a partially concealed cave. They ripped open the mummy bundles, tearing into the ancient and fragile weavings in which the deceased were wrapped, and found each handsomely decorated in gold jewelry, from fine earrings to broad breastplates. Loading their bags with the treasure, they left the remains of the ancient ones scattered about the cave in a litter of torn mantas and broken pottery. They hurried to get home with their heavy loads before dark.

"Along the way the oldest brother began to feel sick, with a severe headache and fierce stomach pains. It must be the dust from those old shrouds, the second brother said, encouraging him to push on and get home for some hot food. By the time they got to the house the oldest brother couldn't walk without help. The second brother collected the three sacks of treasure to hide and told the youngest to get his brother inside. Great was the surprise of the parents when their first-born stumbled into the house and fell dead in his mother's arms."

Angel's youngest girl, Bethany, pressed closer to Steven, scrunching her shoulders and drawing her arms to her chest.

"The parents were inconsolable. The second son was sent to his uncle's house to tell them the boy had died and ask his aunt to come help prepare the body. Meanwhile, the father and the youngest boy made a fire outside to let the village know of a death in the house so they might come to the wake. The youngest brother wanted to tell his parents what they had found that day, but he feared that now was not the time to talk to them of riches. One of their precious sons had been taken from them.

"Worse still was their anguish in the morning, after an all-night vigil around the body, when their second son became ill. They watched helplessly as he writhed with pain and fever, and sent for the curandera to cure the boy. The healer arrived too late.

"As friends and relatives prepared two caskets for the departed youths, the desperate mother clung to her baby, her last remaining offspring, fearing that whatever mysterious malady had befallen her other two sons would claim the last as well. And no sooner were the two elder boys arranged in their caskets when the youngest began to complain of a terrible headache and crippling stomach cramps.

"The young boy knew now that he too would die of whatever had stricken his brothers. Seeing his mother and father kneeling beside him weeping and praying, he decided to tell them of the hidden sacks of gold to comfort them later when they were alone. As the boy began to speak, all those gathered at the house listened, including the curandera, a wise old woman who all along suspected the retribution of some angry spirit in the boys' illness.

"When the young boy finished, the curandera was furious. She told him and his parents that profaning the tombs of the ancients had caused the sickness and deaths.

"'Unless you return what you stole and ask forgiveness, you too will die,' she warned.

"At the supplications of the boy and his parents, the curandera accompanied them and the mourners to the cave, where they gave back the gold and tried as best they could to repair the mummy bundles and restore everything as it had been. Then, on their knees, they begged forgiveness, while a local Quechua priest, the paqo, made an offering of coca leaves, chicha, and tobacco and blessed the sacred site anew. Only then, when all this was done, did the youngest boy begin to recover, and he promised never again to rob graves and vowed to keep the memory of the ancient ancestors sacred."

Everyone was quiet as the story ended. Embers in the fireplace pulsed and cracked in the dim lamplight. The sounds of insects and night birds filtered through the open door. Angel was a marvelous storyteller. Steven wondered whether the tale had been intended more for him than for the children.

The elder daughter, Elsa, spoke first.

"Papa, what happened to the two older brothers? Did they stay dead?"

"My children, when someone is gone, it is forever in this life. We must wait to see them again in heaven."

The boy, Manco, spoke.

"But they could come back for All Souls?"

"Sí, my son, all the departed come back to visit for All Souls. But not as the living. They are truly with us as spirits and we know they are here. These poor parents paid a very dear price for the vandalism of their sons."

Bethany, the youngest, spoke. "Maybe they could keep a little gold because they did not get all their children back."

Angel suppressed a smile and shook his head.

"Ah, my little negotiator. No matter how poor we are, we must never disturb the graves of our ancestors. As the story shows, bad things will happen if you do. But more importantly, my children, what is sacred must be respected always. That is what you must remember. What is sacred must always be kept so."

Señora Dolores took a kettle resting near the embers and poured each of them, including Steven, a cup of warm liquid that smelled like dirty socks.

"Valeriana," Angel said. "It will help everyone rest and sleep well."

A little later Angel and his son walked Steven back toward the plaza to a small one-room house where Señora Eulalia had prepared a bed for him. They followed the road, feeling their way in the darkness without a flashlight or lantern. Tenuous fingers of light leaked from under doorways and a dim glow shone from the tiny windows of a few houses.

They spoke little and concentrated on their steps for the ten minutes it took to walk down the hill to the house. They halted on the road in front of it. The house sat just before the plaza and slightly down the slope toward the ravine.

"It's a beautiful night," Steven said.

Overhead the Milky Way made a bright river of light across the wide ecliptic. Back in New England one rarely saw the starry galaxy. Scanning the moonless sky, Steven found the Southern Cross. He wondered how the Quechua saw the stars, and how the patterns they divined there were reflected in their native mythology. He decided it was too late to start that conversation. He didn't want to keep Manco up any longer than they already had.

From where he stood Steven could see the school. Through the bank of empty window frames a thin line of light outlined the shape of a door inside. The teacher was still there. She was either working late or lived in the same building. He considered stopping in to say good night, but quickly realized how that might seem.

Angel asked if he had a candle and matches in his room.

"I'm sure. Don't worry," he said. "I think I will stay outside for a while and enjoy the stars. Maybe I'll walk around a bit, even at the risk of breaking a leg in some rut."

Angel muttered something, looked at his son, and then stared at Steven as if debating whether to speak.

"Is that not okay?" Steven asked.

The catechist shifted uneasily, and then said something in Quechua to Manco, who moved up the road, a little out of earshot.

"Padre, you should not wander around alone at night. It's dangerous."

"I've got good night vision, Angel. There's starlight. Don't worry. I'll be careful."

"No, it's not that. People here are superstitious. You're a foreigner, a gringo, pale and thin. You'll scare people. They might mistake you for something very bad."

136

"Like what?"

"Padre, right now I don't want to mention these things by name. You can never tell who listens in the dark. Only know this: Evil wanders this land at night."

12

In the morning, Steven celebrated Mass on the plaza. Señora Eulalia draped a striped hand-woven cloth over a small table and set a pair of candles on it. School benches were brought out. He gave a very short homily on the Gospel reading of Jesus being rejected in his hometown and that "a prophet is not without honor except in his own country and in his own house." Perhaps they would connect that with him; but this wasn't his own country and he certainly was honored here. Or, more accurately, his priesthood was honored.

Yet Steven sensed that his words evaporated before reaching the hundred or so villagers who attended the Mass. It wasn't just that most didn't understand Spanish. Some probably understood his straightforward schoolbook Spanish better than they would have the more rapid-fire language of a native speaker. But even Angel's translation into Quechua seemed to provoke little engagement, and no response. What he said wasn't important to them. Only the ritual mattered. Ritual seemed to be the point of much of what he was witnessing at Mass and in the daily lives of the people he was meeting.

As in the few other villages where he had said Mass, parallel liturgies seemed to go on during the service, like miniature sub-Masses among the worshipers. Someone would spread out a manta, much like the weaving on the altar, and would lay out simple possessions: ceramics, brushes, jewelry, photos, and herbs.

The sound of Quechua would move like a crosscurrent during the Mass as people prayed in their own language and in their own time.

Briefly, only briefly, Steven considered suspending the Mass and admonishing them for inattention and for bringing their Andean rituals directly into the liturgy. But if his own catechist embraced native beliefs and rituals, what could he expect of the others? He had not completely resolved his own incertitude about the Catholicism of his youth and that of his ministry, let alone tackle the dichotomy of Christian orthodoxy and Andean animism. Recalling that Angel chided him to listen and receive, Steven continued without pause, thinking as he did that perhaps a hodge-podge of fervently held beliefs was better than the hypocrisy of weekly attendance at Mass as an inconvenient duty. Nonetheless, few took communion, and the teacher was among the abstainers.

After Mass he worked his way over to Cori. It seemed that every child in the village flooded in between them. He was sure he made a pathetic sight wading through a sea of children and responding "Sí, sí" to their greetings and blessing them perfunctorily.

"Miski means sweets," Cori said to Steven when he finally made it to the school veranda. "They want candy, and you keep telling them 'Yes'!"

"Oh, right! I keep forgetting that's what they always want. I never have any either. I can't see winning their hearts, or their souls, by rotting their teeth."

"Well, they don't get very much candy here. That costs money and most of these people don't have it. You have to connect with children on a level that means something to them."

"That's where you're an expert, señorita."

"Cori," she said with a smile, cocking her head a little to the side, much as she had the day before.

"Okay, Cori. Well, I'm afraid I fell flat trying to reach my flock."

She laughed.

"Honored neither at home nor abroad, Padrecito? Many people came today, and that's a good thing."

"Ah, well, the famous Padre Esteban really brings out the multitudes."

"Well then, feed us," she said. "I haven't had breakfast."

"Oops. I haven't gotten that part down yet."

"Ay, Padrecito, you will have to work on your miracles," she said, leaning closer to him and patting his forearm, as one might humor a child. "I guess I will have to do that part. Would you like coffee and tamales?"

"Coffee? That would be great. I always get served herbal teas, like coca tea, or these oatmeal and quinoa drinks."

"I have to have coffee in the morning. I told the children class would start late because of Mass. We have a few minutes yet, so I can invite you to the school patio."

Cori led the way along the portico toward the end of the plaza, where they could get to the courtyard without going through the school. Señora Eulalia intercepted them. Steven already knew she would expect him to have breakfast at her home, and he was right. Like a shadow, Angel slipped in among them to translate.

"I'm going to talk to the teacher and have some coffee. I'll see you afterward," Steven said. He feared the señora would be offended, but she waved him on in a way that told him that was fine. Angel suggested that they meet up later at Señora Eulalia's house.

The patio was cool, shaded by the building and trees, while sunlight played on the bordering foliage, dappling the leaves that stirred in a slight breeze. The morning sun shone brilliantly on the distant fields. Cori offered Steven a seat on a settee in front of a low table with a single wooden chair to the side.

"This is my dining room, living room, and office," she said before turning to enter a small kitchen. She returned, put cups on the table, and sat in the chair, smoothing her lap as if straightening an apron or skirt instead of the jeans she was wearing.

"So, let's see. You are my first guest besides the women who help with lunch and the children who are here during the week. And you are the only American I have ever sat down with, and twice now. I feel honored."

"So you are honored because I'm an American, not because I am a priest."

"Oh, if it's reverence you want, I'll send you back to Señora Eulalia!"

"No, no, no. I'm happy right where I am."

Her face softened. "Me too," she said. "Thank you for coming." She accompanied that with the tilt of her head again and he saw what he liked about it, and perhaps subconsciously why she did it. It was a lovely angle to an already pretty face.

"But why?" She buoyed up. "Tell me what are you doing in Peru? Even more, what are you doing in these mountains?"

"I came here to minister to the people."

"Of course, but aren't you afraid of the terrorists?"

The very bluntness of her question struck him as refreshing. Yet it drew out of him something that had gnawed at him since reading of the growing violence in the newspapers back at the monastery, and now more acutely since he and Angel had run into the soldiers: a sense of dread that went far beyond the vague apprehension he had when he first arrived.

"You think it's getting too dangerous for me here?"

"Perhaps, yes."

"I've just arrived. But the situation does seem to be deteriorating quickly."

She stood up and went to the kitchen, returning with a red plastic thermos of hot water and a small jar of black liquid, "coffee essence" they called it, strongly brewed and concentrated. She poured a little into each cup and added water. Then she brought another couple of jars, one with sugar and the other with powdered milk, and a yellow plastic bag with tamales wrapped in corn husks.

"And you?" Steven asked. "Aren't you afraid of the guerrillas?"

"How political is teaching the alphabet and numbers and wiping runny noses?"

"Unless part of the people's revolution involves seeding the Marxist dialectic in the youngest of minds."

"Ay, Padre, there isn't much dialectic going on with first graders. Here all is memorization. That's our pedagogy. I know what you're saying, but I haven't been bothered, not a bit, since I have been here."

"But what about your predecessor? What happened to him?"

The look that swept across Cori's face reminded Steven of the day they had talked in the restaurant after the robbery on the bus, when all the passengers were in a state of relieved shock.

"I'm not a detective, Padre."

"Steven."

"Padrecito Esteban then. But it seems to me if something bad had happened to him, wouldn't someone know? No one saw anything. Nothing. He didn't turn up hurt or dead."

She dropped her voice to a whisper and leaned over the table.

"So maybe he did run off with a woman, like some people say." She sat back again in her chair. "It's sad that he would abandon these children, if that's what happened. That's a problem for me, trying to catch them up on studies after such an interruption. Even if he joined the rebels, he's gone, and we have to continue with running an education system in this poor country. You can't just abandon everyone because a few people agitate for violence."

"If it is just a few," Steven said.

"This is Latin America, after all. We're more used to changes in political fortune than you Americans are. I've lived through two coups already."

Cori smiled and, stretching her arm across the table, tapped his knee, another of her spontaneous gestures of familiarity that he found himself liking a lot. "Don't worry about me. I'll be fine," she said. "What we have to do is watch out for you."

"What can I do but trust in God? That's my calling. Let's hope and pray that God—and the terrorists—let both of us do our work without interference," he said.

"Amen. Now, is your coffee okay? Have a tamale. One of the señoras in the village made them."

Steven sat back and cradled his cup, sipping the black coffee. He had gotten used to it without milk since arriving in Peru and finding that most milk in the city was canned or powdered. He liked neither.

"The coffee is fine."

"I'm sorry I have no fresh milk, even here in the country-side. The señoras who have cows near the village don't trust me enough yet to sell it to me. They're afraid I'll scald it, which they believe will cause their cows' udders to dry up."

"We wouldn't want that."

"No," she said. "I would love some for café au lait but I don't want to be accused of drying up all the cows in the village. When I go into Ayacucho, I will have some there."

"When are you going? I'm returning to Ayacucho today. If you don't mind the hour walk to my car, I can give you a ride."

"Oh, I can't walk as fast as you. I would hold you up, so don't worry about me."

"No, it would be great to have company, and there's no hurry. I will be leaving late this afternoon. I'll come back for you before I go."

"Thank you. I would like that."

He stood. "Thanks for the coffee."

"You haven't eaten anything."

"Excuse me, please. We both know I'll never escape Señora Eulalia without eating something when I get back there."

"You are a quick learner, Padre Esteban."

Cori went to the classroom, where a few students were drawing pictures on the blackboard. One boy, her best artist, was drawing a condor in flight, and she praised his work, ignoring the cartoonish head on an otherwise masterful work for an eight-year-old. She complimented a little girl on her sketch of a house and a large family of stick campesinos, with the women in hats and very wide skirts. The child corrected her. It was the school. Here's the teacher and these are the pupils! Another boy had drawn a man—she assumed a soldier—shooting a rifle toward the other two drawings. Cori couldn't tell if he was directing his fire at the condor or the people.

As usual she broke the students into groups based on age and ability. Technically her class went to fifth grade, although some of the older students should have been two or three grades higher by now. She only managed it all by identifying "helpers," the three brightest older students—all girls—who assisted the youngest pupils while she was working with the older ones. Today she did her best to give each group enough work to keep them busy and content. The youngest drew pictures of items beginning with the letter C, and the oldest group wrote a summary of a story she had read the day before.

As she walked around the room, looking over shoulders at her students' progress, Cori imagined continuing her conversation with Steven, talking about her life in the village and the travails of getting here, telling this gringo about what must be a million things he didn't know about Peru, filling in his meager knowledge of the food or holiday customs or history, maybe explaining a joke, and hearing about his America. She would have to correct him on that, of course, since everyone born in the western hemisphere is an American. Tell me about the United States, she would ask him. The people couldn't be as shallow as Hollywood shows them to be. And why is it you young foreign priests don't wear collars like the older ones? She tried to picture Steven in a clerical collar and couldn't.

How desperate she was for a deeper conversation than she could manage with the pidgin Spanish spoken in Urpimarca. Steven spoke the language very well for a foreigner. He could converse with her. They might talk about something besides these few square miles of village, and the children, and the weather, and the crops, which is what seemed to dominate every adult conversation she had since coming to Urpimarca. No one except Juan ever sought her out, unless it was to talk about their children.

Cori lapsed once more into an imaginary conversation with Steven. What did he think of the people he had met in the sierra? How were they different, how the same, from the people he knew? Maybe they would have time in Ayacucho for another coffee, in one of the little restaurants on the plaza. She could suggest it when he let her off there. She saw them strolling to a café, and then, intruding into her daydream, a pack of street children, the ubiquitous shoeshine boys, approached. When he didn't pay them any mind, engrossed as he was in their conversation, they began to mock her, as a group of boys had done once after she had started university. That had been the first time she could remember being humiliated about her uneven gait. No one at home ever mentioned it, and her classmates had long ago grown used to it. She had never been taunted about it before that day. Steven seemed to be oblivious to it.

Would he do what Wachi had done once in university as they had walked from class? Just to think about it brought an ache to her chest, and tears welled in her eyes. Passing a group of girls her age, she had lowered her head. Wachi stopped. He turned her toward him, and with just the tips of his fingers under her chin had lifted her head. "I don't want to ever see you hang your head like that again. You are as good—and as beautiful—as any of those chicas," he said. She marked that moment as the beginning of her love for him.

A tear splattered on Cori's hand, and she looked up. One of her young helpers was watching her. Cori smiled to ease the concern on the child's face and went over to look at her work, pulling a tissue from her pocket and dabbing her eyes as she went.

13

The idea of going into the city excited Cori. She felt like a young child for whom any outing is an excursion. She was sorely disappointed. When Steven came for her, she found another passenger would be going with them, and the walk to the car, which took more than an hour, was filled chatting with Lucero, a young woman from the village. Angel had asked Steven to give her a ride.

Lucero didn't look like a typical campesina. Except for the brightly striped manta slung across her back, she was dressed like any college student in Lima, in a sky blue T-shirt, jeans, and sneakers. Her hair was slightly longer than Cori's and a few shades lighter than most other women of the village, except at the part. She was about Cori's age and spoke Spanish, which she had learned as a young teenager working as a maid for a family in Ayacucho. She said she was going there now to sell a few things, without saying what, to help support herself, her mother, and a younger sister.

With Lucero in the car, the banter Cori and Steven had exchanged spontaneously in the morning was impossible. Cori, trying to shake off disappointment and stir some conversation among the three, turned sideways in the passenger seat so she could see Lucero, who sat in back.

"It was nice to have a Mass in the village this morning, no?" she said to Lucero.

147

"I didn't go," Lucero said. "I don't believe in the church."

The abruptness of Lucero's challenge to her host took Cori aback, and she felt embarrassed for blundering into the topic.

"Ah, mind if I ask why, out of curiosity?" Steven asked.

Lucero leaned forward and a bit toward Cori, so that she was looking at Steven's face and he could see hers with a glance to his right. "Why I don't believe in the church? Are you serious, Padre?"

Cori felt her face flush with more embarrassment at the aggressiveness in the other woman's voice. She wished Lucero would drop the subject.

"Or if you'd rather, tell me what you do believe," Steven said.

Lucero sat up straighter, without going all the way back in her seat.

"I don't believe in a rich church and a poor people. The people live in dirt houses and the churches have altars of gold. The priests and nuns and bishops are all fat—well, okay, not you, Padre—but most are. For them the church is just a place to live easy and eat well. The church is just another part of the exploitation of the poor."

She sat back now, crossed her arms and pursed her lower lip, all the while continuing to look at Steven, seeming not to even notice Cori. It was as if she had stated an obvious and unalterable truth and had closed the issue.

"Some of that's true, Lucero. Many within the church would agree with you. Jesus was a carpenter who preached to the poor, the sick, the outcast, the dispossessed, and the oppressed. Too many have forgotten that."

"Exactly," Lucero said.

"It's why I came here to work."

"Padre, that's very good. At least you come out to the campo. Many people are happy to see you. I just don't know what good it serves."

Cori hadn't wanted to butt in, yet couldn't help herself.

"It serves a lot of good for those who might want to go," she said, a little louder than she intended. The other woman just stared at her.

"Lucero," Steven said, "many people get comfort and strength from going to Mass and from receiving the sacraments. They need to be able to connect with God through some physical outward expression, to be able to come together with others in community. That's what the church is, the community of believers. That's what I think the problem is here."

"That is not the problem here!" Lucero said quickly and emphatically. "The problem here is that the church is an instrument of exploitation." She leaned forward, her arms crossed even more tightly over her chest.

"Okay, you have no faith in the church. Even some of us in religious life sometimes have our doubts. But what do you believe in? Do you believe in God?"

Leaning back in her seat again, Lucero appeared to think about this a bit. She shrugged. "Maybe," she said, turning her head and shoulders haughtily right and then left. "And maybe not."

Cori turned back to the front of the car, embarrassed again and getting angry at her compatriot's sassiness. Steven ought to be annoyed, but he didn't appear to be so.

"I know many people in the sierra prefer their traditional beliefs—Pachamama, the apus," he said.

"The campesinos are superstitious," Lucero said.

"That's different," the priest responded gently. "Superstition and faith aren't the same thing, even if sometimes they appear to be. And I don't mean that faith is what I believe and superstitions are the things I don't. You still haven't told me what you do believe, and I'm genuinely interested."

"I don't see much difference," she said. "People believe a lot of things that don't make their lives any easier."

"Lucero, faith gives meaning to our lives and helps us get through the most difficult times. It is something people need, all of us."

"Well, I do not. I only know I have to help feed my family. You're very nice, Padre, but the church has never done anything to help the poor. Maybe in your country, I don't know, but here in the mountains of Peru, nothing. That is all."

Steven seemed about to say more, then hesitated and took Lucero's cue that the discussion was over. He remained silent for longer than would have been warranted even if he were thinking of a response. Cori was relieved. Trying to think of something less charged to talk about, she remembered having provoked this discussion and decided to keep quiet. Eventually, Steven spoke, a note of curiosity in his voice signaling a shift in direction.

"What is it that people fear at night here?"

The two women eyed him with equally puzzled looks.

"I wanted to take a walk last night, and Angel didn't want me to. He said it was dangerous, something about evil."

The women looked at each other, as if trying to decide which one he was addressing. Lucero scooted forward to where her head was close to theirs.

"El pistaco?" she asked.

Cori winced, and shook her hand like she was shaking something off.

"I don't know. I'm asking," Steven said.

"That is real superstition," Cori said.

Lucero said nothing. A minute passed, with Steven swiveling his head back and forth between looking at the road and at the two women, waiting for them to elaborate.

"Well? What is it?" he said.

Cori motioned to Lucero with an open-handed gesture to signal that she had the floor.

"That is what people might think you were if you wandered alone at night in the campo," she said. "The pistaco is like a person or a beast, that is evil, sort of a vampire. Except he sucks people's fat instead of their blood. And then they waste away and die."

"Yes," said Cori, "even in Lima everyone knows what a pistaco is. Children are always afraid of such monsters. I suppose here people really believe in them."

"Do you?" Steven asked Lucero.

They looked at each other in the rearview mirror.

"I have seen people grow thin and shrivel up until they are just bones, and then die. And nobody knows why. What else could do that?"

"Probably any number of diseases—cancer, for sure."

Lucero appeared to think about this, and then said dubiously, "Maybe."

"Anyway," Steven said after a pause, "that's what people might think I was if I just took a stroll to enjoy the stars and fresh air?"

Cori put her hand on the priest's shoulder and leaned closer to him.

"Or, that maybe one might get you," she said in a drawn out whisper.

"Ha! Right!" he said loudly. Steven and Cori laughed and exchanged a glance.

Lucero remained silent. She spoke only when the chuckling had stopped.

"Because some say a pistaco is pale, like a gringo."

Steven and Cori exchanged glances but neither spoke right away.

"So do people talk of pistacos only when there's a gringo around?" Steven asked.

"No, but they think it's like one. Sometimes people say it lives in caves in the mountains and will take people there and keep them and feed off them."

"Maybe that's what happened to the last teacher," Steven said.

Neither woman responded to his attempt at humor.

"Sorry," he said.

Cori sat back in her seat. She gazed out the window and pictured her little room at the school and being alone there at night.

They passed an improvised fence, fashioned from spindly branches and small tree trunks. A house loomed beside the road. Steven slowed the car. He scanned the house and craned his head as they passed, looking toward the rear of the building. He stopped the car and backed up to the closed door.

"I should stop and see these people here for a second, but I don't see anyone. Please wait here."

He knocked at the door. "Señor Pachari?" he called. "Señora Dosia?"

His knocks on the door went unanswered. He got back in the car and they were on their way again.

"The slogans have been painted over," he said. "The soldiers were here yesterday and now the Senderista slogans are gone from the wall and there's no one home."

"The soldiers paint those over, or sometimes make the people do it," Lucero said. "Anyway, the people might be in the field or have gone to market."

"Yes, but I understand the guerrillas kill people for erasing their slogans."

"Not if the soldiers did it."

"I pray to the God you don't believe in that you're right, Lucero."

In Huamanguilla Steven stopped the car at the plaza.

"I need to see a colleague here for a bit," he said. "A bus is idling across the square if you are in a hurry."

"I do need to get into town," Lucero said.

"I don't mind waiting," Cori said.

Lucero got out of the car, thanked Steven for the ride, and said goodbye.

"I need to check in with an American woman who works for a nonprofit group here," Steven said. "I shouldn't be long."

At the words "American woman" Cori wished she had gone with Lucero.

On a side street a few blocks from the plaza, Steven stopped the car in front of a two-story building made of cement block on the first floor and adobe on the second. A heavy cement staircase with no railing cut diagonally across the front of the structure to a door in the middle of the second floor. Steven got out, bounded up the stairs, and knocked. Cori sat in the car, unsure if she should get out. The door opened and Steven signaled for Cori to come up.

The woman he introduced as Judy was as tall as Steven and had straight red hair down to the middle of her back. She wore jeans and a beige T-shirt under a light blue work shirt with rolled-up sleeves, worn unbuttoned like a jacket. She welcomed them into an apartment that was more comfortably furnished than any of the houses Cori had seen in the past two months. The visitors sat on a couch with a dull white muslin cover, while Judy sat in a cushioned chair across a coffee table made of a rough wooden box with a thick piece of glass on top. A thin, striped cotton rug covered the floorboards between the couch and chair. Ceramics in the red, black, white, and clay colors of the Quinua potters adorned the corners of the room, and Andean weavings hung on the walls.

Steven explained to Cori that Judy worked with a nonprofit organization that promoted nutrition, healthcare, and adult education across the region.

"Right now I'm working with some women's groups, mostly mothers of small children," Judy said. "So it's pretty much early childhood development, just making sure the kids get adequate nutrition and see a doctor or nurse occasionally."

"Cori is the teacher in Urpimarca, Angel's pueblo, and I'm giving her a ride into Ayacucho."

"Then you understand what we're all about. I'm trying to help their mothers take better care of them so they're strong and healthy when you get them," Judy said.

"Gracias. Do you know Urpimarca?"

"I've been there. We at ACEP gave a workshop there last year."

Cori wondered what "ACEP" was, and, as if reading her mind, Judy told her.

"ACEP is the Andean Cooperative Education Project. It's the non-governmental organization I work with."

"You know there've been some problems," Judy said to Steven.

"No," Steven said, drawing the word out.

"Some of our instructors were warned the other day that we aren't welcome here anymore. The source of our funding is an issue."

"Warned by?"

"The Senderistas, the Shining Path."

"Wow. What does the warning mean? Do you have to leave?"

"I'm not sure. I know our work just got very dangerous."

The silence that followed made Cori uneasy. She shared their apprehension, yet as a Peruvian she felt guilty by association. The danger came from her countrymen. Right now she identified with her two new friends, but wondered if they instinctively mistrusted her, if only a little bit way down deep. She asked for the bathroom and Judy directed her to the back of the apartment.

Cori took her time refreshing herself. She admired the warmth of Judy's simple bathroom, the walls of which were painted a deep golden yellow, arresting the starkness of the white porcelain toilet and sink and glossy white tiles on the floor and the shower. Even in here Judy had put handicrafts. Hanging on the wall was a pair of chuspas, the little woven bags campesinos used to carry small belongings, especially the coca leaves they so often chewed. Framed black and white postcards of old photos of Cuzco, the still beautiful city from which the Incas had ruled, also decorated the walls. Cori was just getting used to the primitiveness of accommodations in Urpimarca. How this attention to order and aesthetics clashed with the bare functionalism of the campo. She marveled at how this American woman with her stunning blue eyes and red mane had imposed beauty even in her toilet. Cori returned to the others.

Steven was still sitting on the couch. Judy was pouring beer from a tall brown bottle into three small glasses.

"I'm assuming you'll drink some beer," Judy said. "It's the only thing I have right now, unless you'd like some water."

"A little beer would be great," Cori said. She sat on the sofa, as far from Steven as she could.

Judy put a cassette tape into a small stereo and the sound of Andean huayno music filled the room with the high-pitched wailing of a woman singing in Quechua.

"Why don't you come into Ayacucho with us?" Steven said to Judy.

"Thanks. It's tempting, but I have a workshop tomorrow and Sunday. They moved it into Huamanguilla, so I don't have to go out to the campo." She looked at Cori and asked, "When are you coming back from town? Maybe you'd like to see some of our work."

"That would be great. If I can, I will. I'll be back on Sunday."

"If it gets late and you need a place to stay, I have an extra room. It's little, but you are welcome to it if you need it."

"Gracias. Perhaps I will."

After finishing their beers, Steven and Cori went on to Ayacucho, where she asked him to drop her off at the hostel she had stayed in when she arrived from Lima.

Parked on the cobbled street in front of the hostel, where the lights of the lobby outshone the waning brightness of the sky, they sat in the Volkswagen trading comments about things that didn't matter to either of them.

"The evening has turned chilly."

"I hope it doesn't rain tomorrow."

"I need to get an umbrella."

"The hostel looks comfortable."

"It is, for the price."

Cori felt hungry and wanted to suggest they get dinner, but wasn't sure how to ask. She remembered celestial blue eyes, radiant red hair, and long, straight legs. She didn't need to eat. And she felt tired, very tired. An awkward silence welled up between them. She watched a couple of adolescent girls still in their white blouses and gray school jumpers scuffle up the street. A man in a black jacket that was too shiny to be real leather came out of the lobby and lit a cigarette. He scanned the street in an obvious effort not to stare into the car.

"I guess I better go on up and rest," she said. She leaned forward to kiss his cheek goodbye, as any Peruvian woman would a friend of either gender, and then checked herself. He caught her hesitation and he balked too. Their cheeks brushed. Cori grabbed her bag from the back seat and slipped out of the car without looking directly at him again.

"Ciao," she said and slammed the door. She glimpsed a weak wave of his hand as she turned and stepped toward the glow of the foyer.

14

O n his way to the plaza in Ayacucho the next morning, Steven walked passed the Templo de la Buena Muerte— Temple of the Good Death—a small, white, colonial-era church with two square towers and a great arch over the main door. He recalled a prayer from the novena to St. Anne, the mother of Mary, that his family used to pray when he was a child. "Holy Mary and good St. Anne, show yourselves to be mothers indeed by obtaining for me the grace of a good death." The good death referred to was the peaceful passing of the Blessed Mother, and sometimes of St. Joseph as well. The very thought of a gentle ending here only gave greater weight to his fear of meeting the opposite. As much as Steven liked to think his faith exempted him from such fears, it wasn't true. The prospects for a good death here in Peru were growing unlikely.

He planned to get his shoes shined and chat with the street kids who would swarm him as soon as he stepped into the square. He patted the pocket where he kept his wallet with identification and some extra money, a reflex that caused him a twinge of guilt.

The boys mobbed him before he could even cross the street from the cathedral to the park and find a bench to sit on. He usually selected one of the smaller boys to shine his shoes, knowing how the bigger ones would try to squeeze the little ones out of the way most of the time. He would end up buying gum and lemon drops and postcards from the boys selling those and made a point of unloading as much change and small bills as he could. A few kids would stay and talk and ask him to teach them bits of English. They would, if encouraged, tell him their stories. They fell into two groups: orphans on the one hand, and those who might as well have been on the other. They all seemed to live on the street. Those still with parents worked to help support their families. Some were told not to come home at night unless they had made their daily quota.

He selected a boy in a dark green T-shirt, with short, badly cut hair, and a runny nose. The choice earned the kid a cuff on the back of the head from another boy, the tallest of the knot of about six that surrounded him. Steven's reprimand of the aggressor brought a complaint that the shiner had cleaned the padre's shoes just the other day in the morning before he had left with the tall Indian.

Business was bad or this kid was very observant.

"You guys keeping track of me?" he asked.

"Oh no, Padre," several said, but not the one who complained.

"You're getting to be a regular, Padre," that boy said. "You have to be fair."

"Okay." He rubbed the shoe shiner's bristled head with his knuckles. "Next time it's someone else's turn. What's your name again?"

"Antonio," the little one said, just as a loud popping from beyond the far end of the plaza shattered the quiet morning. The boys' heads turned in unison. At first Steven thought it was fireworks and expected to see a procession round the corner and march into the square.

"They're shooting," yelled the big boy, who, with a couple of the others, moved behind Steven and made ready to run.

The sounds, which had been rapid yet distinguishable cracks at first, merged into a roaring crescendo. Then the shots trailed into unmistakable short bursts of automatic gunfire, interspersed with individual shots that punctuated the spaces between the larger bursts. Then silence. Then screams.

Chaos cascaded over what had been a sunny morning of quiet routine. The boys ran. A wave of men and women began to push across the plaza, away from the noise. Out of the side street called Jirón 28 de Julio, at the top of the square and coming from the direction of the market, rushed a stampede of shopkeepers and clerks, women with shopping bags, street vendors clutching their wares, and children grasping bigger hands or hems to avoid being left behind. At shops under the plaza archways, doors slammed and metal security awnings screeched down over windows. Against this tide of people, a couple of soldiers who had been on the plaza attempted to push their way toward the melee. One of the soldiers grabbed the collar of a fleeing policeman, yanking the officer almost off his feet, shaking him, and yelling into his face. The soldier shoved the lawman back toward the shooting, using his rifle butt to prod him forward. Behind the surge of people came the stinging odor of gunpowder.

Steven jumped from the bench and began to pick his way through the rush toward the shooting. As he reached the top of the plaza, the swell from the corner began to subside to an unsteady exodus. Just off the plaza, a few yards down the street, the policeman rousted by the soldier stood, his pistol in his hand, trying to halt the few people seeking to enter the street.

Steven approached him, and before the priest could say anything the officer pushed him hard in the chest.

"No, no! Go the other way! No one's coming back this way," he yelled and raised his arm to block another man hurrying toward the scene.

"I'm a priest," Steven called to him. "I might be needed."

The police officer looked him up and down, peered at his open shirt collar, and shook his head. "Tourist," he said. "No."

Steven grabbed his pocket to show his ID. His wallet was gone.

Another policeman entered the street with arms outstretched to reinforce his harried colleague. A couple more soldiers went by, followed by police in riot gear. Steven stepped back under the archway on the left side of the plaza. Strained faces screamed to know what had happened. Those still exiting the scene shouted over their shoulders, "Atentado! Masacre! Terroristas!" Suddenly a familiar face breached the square from the side street. It was Lucero.

If she heard Steven call her name, she ignored him. He lost sight of her in the crowd.

15

Cori ventured out of her hostel early the same morning, wondering if she might bump into Steven in the market place, and whether he might invite her to lunch. That possibility, improbable as it might be, made her feel less lonely in a strange town.

The Ayacucho market, as expected on a Saturday, was crowded. Shoppers clogged the streets, squeezing between vendors' carts lining the curbs and mingling among the wandering peddlers known as ambulantes, some hawking clothing draped over their arms, others with trays of pastries or baskets of prickly pear or little plastic baggies stuffed with herbs and spices. The few vehicles venturing into the market streets edged their way through the throng of pedestrians. Bicycle-cart taxis moved more nimbly, darting in and out of the swarm with passengers and their goods.

Cori bought a few groceries—rice, flour, spices, and fresh bread—and picked up a few small pieces of pottery in the style typical of Ayacuchan ceramics. One was a group of musicians in a circle, their backs all forming the center, in the red-earth tone, sepia, and white of the Quinua potters. The other was an upright condor, its tail fluted to form a base. Judy's use of Peruvian handicrafts had inspired Cori to improve the aesthetics of her own room.

She came out of the big market hall to look in the small shops and stopped at a cart on the corner for a soft drink. A blue pickup truck crawled by with a dozen police officers riding on benches along both sides of the open bed. One of the last men on the truck looked back at Cori. He was young and light skinned and his eyes were big and bright. He smiled at her. She smiled back. The truck rolled around the corner and stopped at a tangle of bicycle carts. Cori turned to grab her drink and her change from the señora.

When she looked again to see if the policeman was still watching her, she saw an ice cream seller stop his cart behind the truck and reach into his cooler. The policeman was watching him too, and it amused her to think the young cop wanted an ice pop. The ice cream man came up with something dark and bigger than a pop, and the smiling young officer appeared only to have had time to register that it was a weapon before the vendor opened fire. Simultaneously a woman in a pollera and braids stepped out from among the pushcarts along the street and fired into the truck with an automatic rifle.

Cori dropped her soft drink and ducked behind the beverage cart. Police tumbled into one another in front of her. Someone opened up on the trapped truck from the other side, striking two police officers near the front of the bed who were firing at the armed campesina. Other people on the street fell. An officer in the truck cab was leaning out the window firing furiously at the ice cream man. Cori flattened herself to the grimy gutter as bullets ripped into her flimsy shield. Just at the end of the fusillade, she saw the ice cream man's bloody head striking the cobbles.

As she rose from the ground, Cori glimpsed the soft-drink lady lying motionless in a crimson pool. She felt an impulse to stop and help, but fled instead with all the others.

She ran as best she could to the square and turned in the direction of her hostel. With no friends in Ayacucho, she had nowhere else to go. At the hostel, people gathered in the lobby were already talking of a curfew, though none of the others had been at the market. The desk clerk, a woman no older than Cori, brought her tea and held her hand while she calmed herself enough to tell them what she had just witnessed.

"Just rest, dear," said the clerk. "No point in going out. The police and soldiers will go crazy. They'll be grabbing people everywhere. You have your documents?"

"I think so."

She checked her pocket. Her carnet was there. At her feet was the shopping bag she had gripped throughout the ordeal. She opened it. The ceramics lay in shards.

Cori wished she were home in Lima. The curfews she had lived through there as a young girl, first when the leftist generals took power and then some years later when the rightist generals ousted them in turn, had, oddly enough, been good times. Knowing they had to stay put after nine o'clock at night, people had learned to get stuck where they could expect to have the best time. The lockdowns were a motive to party. Her parents' house became a magnet for relatives and friends. They loved her mother's lamb stew, cooked in beer and cilantro, and the large open living room of their home offered guests a place to talk and even dance without worrying about army patrols. How she wished she had somewhere like her mother's to go to tonight.

Sadness swept over her. She should grieve for that young policeman and the others gunned down in front of her. Yet that wasn't the source of the sorrow she felt, at least not the heaviest part of her disconsolation. It was loneliness, a near-panicked sense of solitude. Ayacucho, which had seemed to offer such a well-lit welcome only this morning, now felt menacing, a dark brooding Guernica with angles and points thrusting out at her and monstrous faces leering from gloomy shadows.

Had she only said something to Steven last night in the car that would have left an opening for today. She didn't even know where he stayed—nor had he mentioned it. What if he came looking for her here? Little chance of that. Even if she knew where to find him, how could she? Before the scene even formed in her mind, she felt embarrassed. What pretext would she have to go to a rectory looking for a young priest? Padre, quiero confesarme. He pecado. What sin? Loneliness? Self-doubt. Regretting this whole mad undertaking? Wanting to teach in a rural village to begin with? Not even two months there and already she was feeling isolated and homesick. Night after night she had only that mountain quiet, with nothing outside her window but the silence of an open field in the darkness. Was she sinning just by wanting to talk to this gringo?

But there was the red-headed gringa, Judy. She might be a friend too. She had invited Cori to her seminar, had told her where to find it in Huamanguilla, had offered her a place to stay on her way back to Urpimarca. She would go there.

While Huamanguilla was usually an hour from Ayacucho, crossing the police checkpoint at the perimeter of the city alone took that long, with everyone ordered off the bus to have papers inspected and luggage and cargo searched. Several young men, glum and timorous, were ordered aside and the bus left without them.

By mid-afternoon Cori was at the community center where Judy was leading a workshop on coordination of motor skills in infants and toddlers. Cori slipped onto a bench in the cool room with its concrete floor and fluorescent lights hanging from tree-trunk rafters. Judy acknowledged her with a smile and continued to show the mothers seated on benches how they should take advantage of diaper changing to exercise their babies' legs. A man near her translated what she said into Quechua.

A Peruvian woman came to the front of the room, and Judy passed the presentation over to her. The new presenter said she would talk about developmental stimulation for toddlers. She dumped some plastic vegetables onto the table and began talking about using everyday items to help with their children's eye-hand coordination.

Judy slid in beside Cori.

"You made it. I thought you were coming tomorrow," Judy whispered, so as not to interrupt the presenter, who was setting stones on the floor for a makeshift obstacle course to help toddlers improve their balance.

"Something ugly happened in Ayacucho. An attack," Cori whispered back.

"Oh," Judy said. "Bad?"

"Sí. Very bad. A police convoy was ambushed in the market. A lot of people were killed. I wanted to get out of the city."

"I don't blame you."

Judy put her hand on Cori's shoulder.

"You okay? You're trembling."

"Sí. I'm okay." But Cori knew she really wasn't. She reached her hand over and Judy grabbed it while keeping her other hand still on Cori's shoulder, nearly embracing her. Cori gripped the other woman's hand tighter and, for the first moment since the market attack that morning, felt a little security.

"It was terrible." Cori said. "So terrible."

The woman up front coaxed a few small children from the laps of campesinas to demonstrate how the little ones should walk around and between the stones, and then she asked the older ones to try maintaining their balance while stepping on top of the rocks.

Keeping her eye on the demonstration, Judy leaned yet closer to Cori.

"Many of the children of campesinas don't walk until they are more than two years old, because they spend all that time swaddled and carried in mantas across their mother's backs," Judy said. "We're trying to make up for a year or more of lost development by teaching the mothers ways to stimulate growth and motor skills in their children with things they have right on hand."

Cori nodded. A chubby little boy picked his way over the rocks. He kept putting one foot to the floor to help maintain his balance.

"The lucky ones are the kids who get pushed out of the carrier early by a new baby," Judy said.

Laughter rippled through the señoras as a couple of the little walkers carried off plastic vegetables.

Lunch with the women at the seminar swept away the little doubt Cori had about fleeing Ayacucho to be with an acquaintance she had met only the day before. Tallarines saltado, noodles with stir-fried beef, tomatoes, onions, fresh ginger and cilantro, and lightly seasoned with soy sauce, would have been something she might have ordered for lunch anyway, and at least here she didn't have to be alone.

Most of the people attending the workshop lived closer to Huamanguilla, but several, she was surprised to learn, knew who she was or had heard of the new teacher in Urpimarca. While that made her feel less isolated, she wondered if she was being watched.

The two women went to Judy's apartment late in the afternoon. Cori could sleep in a tiny room parallel to Judy's bedroom, off the combined living room, dining room, and kitchen. Judy opened a bottle of beer and poured two glasses. Cori settled, depleted of energy and enthusiasm, into the cushioned chair, while Judy took the couch. Darkening clouds descended and brought a premature close to the day. Thunder rumbled, and soon the drumming of rain on corrugated metal seemed to seal the women inside their sanctuary.

"So you work with Padre Steven?" Cori asked.

"We don't work together. ACEP isn't a church group, but it takes volunteers from different places. The group that sponsored me funds volunteers, but it doesn't run projects. I met Steven at a conference about a month ago, right after he arrived. Our paths cross a lot."

"I'm not following you about your funding and all that, but I know people in Lima want to work for any group that brings money in from outside the country. They're the only ones who can pay."

"I know. It's sad."

"My country keeps sliding downhill, and the guerrillas keep getting bolder."

"And the very money that makes our work possible is what is now making us targets of the Shining Path."

"Sí," Cori said. She wondered what brought people like Judy and Steven to such a dangerous place as her country had become, but answered her own question by remembering that foreigners just seemed to find Peru fascinating, in much the way she was enchanted by the sierra.

"Steven is very nice," Judy said. "He's a bit lost, though. He's so new here that he's still in what we call the 'National Geographic stage.' Everything is another world of wonder for him."

"Ha! That's funny," Cori said. "But I do understand what you mean. We are the colorful natives. But not for you anymore?"

"People are people. I'm not idolizing now. And I don't think you're a colorful native for him either. You're not a campesina. I'm sure you're a friend, more of an equal, just with cultural and language differences."

"Well, I hope so very much. It is just so good to talk to someone outside of the village. I love being in Urpimarca, but sometimes, you know, it is…I am not sure what I want to say. It is… umm, quiet, maybe even lonely."

"God! No kidding! And you are Peruvian," Judy yelled, sitting upright as she did. "I toyed with the idea of living way out in the campo myself. I grew up on a little bump in the road back home. Huamanguilla is remote enough for my blood. But I feel more secure knowing I can hop a bus and be on the plaza of Ayacucho in an hour. Or the same time to the airport."

Cori nodded. "You keep your passport with you at all times, I'm sure," she said.

"I'm sorry," Judy said after a pause. She dropped her eyes to the table. "I guess I do. Certainly now anyway."

16

Later that morning the radio reported nine police officers dead and four wounded in the terrorist attack on a convoy in the market. Five subversives had been killed, a military spokesman said, claiming several more were wounded. Steven, listening in his room at the monastery, noted that the official report didn't mention bystander casualties. He thought of Cori and hoped she hadn't been near the market.

During lunch, Eugenia came out of the kitchen to talk about the attack. She had heard that a woman she knew only as "casera," a term Peruvians used for a favorite merchant, had been wounded by police during the ambush and was now accused of being a subversive.

"I can't believe she's a terrorist, Padre. She has been there for years. Can you help her?"

She extracted a promise from Steven to see if he could visit the woman. He finished his lunch and then drove through empty streets to the hospital, where he was told they had admitted only one woman wounded in the attack. He was directed to her room, where a police sergeant with a bushy mustache and thick eyebrows guarded her door. This time Steven wore his collar.

"Why do you want to visit the terrorist?" the sergeant demanded, spreading his chest and glowering at Steven.

"A priest visits the sick and afflicted. We don't know that she is a terrorist," Steven said, crossing his hands behind his back in an attempt to ease the tension.

"Why don't you go visit the wounded police at the military hospital?"

"I would like to do that, too, but right now I'm trying to attend to the spiritual well-being of a woman who happened to be selling vegetables on the wrong street corner. She was an innocent bystander as far as I know. Someone said she was hurt in the shooting."

The sergeant stared at Steven, not moving except for the slightest bobbing of his head.

"You foreign priests, you are just apologists for terrorism—sympathizers with communists."

Steven shook his head in disbelief.

"Name one priest who does that," he said.

"Camilo Torres."

"What?" Steven asked. "That wasn't even in Peru. And he wasn't a foreigner. And he was killed decades ago. That's like condemning all cops as corrupt because a few demand bribes. Where does that get us?"

The sergeant stood his ground at first but then stepped aside and allowed Steven past.

"Five minutes," he said. "No longer."

The woman was either asleep or unconscious. Her head was shaven and elaborately bandaged. He guessed her to be middle-aged, but couldn't tell for sure because of her bruised and swollen face. A tag on the bed said "unknown female" and "gunshot wounds."

Steven anointed her quickly, conscious of his limited time, then took her hand in his and bowed his head to pray for her. Even were she an assailant, she was worthy of his intercession. God sends his rain on the wicked and the just. But not knowing which she was left him cold.

As Steven left the room, the sergeant confronted him again.

"Don't waste your prayers on Maoists, Padre. And don't forget those boys at the military hospital."

The man's eyes glistened, and Steven felt a deep sadness for those men and wanted to comfort this one for the loss of his comrades. Somehow, though, he couldn't find the words. He had come to salve the afflictions of one who suffered and was now twice frustrated.

"I won't," he said. "God bless you, Sergeant."

As he left the hospital, he remembered the report that a number of "subversives" had been wounded. He decided not to go back. He couldn't endure another interrogation. He would pray for them back in his room, and at Mass in the morning. He wouldn't go see the wounded officers either. Military hospitals had regular chaplains to see to such needs.

17

Cori awoke repeatedly during the night as her dreams replayed the day before in endless, bloody variations. She was glad she had not stayed at her hostel, was comforted just knowing a friend was in the next room. How nice it would be to share a home with someone. All her life she had lived with her family, and before moving to Urpimarca she had never awoken to an empty house. Over the past month and a half she had believed she was adjusting well enough, mostly because she managed to handle the solitude. Now, knowing that Judy was just beyond the wall gave her a sense of tranquility that she hadn't realized she was missing. What turns her life had been taking lately. Living in the campo, where she was perhaps still in her own *National Geographic* stage, and now falling in with these Americans. They were so open and casual about things. It amazed her that she had been invited to spend the night by someone she had just met.

Cori stirred again when it was full light, as the aroma of fresh coffee wafted into her room. She sat up with a lingering feeling of deep weariness.

Through the doorway she could see Judy in the living room. Still in her light nightgown, Judy stretched in a rectangle of sunlight on the plank floor. She looked like a lioness, her full red mane flowing toward the floor as her back arched, her upturned face focused toward heaven. Cori's eyes traced the athletic shape, the contour of breasts, abdomen, and thighs under sheer, white cotton, translucent in the light. Had great feathered wings grown from Judy's shoulder blades and a sword and shield sprung from her hands, Cori would have believed the transformation real and not her own projection. So strong, so sensual, so purposeful, Judy was like a warrior woman. Cori massaged her aching hip and stretched herself as best she could before tumbling out of bed.

Judy rolled her head from side to side as Cori limped into the room. She opened her eyes, looked at Cori, and stood up, twisting her torso a couple of times before shaking out her arms and legs and then speaking.

"There's coffee," she said. "I've cheese, and bread from yesterday. I haven't gone out yet."

"That's fine. The coffee and company would be enough."

Over breakfast Judy suggested that Cori might incorporate what she learned in the workshop into her work in the village, going beyond mere academics and promoting a complete regimen of development for the children under her care.

"One of my responsibilities is training others to give workshops. You could learn a lot by staying for the rest of the seminar today."

As tempting as it was to stay, to mingle with the presenters again and to have a roommate for one more night, Cori declined. She couldn't pretend things were normal after yesterday, not right away at least. She also feared being lulled into a false sense of comfort she couldn't afford right now. Something her father once told her helped to move her on: Leave early and you'll be asked to return; stay too long and you'll be asked to leave.

"That would be wonderful, but another time. I need to go back today."

"Please come back, then. Feel free to drop in anytime you come through Huamanguilla or just feel like you need to get out of Urpimarca for a while. Mi casa es tu casa."

Another VW bug, this one with so much sand on the floor that Cori's feet slid around beneath her, crept up the hill beyond Huamanguilla and around the arroyos the road skirted on its way to the old hacienda. With the din of yesterday's gunfire echoing in her mind, the images still cascading regularly into consciousness, her destination seemed more welcoming than on her first journey there.

The driver was a quiet campesino who told her no more than that he grew up around Huamanguilla and knew the way. In any event, the road offered few opportunities to get lost. When they passed the house that Steven had wanted to visit, the wall once again bore the red lettering of Sendero slogans. Cori fought to quell a sudden sense of dread, repenting of having left Judy's house, realizing that everywhere in this broad mountain valley was a long way from safety.

They drove as far as the car could go. Cori still had the hour's walk she had made two days earlier with Steven and Lucero, this time uphill. She hadn't thought much about Lucero since they parted. Now she wondered when the woman would be back. It had nothing to do with any feelings of friendship, but with lingering doubts about Lucero. She didn't really seem to belong in Urpimarca. Yet who was Cori to judge who belonged here and who didn't? She hardly knew the elders of the community. To presume to judge Lucero would make her no better than the ministry official who presumed to deem her unfit to be a teacher. Hadn't her own mother done the same to her? Such ugly memories were never forgotten. They always trended homeward in moments of weakness or doubt.

Her mother sat her down one summer in secondary school, on a day when the two of them were home alone. Her brothers and sisters had taken the bus to the beach. Cori had offered to help with dinner, but her mother had said for her to sit.

"Just sit for a bit, because I want to tell you something I've been worrying about for a long time."

"What? What's happened?" Cori dropped onto the couch, while her mother sat in the armchair.

"I don't want you to get hurt, Cori. But you aren't seeing things clearly."

"Seeing what clearly?"

"Cori, you can't expect things to be the same for you as for other girls. I keep praying you will like the sisters at Santa Clara and follow them."

"I don't want to be a nun," Cori said indignantly.

"You need to realize men aren't going to think of you the same way they do other women."

Cori dropped her eyes to her legs, the left tilted sideways to allow her to sit.

"What do you mean?" she asked, sensing in her voice a coldness that she wasn't accustomed to using with her parents.

"They won't. That's all. I tell you this only for your own good. No decent man is going to want you."

The words echoed over her: no decent man. Only the opposite would want her. Only an indecent one would want someone as unworthy of love as Cori.

"Excuse me," Cori said. "I'll be right back."

Opening the faucet over the sink, Cori splashed cold water on her face to wash away the tears. She trembled as she struggled to regain her composure. Words once spoken can never be taken back. Even if her mother had made some effort to correct herself, to correct a thoughtless slip of the tongue, her words were like the ringing of a bell that can never be unrung. A thousand apologies and explanations could not undo them. Rather, it would be a decent man, indeed, who could love her. She dried her face, and in the mirror looked deep into the eyes of the girl who looked back. She returned in a few minutes with as much self-possession as she could muster.

"Fine, Mamá. You say no decent man will want me."

"Cori, I want—"

Cori held up her hand and turned her head away to stop her mother's interruption.

"You're saying no man worth having will want me! Fine. As you say. And when I need affection?"

Her mother didn't answer.

"When I need affection then, I'll go to the barracks!"

Another word and she would break down. She had said enough. The fury in her mother's eyes spoke volumes.

She stormed out of the house, caught a bus, and found herself eventually wandering the path along the cliffs in Miraflores, past the couples necking on the knee-high brick wall meant to keep people from falling off the edge. As night fell she stood alone, listening to the hum of traffic on the coast road below and the rhythmic crash of surf on the beach beyond. Far away, the cross glowed on the point at Chorrillos.

Three boys about her age were hanging out along the wall not far off and glanced her way from time to time. She should have been scared. What young woman would dare to stay in the park alone after dark? That night she wasn't afraid. Maybe she should start with them, with boys, and work up to soldiers. Brazenly, she had walked toward them. They averted their eyes. She walked by, and they did not follow. When she could walk no more she took a bus home.

Her mother didn't ask where she had been, not that time, not any time afterward, not ever again.

As she climbed toward Urpimarca now, Cori felt as she had that night, and it dawned on her what the feeling was: a deep mourning. She hadn't known anyone in the market, yet had lost something there that could never be recovered, just as her mother's careless words had caused her a great and irretrievable loss.

She walked much more slowly now than when she had left Urpimarca with Steven and Lucero, weighed down by much more than the few shattered purchases in her knapsack. As the road's course switched back and forth across the rising ridge, she noticed a lone figure on the road far behind her.

She took him at first to be a local youth, probably heading to Urpimarca as well. But his stride was purposeful, like that of a man rushing across a busy boulevard in Lima, not the easy saunter of a campesino. At each hairpin she saw him drawing closer. She quickened her pace. She heard his approaching footsteps but did not look back as he overtook her a short distance before the top of the ridge. He greeted her in Quechua and fell into stride beside her, catching his breath for a bit before speaking again.

"How do you like teaching in Urpimarca?" he asked her in Spanish without a trace of mountain accent.

"I like it very much," she said politely, noticing as she did that he wore heavy shoes, not ojotas. His jeans were dark and new, so unlike the thin denim the farmers' sons wore.

"It is a very nice village," he said. "You know the history? How it was a hacienda for hundreds of years before they drove off the landlord?"

"Is that where you are going?" Cori asked, trying to remember how close the next house was. "I have not seen you in the village before, have I?"

"I am going beyond the village."

"Where beyond the village?" she asked. "There is nothing beyond Urpimarca."

"Just beyond," he said. "You know, teacher, the work begun by the generals failed to truly reform—"

"But where do you live?" she interrupted.

He stopped and looked at her.

"Teacher, you should—"

"Señorita, por favor," she snapped, hoping she wasn't betraying the fear that hammered in her chest.

His face changed, not to an expression she might have expected—anger or embarrassment—but to a blank coldness, menacing in its simple lack of human warmth. When he resumed talking, his eyes did not focus on her. Rather, they seemed to be reading a well-studied script inside his head.

"The new order is coming, Señorita Maestra. It is time for you to stop filling the heads of your students with the great lies of the past."

He turned his back to her and went up a small path through the brush and over the crest of the hill, leaving her standing alone on the road.

18

Steven said Mass that Sunday morning at the church attached to the monastery instead of the chapel of a barrio on the edge of the city as he had planned. He swapped services with one of the young Peruvian priests, who did so as a favor to Steven. Without his identity card, Steven wouldn't have been able to get through the police checkpoints outside of the city center. After Mass he headed to the plaza, still wearing his black shirt and Roman collar. If he couldn't recover his carnet, the Peruvian equivalent of a green card, he would have to go back to Lima for a replacement. He still had his passport, which he now carried in a pouch under his shirt.

As soon as he took a seat on the same bench as yesterday, Antonio, the little boy who shined his shoes, ran over.

"Padre, you did not pay me for shining your shoes."

"You didn't finish the job."

"I will now then," the boy said, setting straight to work. He opened his wooden box and took out polish and rags, closed it, and tapped Steven's right foot to signal that he should put it on the sole-shaped lid.

"You have to pay double because I am doing this twice now," he said.

"You ran off."

"Everyone ran, Padre. If the terrucos and police start shooting at each other, anyone could get killed."

A few other boys gathered around him, as they had the day before. Among them was the biggest boy, who once again complained that Antonio was getting preferential treatment.

"This is the third time!" he yelled, apparently directing his comments to both the boy and Steven, waving three fingers in the air.

"I'm just finishing from yesterday," the little one said, looking over his shoulder and crouching lower.

"That's right," Steven said.

The older boy snarled something in Quechua to the younger one, who flinched but kept working, picking up his pace.

"Chicos," Steven said, "I seem to have lost my wallet when I was here yesterday. None of you has seen it, have you?"

The boys shifted ever so uneasily in place and traded exculpatory looks, while murmuring, "No, no, Padre." Antonio kept his head down, slapping a rag sharply across the toe of Steven's shoe.

"I need my identity card. You know that's very important. And it's of no value to anyone else. The few notes in the wallet, I don't care about those."

"Sí, Padre," one answered.

"We can ask around," the bigger boy said. "Maybe someone found it. If there's a reward, maybe they will turn it in."

"Maybe? How much do you think?"

The boy named a sum. About ten American dollars, Steven calculated. He suppressed an impulse to grab the boy by the scruff of the neck and slap him silly. He needed his ID, and ten dollars was cheap compared to the cost of an airplane ticket to Lima. Besides, he wasn't going to make headway with these boys by alienating them. He reminded himself that his mission was as much here on the street as in the campo.

He nodded, "Okay."

An hour later he had his carnet, poorer by the reward and the notes amounting to about forty dollars that he had in the

180

billfold. He chalked it up as an initiation fee and left the boys on the square. He walked to the top of the plaza and away from the market, toward the hostel where he had left Cori on Friday.

In the hostel lobby, the man in the faux-leather jacket who had stood smoking outside the other night sat on an upholstered bench near the wall across from the reception desk reading a newspaper. He looked up at Steven with faint interest, and then returned to his newspaper without speaking. Steven asked for Cori at the desk.

"Let me check," the clerk said. "I have been away a couple days." He fanned through the pages of a register.

"The señorita left yesterday," the man on the bench said. "The attack in the market scared her. She was there. She checked out right away."

"She was there? Was she hurt?"

The man shrugged. "Not that I could see."

"Did she say where she was going?"

The man set his newspaper aside and inspected Steven before answering, much the way the police sergeant had at the hospital.

"The little señorita went back to her school."

Of course, they knew her. She had stayed here once before. Steven took a visceral dislike to the man, probably some sort of cheap hotel security. Dealing with police and soldiers and private security guards, little men so smug in their exercise of vicarious authority, was getting tiring. So was this weasel with the conspicuous bulge beneath his sorry jacket. Steven understood the need for security now more than ever, but this guy grated on him anyway. Without saying more, he turned and walked out.

"You are welcome, Padre!" the man tossed after him.

Steven walked quickly down Avenue Mariscal Cáceres, watching his steps on the uneven sidewalk. A couple of blocks from the hostel he knocked shoulders with a man coming from the oppo-

181

site direction and only half turned to mumble, "Excuse me" after the other man yelled, "Hey, Padre. Be careful."

At the monastery Steven blew down the hallway past the dining room entrance, where he glimpsed Father Jaime talking to Eugenia as she set the table for lunch. He cut through the courtyard to his room, where he stuffed a change of clothes into the overnight case he called his "toolkit." He grabbed the toolkit, a jacket, and his car keys, and left the room.

He entered the dining room through framed glass doors that slid on worn wooden tracks. He left them open behind him to let in the breeze. Eugenia usually kept them shut tight. Father Jaime sat alone at a table in the otherwise vacant room, a book in his lap.

"You're just in time for lunch," he said, his face lighting up as the younger man entered the room. Looking at Steven's valise, the older priest added, "You're off again."

"Yes, I need to see someone who's distressed about the tragedy in the market. I'd like to stay, but it's a long drive."

"Sit, Steven. Sit," Jaime said, patting the air with his palms and signaling his colleague to calm down. Steven glanced at his watch but obeyed. He had come in to excuse himself from lunch, but felt obligated to hear the older priest out.

"You are so inquieto," Jaime said, using Spanish the way so many English speakers here did, adopting certain words and phrases that were more expressive than their closest English equivalent. Yes, he was unquiet—restless and anxious, to be sure. And why shouldn't he be? He didn't have time for Jaime's pastoral advice right now. He said nothing, though.

"You need to be careful that you don't burn yourself out," Jaime said. "You know, even when I got a car, I kept to the pace I established before. I had a schedule, a circuit like the preachers in the Old West, or maybe more like a wandering Dominican friar of the Middle Ages. I ministered to communities one at a time, each in turn, in its time. Keep that in mind."

Steven nodded, understanding but not necessarily agreeing.

"It's the only way. There will never be enough willing priests to attend to all the parishes in the campo as the church would like. That's why people hold to their traditions, their paganism if you want to call it that. Before the Second Vatican Council these questions of orthodoxy used to be an even bigger challenge. Now, we recognize the campesinos' genuine impulse to seek the divine. We approach their beliefs with respect, in the spirit of Vatican II. God is also their final goal. We're not rejecting anything that is true and holy here by succoring their attempts to find their way to goodness and to God. The religious impulse is strong in the campesinos, so they cling to their apus like an Irish grandmother clutches her rosary."

"I admit I am struggling a bit with the mixing of beliefs," Steven said, reaching into the right-hand pocket of his black pants and pulling out his own rosary, a single decade of bogwood beads from Ireland. He held them out to show Jaime, who smiled and nodded.

"Today, Jaime, I'm worried about a single person who got caught in the attack yesterday. I feel responsible for her."

"I understand, Steven. There's neediness wherever we serve. Our role, yours and mine, is not to fix every crisis, to jump up from our chairs and run out to the campo to soothe every heartache. That will consume you.

"We bring the Word, which is like stoking coals," Jaime continued. "The fire is already there, and it's the spirit that we're fanning. They experience it differently from the way we do and so its expression varies from ours. That's all okay. We simply bring the Word, which is what really counts. In bringing our vision of the holy to theirs, we're being true to our faith—if that is what's worrying you. You respect their relationship with God and share yours. And we have to be content to spend some time here and some time there across a huge territory. Slow down. Today, after what just happened, everyone's on edge. No one knows what's next. Don't rush off to the campo. Stay here in Ayacucho today."

Steven rose. "I have to see if someone's safe. I'm sorry. I have to go."

If Cori had stopped in Huamanguilla, as she had discussed with Judy, Steven thought she might still be there. He could drive her out to the village and talk about what had happened on the way. If she was already gone, he would drive on to Urpimarca and seek her out there. Tomorrow he could backtrack from there and continue on to a couple of communities he and Angel hoped to visit this week. Either way he would see Cori again. She must have been terrified. For his own peace of mind he needed to make sure she was all right.

At Huamanguilla he stopped at the workshop and learned from Judy that he was too late. Cori had already headed back to the village. Before he could continue on his journey, he was beset by a friend of Judy's, who told him her son was seriously ill. She begged him to come to her house to see the young man.

Steven looked to Judy.

"Her oldest son has been sick for a while and they don't know what he has," Judy said. "He was working in Ayacucho but now he is home, bedridden, wasting away."

"Has he seen a doctor?"

"Yes, but the doctor said he didn't know what was wrong and sent him home."

"No tests? No follow up? Wouldn't he be covered by the national healthcare system?"

"That's the way it is a lot of the time," Judy said. "Resources are scarce and doled out inequitably. He's just a campesino. He doesn't have the money for a specialist. He can't even afford the simplest pain medication. Can you go see him?"

The woman led Steven to a house much like Judy's, adobe on cinder block. The family lived in part of the first floor, where the concrete chilled the room even as the sun warmed the earthen bricks above. The son, Tomás, was in a bed beside an uncurtained window in the one-room apartment. The unfiltered light amplified the starkness of the gray walls and floor. Tomás perspired beneath layers of dark blankets. Only his gaunt head, with sunken cheeks, sparse, unshaven whiskers, and disheveled mop of black hair, was visible on a sweat-stained pillow.

"Good afternoon, Padre."

"Hello, Tomás. How are you feeling?"

"Not so well as you, Padre," the boy said with a weak smile.

"I'm sorry to hear that. I think you need to see another doctor, a specialist of some sort."

Tomás smiled wanly again.

"Even the curandero says there is nothing more to do. He passed a cuy over me and it came out clean. My time will be better spent with you, Padre."

Steven had never seen a curandero pass a guinea pig over the body of a sick person, a common procedure used by medicine men and women to diagnose illness. After moving a live cuy over all parts of the ailing patient, the curandero would kill and dissect the animal. The malady sickening the person was supposed to be mirrored in the rodent. Tomás was saying the cuy used on him showed no disease. This man's faith was in the curandero, not city doctors.

"So why are you sick?"

The youth looked around the room to where his mother was sitting, just out of earshot if he whispered. He leaned his head closer to the priest.

"Padre, this is a confession that I'm very sorry to have to make."

"It's okay, Tomás. Go on."

"I worked hard in Ayacucho to earn money for my mother and my brothers and sisters. But sometimes I spent some of it. You know, on drinking, and a few times on women you can find there."

Steven nodded. "And you think God is punishing you for this?"

"It's not that. I was more foolish than even that. One night, I was coming home from working all week in construction, bringing money to my mother because my father isn't always around. I met some friends and we decided to go to a chichería on the way, you know, to just drink chicha and relax after so much work. We drank lots of chicha, then some cañazo, and then more chicha. When I was very drunk, I went outside to pee and my head was spinning so badly I just wanted to go home. I took a shortcut across the fields, but was too drunk to find my way. Finally, I just passed out somewhere. When I woke up in the morning, I was sick and dizzy and I had scratches on me and had been bitten by what I thought were insects. And that was the beginning of all this. I have never felt well again."

"And you think your illness is God's answer to your foolishness?" Steven asked. "That this is God's work?"

"Not at all, Padre," the young man said, pulling out a near skeletal hand and signaling for the priest to come closer. When Steven leaned in Tomás whispered, "It is the work of el pistaco."

19

The better part of the afternoon was gone before Steven got back on the road. It would take a couple of hours to get to Urpimarca, and he wasn't looking forward to the probability of being out there on an impassable road on foot in the dark.

He pondered how a phantom like the pistaco could be so inculcated into the psyche of a people with access to modern medicine, however meagerly portioned. Then again, that was the point. The young man was doomed. Neither Western medicine nor Andean folk remedies offered any hope, so superstition took over. Evil was clearly present, and so commonly triumphant, in our daily lives. He remembered the woman in the hospital and the police officers ambushed in the market. Discovering incarnations of good and evil in the world was a universal practice. There was no mystery here for the youth. There was a simple enough explanation for his predicament, el pistaco.

About midway through his drive, the Pachari house, where he and Angel had their encounter with the military, came into view. Without someone to interpret there wasn't much sense in stopping, except he wanted to know if the army had taken the young man. He hoped the old couple had prevailed upon the soldiers to leave him alone, but doubted it. As soon as he approached the house, he knew something was terribly wrong. The graffiti was back—bolder and more frantic: *Viva Presidente*

Gonzalo! PCP! Stoolpigeons! A large red hammer and sickle defaced the whole front of the house. It was like a graphic obscenity scribbled across a picture-book pastoral.

The door was ajar. Steven killed the ignition and stepped cautiously out of his VW, calling, "Good afternoon."

No one replied. Even the yard was still. He went to the door and spoke into the dark crack, "Hello? Señor Pachari? Señora?"

He pushed the door just a little and called again. Flies buzzed in the harsh gash of light falling into the room. He swung the door fully open and peered inside.

The son hung by a rope from a rafter. A blood-splattered paper sign around his neck read "Informer." The lifeless bodies of the mother and father lay face down on the floor beneath him, their hands tied behind their backs and leather strips wound around their necks.

Steven bolted to his car. He pressed his forehead and palms to the hot metal roof. He snorted to get the stink of the hut out of his nose. A fury rose in him and he pounded the top of the car with his fist making his hand tingle and ache. Turning around, he slipped to the ground, tucked his knees up and rested his forehead on his folded arms.

He had seen death before, had anointed the dying and blessed mangled bodies pulled from car wrecks and charred ones from fires. But he had never seen an execution, never encountered such a gruesome display of abject cruelty, never stepped so close to evil incarnate.

He sought in vain at first for a prayer to abrogate the presence of such evil. He struggled to summon words he had never truly needed until now. As they came to him, he rose to his feet. "Saint Michael the Archangel, defend us in battle, be our protection against the wickedness and snares of the devil. May God rebuke him, we humbly pray, and do thou, O Prince of the heavenly hosts, by the power of God, thrust into hell Satan and all the evil spirits, who prowl about the world seeking the ruin of souls. Amen." Taking a deep breath, Steven headed back to the house, putting his faith above his fear that the killers might return. He stepped inside to bless the remains and pray for the souls of the departed.

Steven rejected the idea of going back to Huamanguilla to report the killings. The people in Urpimarca were closer and were their neighbors. They needed to know. And he needed to check on Cori. He couldn't help this unfortunate family any more than by commending theirs souls to the angels and to everlasting peace with God. Whose God, he wondered, theirs or his, abandoned them to this barbarity?

Steven prayed continuously as he drove toward Urpimarca. His hands trembled on the wheel. His body and legs seemed disconnected. His head spun in vertigo and the road seemed to plunge into an endless pit before him, regardless of the grade of the terrain.

As he approached the house where he had left his car in the past, he feared another atrocity, but no one was home and he found no signs of any disturbance. He zipped up his tan jacket against a cool breeze, slung the strap of his bag over his shoulder, and began to walk.

The shadows were already long as he began the hike to the village. He had forgotten to bring a flashlight. At least the way was unmistakable. He only had to keep to the old hacienda road. The faintest breeze carried the fragrance of burning eucalyptus from fires in huts somewhere out of sight beyond the darkening hillsides.

Fresh air and walking seemed to steady him. His lightheadedness lifted as he walked deliberately on the uneven path, though the tread of his steps seemed loud in the deepening gloom. In the distance a dog barked. Over the ravine to his right a night bird trilled eerily as it plummeted through the twilight. Bat silhouettes flitted overhead.

Before long, Steven was stumbling beneath the thinnest crescent moon. He had never walked alone at night in countryside or woods. As a boy he had remained fitful in his scout sleeping bag in predawn hours, holding in his urine rather than abandon the sanctuary of his tent and go out into the dark alone. Now he tried the impossible—not to see the face of the young man hanging from the rafter, puffed and blue.

Something rustled in the brush ahead. Steven felt a jolt of adrenalin. His instinct was to flee. But to where? Pitch headlong into the darkness and perhaps over the mountainside? Go back toward the bodies in the house? He stopped to listen more closely. What moved in the bush sounded small and seemed to move off. Perhaps an armadillo or some rodent, more frightened of him than he was of it. As he pressed on, he again heard his own steps, louder now, seeming to drown out other sounds in the night, as if he were announcing himself. He slowed down and stepped more softly. It would take twice as long to get to Urpimarca this way, but it seemed foolhardy to be stomping down the road when he should be alert and listening. Carefully, to minimize even the sound of his hand brushing fabric, Steven reached into his pocket and drew out his rosary. He skipped the introductory prayers and started right in with an Our Father..."who art in Heaven"...mouthing the words only, and then began the ten Hail Marys..."full of grace, the Lord is with thee...now and at the hour...the hour...the hour of..." He stopped. He didn't even want to say it. But then it rushed into his mind—"hour of our death! Amen!" He stopped. Frustrated by the very prayers that usually helped calm and center him, such as when he flew and unobtrusively fingered his beads on takeoff. He trod quietly for a bit, trying to think of nothing.

Still, the bloated faces of the Pachari family intruded. He

shook his head to dispel the image, only to find it replaced with the gaunt skull of Tomás. "It was the work of el pistaco," he heard the dying man say. Steven stifled a nervous laugh at his own foolishness, his own superstition. Yet again he sensed, as he had at the Pachari house, the presence of evil, and he felt distinctly as if something followed him.

Willing himself to calm down, he stopped abruptly, rested his hands on his knees, and took a few deep breaths. He sought his rational side, where reason and experience and science might protect him from the haunts of his imagination. It failed him. That evil manifested itself in human action was undeniable. Nor could he limit his conception of evil to random acts of cruelty without denying God. How can one insist on the personification of all that is good, but deny the personification of evil? Where there are angels, there are surely demons.

If the original shape-shifter, the master of all deception, could take form to tempt even Christ, who was to say it couldn't wander camouflaged as this vampire of the Andes? Evil will take form in whatever trappings suit the sensibilities of time and place. Evil could stalk the night, in human form or not, and he had been foolish to ignore local wisdom.

Oddly enough, admitting his fear helped. He resumed his walk, stepping up his pace just a bit. He settled on repetitions of The Jesus Prayer, "Lord Jesus Christ, Son of God, have mercy on me, a sinner." It was short enough to focus him and keep other thoughts at bay. He was determined to continue on to the village unless physically overwhelmed by someone—or something.

After a time he left off the prayer and began to hum a hymn he so often heard during Mass since his arrival in Peru, and then, ever so quietly, began to sing the words:

O, Lord, with your eyes set upon me,
gently smiling, you have spoken my name;

all I longed for I have found by the water,
at your side, I will seek other shores.

"You sing that beautifully, Padre," a voice said just beside him.

Steven screamed! He fully expected to see the phantom of the sierra with the bulging face of the dead youth.

Instead, a teenage boy and girl stood in deep shadow where a path joined the road.

"I'm so sorry," the boy said. "We didn't mean to frighten you. It was you who scared us, coming down the road."

"Until we heard you singing 'Pescador de Hombres.' Then we knew it was okay," the girl added.

"You scared me half to death!" Steven protested.

"We're very sorry, Padre," the girl said, cowering behind her companion.

"Padre, why do you come at night, and alone like this?" the boy asked.

"I was delayed on the road."

"The village is just ahead," the boy said. "Something has happened. We are going there to see."

"Vamos," Steven said.

Surprised to find himself so close to the village, Steven was even more amazed to find the community astir. Rather than turn right toward the plaza, he and the young couple cut straight up the grassy ridge that formed a saddle between the two high ends of the village, to a point where the whole panorama of the plains to Ayacucho lay spread out beneath a heavy mantle of stars.

A couple dozen people stood looking into the night. A few shifted nervous glances at the newcomers joining them before turning their gaze back to where the black night sky melded into the horizon. There, midway between Urpimarca and Ayacucho, where in daylight the dusky hills would have been visible, burned a hammer and sickle.

20

Urpimarca slept little that long night. Heavy-set señoras clutching machetes posted themselves outside their homes to await the dawn, wrapped in shawls and mantas and perched on blocks of wood or bundles of straw. A few men armed with old rifles and cloaked in the darkness kept vigil on the road where Steven had encountered the young couple. Others scanned the broad, sloping fields from the heights above.

Steven pulled Señor Huanta aside. The mayor absorbed the news of the butchered family with typical stoicism.

"Where do we go if we are the battleground?" he said, more to himself than to Steven as they watched the lights of the hammer and sickle stir chaotically and then go out. "The soldiers can stomp out little cans of kerosene, but I'm afraid that to get to the fire-starters they will trample on us the same way." The old man turned abruptly toward his house and walked away shaking his head.

Steven declined an invitation for dinner from Angel with a promise to meet in the morning. His one desire was to find Cori. As he neared the plaza, he ran into Señora Eulalia, who said she would hurry to open the little room for him. He ignored her scowl as he gravitated toward Cori, whom he found in front of the school reassuring three adolescent girls who likewise were worried about their teacher.

"I'll lock my door and hide under the blankets," she told the girls as she dispatched them with brief hugs. "Go on home. Everything will be fine in the morning."

She looked up in surprise when she saw Steven coming toward her.

"Esteban," she said. "What are you doing here?"

"I had to know you were all right."

Cori looked at him as if she didn't understand what he was saying.

"I heard you were in the market," he said.

"And you came all this way again," she said, stepping closer to him.

She looked intently into his face, though he doubted she could see him any better in the darkness than he could her. She took his hand and squeezed it. "Come have some tea."

"I was going to ask for a cup of coffee," he said as she turned and led him toward the patio.

"If you'd like, but herbal teas are better for you in the evening."

She directed him to the settee, refusing his offer of help, and went into the kitchen. She brought a tray with candles, a few patties of cheese she said were made by a villager, and some bread she had bought in Ayacucho. She went back and returned with a thermos of hot water, a jar of coffee essence, and packets of anise and of chamomile.

"On cool nights in Lima my father pours a shot of a pisco into his tea. It's called té piteado," she said. "I'm sorry I haven't anything like that to offer you."

"I'm the guest. I should have brought you something," he said. "I'm fine with coffee."

She joined him on the seat and made him a cup of black coffee. She prepared chamomile for herself and set it to steep. She turned to him.

"I saw the whole awful thing," she said. "I saw people killed right in front of me. It was horrid." She took a couple of deep breaths.

"But you're all right?"

"Yes," she said, yet she shook her head as if denying what she was saying. "That, and now this." She motioned toward the hills where the hammer and sickle had burned.

"I know. I know. Everything is crazy. Do you remember the house where we stopped yesterday?"

"You knew some people there. No one was home."

"Yes, the Pachari family, an old couple and their son. I found them all dead there tonight."

Cori closed her eyes and sank back into the bench.

"Sendero?"

"Yes."

She opened her eyes and reached for her tea, grasping the cup without drinking.

"What will you do?" Steven asked, picking up his coffee.

"Me? Stay, I think. I don't know. I can't just leave these kids without a teacher again."

"It is too dangerous. I have been very worried about you."

Cori tilted her head up to look into his face again, and this time, even in the dim candlelight, he could tell she was peering into his eyes, searching.

"It is much more dangerous for you," she said. "Everyone on that bus up to Ayacucho when we met was worried about you, Esteban. You're an obvious target."

Steven drank some coffee and then looked into his cup. He couldn't think of a rebuttal to something so obvious. A long silence passed between them before he looked at her again. She was still watching him. She raised her eyebrows and smiled.

"If we both leave, people might think we ran off together," she said. "You don't want scandal, do you, Padrecito?"

"I guess not," he said, allowing himself a short laugh. Perhaps it was inappropriate, given recent events, but it seemed a fitting, even necessary, antidote to anxiety. A yearning for comfort was an unfamiliar impulse for Steven. At the moment it was compelling.

"It's chilly," Cori said. "If I'm going to sit out here in the cold, I need something warmer."

She went inside and returned wearing a dark blue sweater and carrying a gray wool blanket.

"I don't want you to be cold either," she said placing the blanket over him, covering him from chest to knees. She sat beside him, closer.

"It's big enough for us both," he said, tossing part of the blanket over her lap. His fingers brushed her arm, and simultaneously they slid to where their thighs just touched. Cori pulled her section of blanket higher. They leaned together, shoulder to shoulder. Their eyes focused on the flickering candles.

"Are you going to behave yourself, Esteban?" She kept her gaze forward.

"I don't know," he whispered as he turned to look at her. "Maybe not."

Cori lifted her head, and the candle flames danced in her eyes. He couldn't say whether he kissed her or she him. The touch of their lips was soft and brief, steeped more in tenderness than passion.

He put his arms around her and she settled back into his embrace, their hands clutched together on her lap. They stared into the tongues of candle flames that only intensified the darkness around them. Steven felt contentment unknown to him before, a sense of being needed and of being a protector. He squeezed her tighter.

Cori turned toward him again and there was no doubt who kissed whom this time. Steven had never before been kissed with such hunger. Had they not been so exposed, had walls rather than trees sheltered them, he could not say where it might have led. Slowly, very slowly, because he wanted it to linger, he broke the kiss. She rested her head against his chest. Neither sought another kiss. He didn't dare. After a while, she fell asleep in his arms.

The intensity of his emotions nagged at and confused him. He brushed it aside, refusing to deliberate on it. Not tonight. Not with this woman he cared for curled in his arms. Something inclusive and all-encompassing outweighed it, something bright and warm that made total sense of it, the undeniable rightness of this embrace. He rested his chin atop her head and must have dozed.

He woke to see the stars fading overhead. He could just make out the melted stubs of candles on the table. As he lifted his eyes toward the coming day, he caught the figure of a man stepping away from the opening in the brush—unhurried and apparently unconcerned that he had been caught spying.

21

Cori sat up and wiped her eyes. She found Steven watching her. She had spent the night wrapped in his arms, reclining on a bench in the cool night air, and he had held her, guarding her while she slumbered. For the second morning in a row she felt completely rested, when by all rights she shouldn't have been.

The terrorist attack still churned in the back of her mind, as did the images of the scrawled guerrilla slogans, the flaming symbol of defiance, and the young man who had threatened her on the road—something she had not mentioned to Steven. Yet the nightmare was ameliorated by a dream, a buffer of space and light that stood between her and the horror. In that safe place resided an abiding warmth. It felt to her like coming out of chilly shadow to sit on sunbaked rock radiating a steady heat.

Leaning over, she kissed Steven on the lips with deliberate ease, an endearment, a simple affirmation of the new intimacy between them. He didn't respond. Cori pulled back and looked into his eyes for an answer. His hand swept stray strands of hair from her face and stroked the rest into place as if his fingers were a comb.

"I just saw someone watching us, maybe a villager. He headed around that way toward the houses."

A sense of relief came over her. He was only worried about an observer.

"Tall and gangly?" she asked.

"Yes."

"Juan. He is like the caretaker of the school."

She sat up and stretched her arms around his neck and gave him another kiss. This time he responded and they held it briefly. Putting one hand on the armrest of the settee, she pushed herself to her feet and stretched again.

"Juan is the only one around here who looks like that. He is harmless. He is just protective of the school."

"And of you?"

Cori laughed and cocked her head with that endearing little shrug she used to great advantage, and widened her eyes.

"I hope so," she said in a lilting voice.

Cori went to make coffee, and when she returned she found Steven in a pensive state on the bench. He set aside the cup she handed him and took her hand.

"What are we going to do?" he asked.

"About us? Or about the terrorists?"

"Us—for the moment."

She leaned forward and kissed him again. "I'm happy in the moment," she said. "I feel safe with you. The question is, what are you going to do, Padrecito?"

He nodded, but looked unsure. He folded his hands together and pushed them between his knees, scrunching his shoulders. Cori sat down in the chair opposite him.

"Your coffee will turn cold quickly out here," she said, taking a sip from her cup.

"Yeah," he said, reaching for his cup. "Of course. Thank you."

Steven left after coffee, and Cori busied herself around the patio. The cloudless blue sky promised a brilliant, sun-drenched day. The brightness and clarity of the morning mirrored her feelings. The shadows and her fears diminished.

She tried to ignore a droning uneasiness, a simple note that was badly off key in the resonating excitement, an emotional minor chord to her symphony of allegria. She was falling in love with a priest. She feared he was already repenting of last night and wondered if he was blaming her. Was she to blame? Abruptly, she sat down on the settee. Love was not the problem, and it was not just sentiment and desire. Had it been, she would never have left Wachi, would never have sealed away all her yearnings for him, would never have freed him from the unhappiness she believed she would have inevitably brought him. For Cori, love was the forging of feelings and desire into action. It was a decision. And she had made hers.

Of course, impulses of the heart ruled her right now. Unless she could see how simply loving Steven would hurt him, and she couldn't, there was no reason to stop it. She had walked away from one man she loved because to do otherwise would have eventually broken her. Wachi, she was sure, would have one day needed the one thing she couldn't give him, a child. She knew it. She wasn't going back to a doctor to have this confirmed. The last time had been too painful. But Steven shouldn't need that from her. He had already made a commitment to life without a family, without children. Why did that have to mean without love?

More certain of herself, Cori got up to go out to the plaza and perhaps wander around the village, hoping to meet some children, who might need reassuring after the fearful events of the last few days. Rather than cut through the classroom, she turned the corner to go behind the building to the far end of the square and almost walked headlong into Juan.

He wore a straw sombrero, tightly woven and supple, like those donned by the horsemen of the coast in parades and festivals when they showed off their paso ponies, the loping-gaited breed descendent from mounts that the Pizarro brothers rode over the backs of Inca foot soldiers. His boots, cracked at the creases and heavily worn at the heels, were freshly shined. The bottoms of his pants were tucked into the tops of the boots and a dark poncho covered all but the collar of his frayed shirt.

"Juan! I hardly recognized you."

He stood up straighter.

"I want to talk to you," he said.

"Right now?"

"Please." His shoulders sagged a bit.

"Are you going somewhere?"

"I want to show you something. Come on."

He led her out the open end of the patio to where the fields began and then away from the plaza to the hillside where she had first looked over the plains tumbling to Ayacucho. She worried that he would show her another sign of rebellion, a symbol somehow visible in the distance even in the glare of mountain sunlight, or perhaps something worse, another act of violence, and she balked at that.

"Juan, if it's something terrible, please, I don't want to see it."

Shaking his head, he glanced over his shoulder, assuring himself that she was still following and continued by the chapel on the path that she had taken her first day in Urpimarca.

They stopped before the manor. She had never been inside, despite her occasional walks along the path that neared it. Apparently, no one but Juan bothered with the place, so hidden in overgrown vegetation that it seemed spectral. For Cori the house had felt off limits from the first time she'd seen it. If not haunted, it was nonetheless enveloped in some malediction. She recalled her first reaction to it, a concurrent sense of revulsion and fascination, as if it might somehow pull her in. She remembered the villagers' mockery, the scoffs that denied the place venerability. Only Juan seemed caught in the manor's spell, to defy the communal will that it be forgotten or ignored.

When Cori reached the top of the two stone steps, Juan tugged on the heavy door that swung out with a grating of dry metal. Crossing the high sill felt like stepping into an icy pool. The black and white tiles chilled her feet and ankles as she stood in the dim entry while her eyes adjust to the darkness. She shuffled in a few feet as Juan came in behind her and closed the door, cutting the beam of sunshine from outside so that only filtered light illuminated the entrance hall.

The wall to her left was blank to a point midway down the hall, where an arch the width of two doors opened to a room brighter than the entry. Straight ahead another arch led to what appeared to be a center hall. To her immediate right was an iron-hinged door of black wood with an arched top. Juan opened it unceremoniously.

"The study," he said.

It was empty and no larger than her bedroom at the school, though square rather than rectangular. Grungy windows on the side and front of the room made it possible to see the outline of vacant bookshelves built into the back wall.

Mutely, she followed Juan out, down the hall and into the archway on the left.

"The reception hall."

The room was long, three times the size of the study, and likewise empty. It too was lit by the front windows, as well as by a tall window opposite the doors. Cori could see nothing through either. Filmed with dirt, they diffused the sunlight so that the whole chamber seemed blurry. She couldn't help but imagine a colonial gala of gentry from God-knows-where, other haciendas she supposed, some out from Ayacucho maybe, celebrating and mingling, discussing the state of Peruvian and world affairs. So close to the great battlefield of Quinua, the hacienda might even have played some role in the revolution against Spain. The very smoke and cry of clashing armies could have been planned and commanded from a place such as this. Shouts of victory, too, might have resounded within these walls.

She looked at Juan, so rustic, so uneducated, so buffoonish in his aspirations. Did he have any sense of what so probably occurred here?

Juan evidently took her silence as a sign to move on and stepped back into the corridor. From there they entered the mansion's center. A curved wooden staircase swept up the right side of the room to the second floor, its dark railing swirling with it, then straightening along three sides, past doors to rooms on two of those walls and a balcony opposite the stairs. Above the staircase, a six-foot stained glass window showered the hall in a prism of colors, its symmetrical design coordinated around a large claret circle with a golden letter H in the center. The globe and initial were intact, unlike parts of the rest, which had been repaired with bits of colored cellophane affixed over breaks in tinted glass. A lone straight-backed chair under the staircase was the only furniture in the room.

Juan crossed the hall and passed under another arch, the thick doors of which were pinned back to either side. There an old table, its rugged planks two inches thick, filled the room. Interior shutters, rough-hewn and heavy like the doors, covered windows on the far wall.

"They took the chairs—all but the one," Juan said. "They took everything but this. It was too heavy."

"This building is beautiful, Juan."

"Part of it is very old, and part of it my father and grandfather rebuilt."

How odd that Juan should speak of the old hacendados as if he knew them and was a part of their family, an heir to their estate, not the disavowed child born of a household servant.

"So strangely out of place," she said, walking back to the center hall, scanning the open second floor and settling her gaze on the blazes of colored light spattered on the walls and floor.

"No! It is not out of place," Juan said loudly. "It is the heritage of Hacienda Hurtado. It is my inheritance!"

"Juan, I mean it is so unlike everything around it, unlike the whole village."

"The village is the hacienda, too."

"Not is, *was*, Juan. Not now," she said.

"It will be again," he said. "The military dictators drove my father off. But he will come back, with my brothers, and when they do, they will see that I protected the house from vandals and weather. They will see that I am also a true Hurtado, and my father will acknowledge me as his rightful son."

Cori said nothing.

"Please, sit," Juan said as he pulled the chair to the center of the room, into the shattered rainbow.

She obeyed, hoping as she did that she had not badly misjudged this deluded loner by coming with him to this lair of sad dreams.

"It will happen," he said, dropping to one knee before her so that their faces were nearly level. "When it does, I will live here in this house, and those peasants who snicker behind my back and call me 'Hacendadito' will be sorry."

"They are mean, Juan, but maybe they are just being realistic about this place."

"No. Listen. I will live here. But when they come back, they will find a bumpkin and will be ashamed of me. I have to do something before then to better myself. And you...you..."

"If you want me to teach you, of course I will, Juan. I've told you that before."

"No. I mean, yes, I want you to teach me, but not like the little kids." He leaned closer to her and set his hand upon her knee. She moved her hands to lift his, and as she did, he caught them both with his free hand and brought them down as a net would fall upon a fluttering bird, trapping them between his strong hands.

"Juan," she pleaded. She tried to pull one of her hands free, but he held them fast.

"What I am saying is, I want you. I love you! You are what I need to make me more like them. Then we could both live in this beautiful place."

"Oh, Juan, please. You are sweet and that is flattering. But we are not a couple. That is not what is between us. I appreciate all your help, but we are...colleagues."

Juan opened his hands, freeing hers. He leaned back and crossed his arms. Cori looked down the hall, measuring in her mind how quickly she might run in her hobbled fashion to the door and outside, where she might scream for help.

"You too think I am a clown."

"No, I don't, Juan," she said as kindly as she could. "I don't treat you like that. You know that."

"Then it is the priest, isn't it?"

"Juan, I know you were watching this morning." She reached out and put her hand on his shoulder. "Please try to understand. You and I are friends. I'll help you to better yourself if I can. I will. But as a teacher, not as your wife."

She waited for him to respond but he seemed to look past her into the dark recesses of the room.

"And please, don't ask me about my feelings for someone else," she said. "It's just not appropriate right now."

Cori got up to leave, and Juan did not try to stop her. His anger seemed to have abated, and she felt guilty leaving him there this way. She wished she didn't feel so relieved to be away from him. Yet she did, especially after hearing him mutter, just before she stepped again into the sunshine.

"What is going on with the priest is not appropriate, either."

22

Steven went straight to the mayor's house from Cori's patio. He sheepishly passed the little house where he had been expected to spend the night, and was thankful he didn't encounter Señora Eulalia. Don Javier answered his knock immediately and stepped outside, setting his fedora on his head as he shut the door. He told Steven he had already informed some of the Pachari family's relatives in the village of the deaths. Steven followed the mayor, who led the way to a stand of houses up the hill past the turn in the road to Huamanguilla. Don Javier rapped at the door of a low house that Steven at first mistook to be a hut for animals or storage, and spoke with two somber men who emerged in tire-soled sandals and dusty black pants. One man was about as old as the mayor and the other close to Steven's age. All four stood for a few minutes, with only an occasional brief exchange in Quechua between the men and the mayor. It finally dawned on Steven that they must be waiting for him to speak.

"We are all going together?" Steven asked Don Javier.

"Yes. They are relatives, Cansio, here, and his son Jacinto. The dead are Cansio's brother, sister-in-law, and nephew."

"Please tell them I am very sorry, and will pray for the departed. Anything else they need they should ask."

The mayor translated for the men, who in turn nodded and thanked him with a simple, "Gracias."

"We need to get Angel," Steven said.

Don Javier spoke to Jacinto, who ran off up the ridge toward where the catechist lived. While they waited, Steven looked across the countryside and could see the hills where the hammer and sickle had glowed last night. The day was as clear as freshly cleaned glass, and the nearest slopes across the long incline of fields and beyond the valley stood in stark outline along the horizon. In the light of day he couldn't tell which ridge had served as a beacon for insurrection. Don Javier came alongside him and followed the priest's eyes.

"That was for Ayacucho," he said.

"And anyone else who could see it, I imagine."

"True. I just don't think it was aimed at Urpimarca. If they want to send us a message, there are easier ways."

"Like scrawling slogans on walls."

"That too. But people say when the terrucos want to be clear they usually send a messenger to the person directly, or to someone else to relay it. They send a warning, just one, but not always."

"Have you gotten a warning?"

"Not yet. Near Huancayo they warned a mayor to resign and he didn't. When they came, they tied him to a post in the square. The villagers' pleas were useless, as were the tears of his wife and daughters. They stabbed him in the heart."

Angel and the other man strode into view higher up the hill and descended with halting steps over the stony path.

"Would you resign?"

"I don't court mining engineers in hopes of attracting jobs as he did. We are simple farmers here, who grow little more than we need. I don't think they care what we do here."

Angel greeted Cansio solemnly, and was courteous, if reserved, with the mayor, but he grabbed Steven in his typical abrazo, slapping the priest's back with both hands.

Don Javier and the other two men walked quietly ahead as

they left the village on the road that skirted the ravine. Steven and Angel lagged behind.

"Those two have had a very tough night," Angel said. "They are afraid of the souls of their murdered relatives. They heard the cries of the dead last night."

One of the first things Steven had learned in the sierra was the Andean belief that after death the soul wanders for eight days before its appointment with God, when it is judged and dispatched to either heaven or hell.

"Jacinto told me it was a terrible, angry racket," Angel said.

When the men reached Steven's car, after a mostly silent hike, Don Javier joined Cansio and Jacinto in the rear seat out of deference to Angel's long legs. Steven rolled down the window on his side of the Beetle, which felt stuffy, packed with five grown men.

"Todo está bien, señores?" he said slowly, unsure if the mourners possessed even elementary Spanish.

"Está bien. Gracias," the mayor replied.

Angel rolled down the front passenger window as well.

Steven glanced at Angel, wondering about apus and what role, in his friend's mind, they played in the tragedy these men must now witness. Did Angel find the apus to be participants in the cosmic struggle between good and evil, or dispassionate spectators to an internecine drama, a black comedy among wanton mortals?

Steven didn't want to dwell right now on their destination. He could not shake off the grisly images in that farmhouse. Everything today seemed to lie in the shadow of that grotesque display, even the embraces he had shared with Cori last night. The feel of her hand in his, the weight of her body as she rested against his chest, the faint tickle of her hair against his cheek, the scent of shampoo mingled with the smoky aroma of the countryside. Such sweetness paled beneath the macabre mural of hate they were driving toward.

He tried to let the feelings of tenderness linger. He had never felt so comfortable with a woman. More than that, he felt complemented. The emptiness he had felt for many years was now being filled. It wasn't about sex, though it was inarguably physical. He couldn't deny that. Her offer of intimacy, the way she placed her hand on his shoulder or his arm—unassuming, uncalculating—stood in contrast to the deference he had received from most women, young or old, since his ordination.

A knot in his stomach, though, gave him pause, the nagging concern that he feared was going to grow into full-blown remorse: the contradiction of his vocation and his feelings for Cori. He recalled the look on her face when he failed to kiss her back this morning. The hurt in her eyes pained him. He remembered the longing gaze of another woman who pushed him to Peru.

As the adobe house of the Pachari family came into view, Steven said a silent prayer that someone else had by now dealt with the tragic mess. A man and woman squatted beside the house, with a small black dog sprawled beside them. Steven and his passengers got out of the car and greeted the man, who rose to his feet at their approach and spoke to Don Javier in Quechua.

"The bodies are still inside," the mayor explained to Steven, "just as you found them. These people are neighbors. They sent a son to Huamanguilla this morning to find the prosecutor. Until he arrives, no one can move the bodies."

"We don't need to stay, Padre," Angel said. "They don't expect you to stand around out here for hours waiting for the officials."

"That's all right. I don't mind, if they want me here. We should pray."

"Yes, we can, but they won't put much value on it. These dead must wander their eight days, returning to places they visited in life, picking up their footprints and saying goodbye."

A Mass on the eighth day, Steven already knew, would be the best he could offer this family, on the day when their loved ones' spirits departed this world for their great reckoning with God. While the notion of the wandering soul didn't fit Catholic orthodoxy, the church had somehow come to terms with it here in Peru. Or perhaps, it had just given up. No relative or friend would bother to attend a funeral Mass before the eighth day. They saw it as futile. A Mass on the eighth day, however, was a faith-filled and indispensable appeal to God that might yet save the sinner's soul.

They prayed together anyway, and when they were finished Steven and Angel set out toward Huamanguilla.

As he backed the car onto the road, Steven noticed Cansio and Jacinto leading the black dog by a leash behind the house.

"What are they doing?" Steven asked. Angel turned to look.

"The dog belonged to the dead. These men are going to send it on with its owners."

"What?"

"It's all right, Padre. The dog will guide them on the narrow path and help them cross the river that is between this life and God. If they miss their appointment, they might never move on and would haunt their family forever."

23

Cori's job got harder after her rejection of Juan because he stopped taking care of the school. He hadn't disappeared. He simply steered clear of the school on his ambles to the manor. Some mornings she would see him moving along the field edge beyond the patio, pretending he didn't see her. She suspected that he still spied on her and lurked among the undergrowth, as he had the night she slept in Steven's arms.

She now rationed her kerosene, since what Juan had done unbidden she would have to find someone else to do. Likewise, if something needed repair she would have to approach Don Javier, or perhaps one of the village men with children in the school. Either way, it was obvious that she had fallen out with Juan, and people were probably speculating about why. She could only imagine what kinds of rumors might be developing, or what Juan might have said. Her consolation, sad as it might be, was that no one in Urpimarca took Juan seriously.

In the weeks that followed the events that had exploded around it, the village settled into a quiet that reminded Cori of the silence in the marketplace in Ayacucho after the last shot had been fired and before anyone dared breathe, when it seemed as if her own heart had been stilled. Recalling the chaos that broke as people fled seconds later, like an explosion itself, Cori braced for the aftershock that could be as deadly as the first temblor. A sweet yearning sharpened her anxiety. In waiting, in a village without a telephone or post office and without anyone in whom she could confide, Cori took it on faith that Steven could be neither shallow nor capricious. If he couldn't get to Urpimarca soon, and a priest's visit was rare enough, then she would be going into Ayacucho at the end of the month to get her salary from the ministry. Somehow, through Angel or Judy, she would arrange to see him.

Angel had returned after a couple days in the city, and if he guessed the depth of her feelings for Steven or his for her, the catechist didn't let on. Nor did Cori attempt to talk with him and ask casually how her gringo friend was or when he might be back. Angel and the other villagers were beginning the harvest. Their energies were focused on their crops, on pulling from the black earth the tubers that would nourish them over the winter. In their view they were receiving from Pachamama the fruit of her gestation, the great gift of life. Sometimes so few children came to school that she spent the day reviewing past lessons, unwilling to teach anything new until all her charges were back.

One Sunday morning, Cori stood in the tiny school kitchen, sheltered from a wind that blew through the patio, sipping her coffee and planning the day before her. When it warmed up she would walk off some stiffness the cooling weather had put in her hip. The tricky part was not overdoing it and ending up lamer than before.

"Teacher?" someone called from outside.

Peering through the doorway, Cori was surprised to see Lucero standing on the flagstone. Remembering Lucero's rudeness on the ride to Huamanguilla with Steven, she wasn't totally pleased to see her.

"Sí? How are you?"

"Fine. You?"

"The same."

"Am I interrupting your breakfast?"

212

"No. I was just having coffee. Would you like some?"

"Sí. Gracias. That would be nice."

Cori grabbed a cup and poured coffee essence into it, then added hot water from a thermos.

"Come in," she said handing the cup to Lucero and signaling with a wave of her index finger the jar of sugar.

The two stood face-to-face, squeezed into the tiny cube of the kitchen.

"I came to see if you would like to go with me up the hill beyond the other side of the village today."

"I was just thinking of walking a bit, but I am afraid I might not be up to so ambitious a climb. Thank you anyway."

"You don't have to climb. I have a burro for you."

Lucero didn't seem like someone who went out of her way to do nice things for others without expecting something in return, and Cori was tempted to ask what it was going to cost her, but she decided rudeness wasn't warranted. Lucero was one of the few other women in the village Cori was sure spoke fluent Spanish. Had it not been for Lucero's tone in the car that day, Cori might have warmed to her as a friend here. Perhaps Lucero recognized that.

"I have never ridden an animal."

"It's easy, and there's a saddle, an old one, but good enough, I think. Why not give it a try?"

Not until they were out of sight of the village did Cori climb into the saddle on the brown donkey. Unable to bend her left hip, she was positioned awkwardly, only half sitting. Lucero lengthened the stirrup on one side to help Cori sit more securely, and then walked ahead, leading the animal into a plodding gait before dropping back beside Cori as the beast trudged along the path circling the mountain.

"The path leads all the way around the hill, but smaller trails branch off up the slopes past the trees," Lucero explained. "It is probably too steep for you to go to the summit on the donkey, but if you dismount we can walk there."

Ahead Cori could make out some structures on the downside of the path, and as they drew nearer, she could see it was the cemetery.

"My father is there," Lucero said. "He died when I was very little."

"Oh, I'm sorry. That must have been hard."

"He was murdered."

Lucero stepped in front and stopped the burro. She grasped the animal's throatlatch and looked at Cori as if searching for a reaction.

"Murdered? That's horrible, Lucero."

"He was too prosperous. We had two houses, one here and one higher in the mountains, where we grazed sheep. People in the campo are envious of anyone who gets ahead. He was found dead up near where he watered the sheep. My uncle, who saw the body, said my father had been poisoned."

Lucero scratched the burro's head. Cori wondered if Lucero wanted to visit the grave, but she resumed talking without moving on.

"Some time after my father died, my mother took up with another man. That left little room for me. I was rebellious and refused to do chores. So my mother decided I was unfit for the campo and sent me to work as a housekeeper in Ayacucho. My employers wouldn't speak Quechua, but they understood it.

"I was ten years old. They were not so rich, not so white, and not so nice. The señor owned a little store. When I was fourteen, the señora went away for a few days to visit some relatives with her two sons. They were just a little older than me. I had a room on the roof, and that night the señor came up there. I was so naive that I didn't even know what he had come for until he started touching me. And then I couldn't stop him. I didn't know what to do. I just froze. Those were the worst few days of my life. He came for three nights, and each time was more demanding."

Lucero stared into the back of the donkey's head, which the animal had pressed against her chest, like it wanted petting. Cori couldn't see Lucero's eyes, but neither the tone of her voice nor the slightest tremor of her lips gave any hint of tears.

"He said he would kill me if I told the señora, but she didn't go away again so maybe she suspected. I don't know. Then his sons started coming to my room at night. But I had gotten a lock for it and wouldn't let them in. I told the señora her sons were pestering me at night." She looked up at Cori.

"What did the señora say?"

"She slapped my face and called me a chola for tempting them!"

"That's horrible!"

"She asked me who I thought I was. She called me conceited and ungrateful. She kept repeating chola, chola, chola, each time in a way more ugly than before."

"What did she expect you to do?"

Lucero just looked at her, and now it was Cori who felt naive.

"I came back here. My mother's new man had already found himself a younger woman, so I stayed with my mother and my sister."

Lucero turned quickly and led the burro on, staying out front this time.

Cori wanted to say something, to offer some comfort, but Lucero hadn't given her the opportunity to express pity. Everyone in Peru knew that empleadas were often sexually abused. That was nothing new. People just didn't talk about it.

Shortly past the cemetery the path turned left, uphill, and soon lost the cover of trees and shrubs, breaking into an alpine terrain, sparse and rugged. On this side of the hill, the land lost the gentle sloping grace of the village side and the trail followed the narrow edge of a steep ravine. From here, Cori knew, the mountains dropped precipitously to the high cloud forest and gave way to the vast jungle that extended across the continent. Though the path was smooth, and the donkey tranquil and sure-footed, she felt off-balance and imagined herself falling off the burro and tumbling out of sight.

Cori leaned into the burro's neck.

"I'll get down now and walk," she said.

Lucero brought the burro to a halt. Cori slipped off. Solid ground felt good, and she steadied herself there for a few seconds, one leg asleep, holding onto the burro's back.

"Just a little way ahead and we can leave this fellow. There's a good trail that goes to the top."

The place Lucero indicated was a wide junction where the path branched, the main trail steering up the grade yet again and disappearing around a bend while another followed a spur down the mountainside to the right. A separate and narrower trail shot up to the left and would require them to climb a short bank to reach it.

Lucero tied the burro to a rock, and then signaled Cori to come to where she stood.

She prodded something with the toe of her shoe. On the ground was a small pile of leaves that looked a lot like small bay leaves, some of them chewed up.

"Coca leaves," Lucero said. "The people leave them when they pass by here as an offering to the apu of this hill. It's disrespectful not to leave something, and they're afraid the apu will punish them if they don't."

"Punish them how?"

"Make them sick, mostly, or something bad might happen, one of their animals could die maybe."

"Should we leave something?"

"Ha! Vamos." Lucero started up the bank to the trail on the

left, waiting part way to offer Cori a hand up.

Cori dug into her pocket for an offering of lemon drops, but finding none turned and followed Lucero up the hill.

The new path led around the face of the hill in the direction they had come. After walking some fifteen minutes they returned to the panorama that Cori was used to seeing from the village, only the higher vantage point opened the vista even wider. She looked across the countryside on a new level, with the hills in the distance and a great unbroken vault of sky all around them.

Lucero sat on a rock and Cori joined her.

"This is what I wanted to show you," Lucero said.

Cori nodded. The view spoke for itself.

"You can see the Pampas de Quinua from here," Lucero said.

"I want to visit it one of these days."

"It's just a big field with that obelisk in it."

"Oh, go on! It's the most important battlefield in South America. That is what I teach the children, anyway. It's Peru's contribution to the liberation of Latin America."

"It is a monument to continuism!" Lucero shot back. "The Spanish were defeated, but for the peasants nothing changed."

It was clear to Cori that Lucero hadn't learned these ideas in a shopkeeper's house in Ayacucho. Cori had heard this kind of talk before, and the direction the conversation was taking made her nervous.

"Lucero, what that man did to you was rape, you know that, and you were young. You were right to get away."

"He treated me like his property." Lucero's tone was argumentative, much as it had been in the car ride with Steven. "That's what the woman's role is in this society, and worse if you are a campesina, an Indian, a chola. The oppression of women— of poor women especially—is founded on the concept of private property. Whether a woman is working for someone who abuses her or is in a bourgeois marriage, it's all the same thing."

"Oh, Lucero, please. What happened to you as a young girl wasn't political. It was criminal. Don't let bitterness get you mixed up in Marxism. Look what it's leading to. Look at the violence. That isn't going to help anyone."

Lucero stood up. She breathed deeply, looking down at Cori and speaking more calmly. "You people who are educated are so gullible. Why is that? In Ayacucho I went to secondary school at night but didn't finish because I came back here, yet I know more about life than you ever will. Here we live in semi-feudalism and the so-called agrarian reform that broke up the hacienda did nothing to better the life of the peasants. Why? Because all economies maintain a class system, the same as always, Spaniards or no Spaniards, hacendado or no hacendado."

Cori hated politics, and here she was, being lectured to by a woman whom she had hoped only minutes earlier might yet become a friend.

Looking up at Lucero, Cori squinted into the sunshine. The young woman stood in sepia silhouette against the light. Her Andean physique, broad through the chest and square through the hips, was fringed by a glow that gave way to a cloudless blue sky. Her arms were muscular and scalloped, like a man's. Cori had a hard time imagining her as a pliant adolescent whom a grown man had forced so easily to comply. Lucero crouched down and her face again took on the color and texture of live flesh.

"Listen, the last teacher here understood this. He was a good teacher, and those of us who listened learned a lot from him."

"And what happened to him?"

"You already know. He disappeared after the soldiers came through one time."

"Is that what you want to have happen to me, Lucero?"

"Teacher, listen closely, understanding sometimes takes a while, especially if someone hasn't had the opportunity to learn correctly. That's okay. The important thing in the meantime is not choosing the wrong side."

Cori didn't want to listen to this diatribe anymore. She turned toward Ayacucho, in the direction where she knew it lay. She imagined going into the city and meeting Steven in a café on the plaza.

But Lucero refused to let Cori daydream.

"As women we must be motivated by logic, not feelings, which is what allows men to use us at will," Lucero said. "We must be as politicized as men and be as indispensable in the people's war."

Lucero took Cori by the shoulders, forcing her to turn face-to-face.

"This is a momentous time for the Peruvian woman, the campesina woman. We must all be Micaela Bastida!"

At this Cori stood up, gripping Lucero's arm to steady and pull herself to her feet. The two women stood in an awkward embrace, Cori with her hand still on Lucero's firm bicep and Lucero with her other hand on Cori's shoulder.

"Lucero, the Spaniards cut out Bastida's tongue and chopped off her head with a dull sword. They made her husband watch, and then ripped him apart with horses. Micaela and Tupac Amaru are our heroes, but they died horribly—and their insurrection with them. The generals today will be just as cruel, just not so public."

"This time, so will the cholas."

24

Steven stayed away from Urpimarca in the weeks that followed. He went out to other villages, but he didn't go near the old hacienda.

He yearned to go. Yet the pin jab of doubt he felt when leaving there had swollen to a pulsing wound. He struggled. Even trying to just let it go, turning his long history of doubt and uncertainty over to God, didn't work. It seemed as if God handed it right back to him and said, "No, you deal with it." And now Steven had upped the stakes in his old quandary. He was falling in love.

Had Steven wrestled with these demons earlier in life, before ordination, he might have reconsidered his vocation. He never did. His ability to handle what was expected of him, to overcome whatever challenge came next, made his calling clear—or so he thought. That he liked women was undeniable, but it had not been the kind of obsession that tormented many of his fellow seminarians. That came later for him.

So he stayed away from Urpimarca. And he felt terrible about it. He should have contacted Cori, if only to let her know that, despite the confusion he was feeling now, what had passed between them had been real, and he ached to be with her. So how could he put into words or writing his conclusion that they could never allow such intimacy to happen again, that he needed to remain true to the commitment he had already made in his life? He didn't want another way of life. He didn't want to be anything except a priest. Still, Cori dominated his thoughts even more than his mounting fear of the guerrillas.

Just set her down again, Steven told himself as he neared Huamanguilla one afternoon. Stop carrying her around all day. But he couldn't.

He came into Huamanguilla, passing through on his way back to Ayacucho, and turned his VW up the street toward Judy's. He needed to talk, and maybe confide in someone. Judy wasn't Catholic, but was American and might understand him. She wasn't home. He left a note saying they should get together soon.

He stopped the car at the bottom of Judy's street. Left was the road back to Ayacucho. It was late and he should go that way. Right would take him to the plaza and from there to the dirt road that would eventually take him to Urpimarca. He waited. And he waited. The engine was running. In Ayacucho he would have dinner with the priests at the monastery, or he would go out to a restaurant, and later he would have a well-deserved beer after a day in the sun and dust of the mountains and watch some television. Still, that all seemed so empty. The engine idled on. He would end the night in his room reading. Restlessness would keep him from concentrating and it would be a wasted effort. He could make himself a stiff té piteado with an extra-large shot of pisco, and try to sleep—try to sleep and forget about Cori. He smiled to himself as another idea occurred. He could take some pisco to Urpimarca. He pictured the two of them on the school patio, snug beneath a wool blanket, vapors rising from the hot tea and the flavor of pisco on her lips.

Steven turned the car toward Urpimarca, drove to the plaza, and stopped in front of a little shop that would probably have a bottle or two of pisco. He sat there. The engine idled. It was getting late. He would have to drive past the Pachari farm in the dark. The ghastly face of the youth hanged from the rafter came back to him. The terror he had felt on the road alone, the sense of being stalked, the premonition that the pistaco was real, came back in full measure.

What was he doing? Plotting to sneak out to a village at night with a bottle of liquor to see a woman? How was he supposed to explain that to the villagers? How would he explain it to Cori? Here, liquor's quicker? The very thought was humiliating—and disrespectful. He was deluding himself. He was a fool.

He pounded the steering wheel with the heel of his hand, and with a squeal of tires he hurled the car around the plaza and headed back to Ayacucho.

25

Steven met Judy in the foyer of the monastery. He knew something was wrong as soon as he saw her. He led her to a waiting room just off the entry.

"Is everything all right?" he asked as she took a seat on a couch. She shuddered.

"What's wrong?" Steven asked.

"I came this close," Judy said, holding her thumb and forefinger almost together, "to being killed two days ago by the Shining Path." She breathed deeply and let out a long sigh.

"We had a training workshop at a private compound in the campo near Huancayo over the weekend. I wasn't feeling well, so I skipped supper and went to lie down. They surprised and disarmed the guards and must have gone right past my room. Thank God I didn't have the light on or anything. They marched right into the training session. By luck all the rest of the ACEP staff were Peruvians—but I should have been in there.

"They told everyone they were the Communist Party of Peru, the fourth sword—Marx, Lenin, Mao, and this Peruvian maniac Gonzalo. They surrounded the room and hung up a banner with Gonzalo's face on it. They checked everyone's ID, especially a couple of lighter-skinned kids from Lima who they thought might be foreigners, and they interrogated the entire group like they were criminals. They harangued the staff for an hour. They made them sit through a rambling economics lesson and denounced the semi-feudalism of Peru. They launched into the United States, saying that all the aid we give is just intended to perpetuate the powerlessness of the people while international companies siphon off Peru's wealth. They accused everyone in the room of being collaborators and threatened that this would be their only warning."

"Good Lord," Steven said.

"Then they wanted to know where their American bosses were hiding."

Steven shook his head incredulously. "No one said anything about you?"

"Not a word. Someone tapped at my door right after they came in and whispered that the terrucos were here and to stay put. I was never so terrified in my life. I actually hid under the bed."

"Thank God you didn't come out. Nobody was hurt?"

Judy closed her eyes and didn't answer immediately. When she opened them again, she looked at the ceiling and her voice was thick.

"The director, José Mejía," she said. "He just walked in on them. He told them he was the director and then they questioned him for a long time with loaded questions, like why did he prostitute himself to the foreign exploiters. They called him a traitor."

"They shot him?"

She shook her head furiously, not only denying Steven's conclusion, but as if trying to shake off the memory.

"Not shot. They dragged him into the yard and smashed his head with rocks."

Judy grabbed a tissue from the end table and wiped her eyes and nose. She took a breath and continued.

"They blew up two of our vehicles and painted slogans on the walls. Even when folks told me it was safe to come out of my room I was afraid to move. I didn't sleep the whole night and didn't come out of my room until morning. I just grabbed my pack and left. I didn't see his body. They said I should wait for the police. I couldn't. I went out to the road and caught the first bus. I was hoping it was going to Lima, but here I am."

Steven pressed his palms flat together, his fingers to his lips, like a child learning to pray. He lowered them to speak.

"They would have killed you for certain."

"The same way, or worse somehow. I can't even imagine."

"How is it that Senderistas show up at a workshop where you are the only gringa, and you aren't in the room?"

The first hint of a smile curled from Judy's mouth. "My mom and dad are Southern Baptist evangelicals and they get down on their knees and pray for me every day."

"Tell them, don't ever stop," Steven said.

Judy let out a nervous laugh that dissolved into tears. Steven stood and she stepped up and into his arms and he hugged her, patting her back as she regained control.

"You going to be okay?" he asked.

"Yeah," Judy said, stepping back. "Give me a minute. Which way is the ladies' room?"

Steven directed her down the hall.

She returned looking somber but clear-eyed. Steven had two cups of coffee and some rolls waiting on the coffee table. They sat down together on the sofa.

"Too early for something stronger, I guess," she said, reaching for a coffee.

"I could find something."

"Nah, just joking, sort of. It is too early, even under present circumstances."

"What will you do now?" he asked.

"I've no idea. I got into Ayacucho yesterday, and I was at the office today. People thought I was already on my way home.

225

They're bringing José's body back today. I haven't heard any plans for the funeral yet. After that, I don't know what's going to happen. I probably have to leave. This carrot top of mine is kind of hard to hide."

Steven sat back in his chair and sipped his coffee, watching Judy twirl an unbitten roll in her hand absentmindedly. His sister had red hair like Judy, but not so intense. Picturing Rosemary trekking across the Peruvian Andes in three-inch heels made him smile.

"Well, it is," Judy said.

"It wasn't that. I was thinking of my sister, whose hair is red, too. But that's as far as the comparison goes. She isn't an adventurer like you."

"I wasn't at first, but then I grew into it. In the Peace Corps, in Ecuador, I was a babe in the woods. But after a couple years there I became smitten with Latin America and wanted to keep working with indigenous people. I seem to scare the bejesus out of the men, but make friends with the women easily enough. There's a definite gender bond. Even though they think I'm strange because I don't have a husband and kids, we connect on the level of caregiving, I think. You don't have to be a mom to nurture. They see that in me. They know I'm trying to make their lives easier with all the new ideas I bring, and they dig that."

"I hate to say it, but I don't think staying on is going to be an option," Steven said.

"It isn't safe for any of us to wander out in the campo anymore, Padre. Even you."

"I'll be all right. My ministry is pastoral. But if all the foreigners leave the highlands, it's going to get a lot lonelier. The only other American I know here is Father Jaime. But I guess if I wanted to be surrounded by American friends, I could have stayed in Lima. Here my friends are basically you and Angel."

"And Cori."

Steven felt himself flush.

Judy laughed out loud, and in a needling tone added, "Gotcha, Padre!"

"Okay, you got me. But let's drop that line of inquiry," Steven said with a tone more plaintive than commanding.

Judy's laughter trailed off into an approving smile. "Hey, she's cute and sweet," she said.

"I know."

"So what is a priest supposed to do if he's attracted to someone?"

Steven stared into his coffee as if willing some clarity to emerge from the reflections playing on its dark surface.

"I used to have an answer for that," he said.

26

When the soldiers came into Urpimarca, Cori saw them first through the windows of the classroom, where she was in the middle of a lesson. They marched onto the plaza and stopped directly in front of the school.

They didn't knock. The door opened and a lieutenant with a sidearm on his belt entered, followed by two soldiers with rifles. The children turned as the soldiers filed across the back of the room, and some of the smaller children hurried over to older siblings. One girl ducked behind Cori.

"Good morning, teacher," the lieutenant said tersely. He was muscular and thickly built, with a heavy but neatly trimmed black mustache.

"Sí? Good morning. Can I help you?"

The lieutenant scanned the walls, peering at the alphabet and numbers charts and the lesson on the chalkboard, and then ran his gaze over the rows of students sitting on benches. He motioned to his men, who slung their rifles over their shoulders.

"This will not take long, and it will help if they take out their notebooks as we go around." The officer put his hand out toward a girl in front of him. The child looked first at the hand and then at Cori.

"Your notebook!" the lieutenant snapped and pointed to the book on the girl's lap. She handed it up without looking at him. He flipped through it, occasionally stopping to read something before turning a page. The soldiers collected others and followed suit.

Cori turned to the girl behind her. "Go get your notebook and bring it to me."

The child ran to the bench where she had been sitting and returned with the book, slipping back behind her teacher again.

After giving back the notebook he was inspecting, the officer stepped over to Cori, who handed him the little girl's work. He seemed to review it perfunctorily.

"May I ask what you are looking for?" Cori said.

"That should be obvious. We have a duty to ferret out communists."

"These are just children. You're upsetting them."

"It has to be done. We'll be finished soon enough."

However much she resented the intrusion, and despite what pretense she might attempt, Cori knew she had little authority. This inspection was more about her than the students.

"What is this?" one of the soldiers asked heatedly. He was looking down at one of Cori's helpers, a fifth grader named Pilar. The lieutenant strode over and looked at her notebook.

"Stand over there near the wall," he told the girl. Tears filled Pilar's eyes as she did what she was told. The lieutenant brought the book to Cori.

"Can you explain this?"

On one page Pilar had drawn a hammer and sickle. On another, in the margin among geometric scribbles, drawings of flowers, and bordering reminiscent of patterns in village weavings, were the words: Viva Presidente Gonzalo! PCP!

"She is bright—and bored. She doodles."

"Why this stuff?"

"She scribbles what she sees. They all saw the hammer and sickle lit up on the hillside and the words painted on buildings. You see that even in Ayacucho."

229

He looked at her skeptically, as if insulted by the simplicity of her answer. Tucking Pilar's notebook under his arm, the lieutenant continued around the room, looking at the work of other students.

When no further evidence of indoctrination was found, the lieutenant motioned for Pilar to follow the soldiers out of the classroom. He nodded abruptly to Cori and headed toward the door.

"Where are you taking my student?" Cori demanded, stepping toward the door.

"What?" he said, with a flash of anger.

Cori stepped back as if pushed and dropped her gaze before responding imploringly.

"Please, she didn't do anything."

He pushed Cori aside and led the girl out to the plaza. The door remained open. Cori stayed with the other children.

When the soldiers were gone, some of the children began whimpering. With hugs and cooing, Cori tried to calm them as best she could. "It's okay. It's okay. They are just making sure we are all safe." As she comforted them, she watched through the window the drama unfolding on the plaza.

In the center of the square, Pilar hung her head as the lieutenant harangued her. Cori couldn't hear his words as he stabbed the pages with his finger. Villagers were beginning to file into the plaza, hanging back from the soldiers and watching the inquisition with growing unease.

"Papá!" shouted a boy who was standing on a bench to see outside. He bolted and ran out to his father. Other children stood on benches to see and two more went out.

"Unless you see your father or mother, stay here!" Cori yelled as some thirty children stirred like a herd of deer, nervous and ready to break in panic. She stepped toward the door to shut it. She saw the lieutenant rip pages out of Pilar's notebook and hand it back to her. He pointed toward the school. Pilar walked in her direction. Cori met her at the door.

"He wants everyone outside on the plaza," Pilar said in a voice smothered in sobs.

"Vamos," Cori told the students. "Hold hands with your partner and stay near me."

Her instructions were largely futile. As soon as the children saw any relative, they rushed to join them. Cori remained with about half of her class on the veranda in front of the school windows. The square filled with villagers, now corralled by soldiers who stood around the perimeter. Most of those assembled were elderly, mothers with young children or campesinos who had been working in the fields close to the village. A few of the men tried to talk to the soldiers. They got no response. Cori looked around for Lucero but didn't see her. Neither was Angel there. Don Javier came down the road with three other men in front of a soldier with a rifle pointed toward the ground at their feet.

Don Javier approached the lieutenant and the two conferred before turning toward the crowd. The lieutenant motioned for people to step back. They obeyed. A little boy stepped on Cori's foot. She propped herself against the wall and gathered the nearest children even closer.

"I am Lieutenant Alejandro Osorio Sanchez," the lieutenant shouted in Spanish. "My job is to find and arrest terrorists."

He waited while Don Javier translated. No one spoke. Most merely looked at the officer. Some stared at the ground. A few shifted their weight from foot to foot. Don Javier watched the lieutenant, who used the pause to look into the faces of individual villagers. Finally, he continued.

"If you know someone who's a terrorist, it's your patriotic duty to tell us." Again he waited, allowing the mayor to translate it into Quechua and letting the villagers ponder what he said. "Rebels, guerrillas, terrorists, they are all the same. And anyone

231

who harbors one, is one!"

He underscored the last sentence with an angry tone. Don Javier didn't bother with the emphasis.

"Communist, Marxist, Maoist, Senderista. It's all the same. Some of you know them. If you don't report them, you are with them! If I don't have names by the time we leave here today, I will know where Urpimarca's loyalties are, won't I?"

Cori's ears burned. She panned the crowd again to see if Lucero was present. She could no more betray Lucero than she would one of her own students, yet she couldn't help but look for the young woman. People on the plaza shifted nervously. Some murmured to neighbors. An elderly woman spoke out, and Don Javier translated.

"This is a peaceful village. Everyone just wants to tend their crops and stay out of politics."

A chorus of affirmation followed.

"Mamita," the officer said, taking a gentler tone with the woman, "I would like nothing better. But the terrorists are not going to let you be. They are already here."

Cori wondered again where Lucero was. In town, perhaps. Who knew? Had she spoken to others as she had to Cori that afternoon on the mountain? She hadn't mentioned the Senderistas by name, but Cori was sure, in her gut, that Lucero was one of them.

Lieutenant Osorio spoke again.

"You don't have to speak publicly. We will be questioning everyone and taking a census of who's here and who's not. Some of my soldiers speak Quechua, so I expect complete cooperation."

He turned to Don Javier, who looked embarrassed at realizing his services as translator had been a test. The lieutenant spoke to the mayor in just as loud a voice, for everyone to hear.

"You need to appoint men to a self-defense militia to protect the village from the guerrillas. I want Urpimarca on our side.

How much we can protect this community depends on how much we can count on it."

He turned and walked a dozen paces toward the main road, where he stopped. The soldiers had set up a checkpoint where he stood. For villagers to return to their homes and fields they needed to filter past it. They began to queue up across the plaza.

Rounding up as many of her students as she could, Cori returned to the classroom. Fewer than half of them rejoined her. The lesson plan was shot for the day, anyway, so she spent the rest of the afternoon distracting the students with storytelling and by coaxing from them the folk tales they heard at home. When the last story was told, she dismissed the children and watched them from the plaza as they ran home. She could see soldiers still going house to house.

She turned at a sound from the path that led up to the mansion, and found Lieutenant Osorio and two of his men approaching from the knoll.

"It's a shame no one uses that old house," he said to Cori.

"The villagers don't want anything to do with it."

"All but one, I gather."

"One of the men takes care of it. He believes the hacendado will return one day."

"A strange man, I am told."

Cori didn't comment, but stepped aside as the officer and his men strode into the classroom again. She followed.

"Find Carvallo and help him search the houses on the hillside," he instructed one of the men. To Cori he said, "I need to see the rest of the school. What is in this closet?"

Cori opened the storage closet door without responding. It held some paper, unused notebooks, and a couple of textbooks. The other soldier knelt down, pulled them out and fanned through them rapidly.

Osorio went to the far door of the classroom and opened it.

"Your office and dormitory?"

"Sí. I am the only teacher here."

"I am well aware of that."

This statement chilled Cori, and she followed him in. He opened the wardrobe, passed his fingers through her coat, a sweater, a blouse, a few skirts, and a couple of pairs of slacks that hung inside. Then he opened the single bottom draw, where Cori had put her underwear, socks, T-shirts, some folded blouses, and a pair of jeans. Bending down, he felt among the clothing, pausing as he rubbed a pair of panties between his fingers while looking her up and down. Her stomach tensed and she caught her breath. He left the apparel disarrayed and the drawer open. Half a dozen books were arranged on the window shelf. He picked up one with a red cover, a shiny metallic wrapping paper she had used to protect it.

"Chairman Mao's Little Red Book?" He didn't look inside.

"Poetry."

He opened up the book to the title page: *The Poetry of Cesar Vallejo*. He set it on the desk and went out the patio door. From there he sent the other soldier to search the kitchen and the storeroom, where Cori kept powdered milk, cooking oil, and dry goods for school lunches.

"This is the nicest place in the village, after the mansion," he said.

"Yes, it is nice."

"Your own little courtyard, with flagstones even."

"It's a functional part of the school. We make school lunches in the kitchen. Unless it's raining, or too cold, the children pull the benches out here and eat."

"You are the only outsider here, no?"

"Living here, yes."

"Who comes who is not from here?"

"A priest comes occasionally."

"The American?"

"Yes. But I would not know if the villagers have other guests, like relatives or friends, unless they told me. They have not said anything like that."

"You know the last teacher here was a communist?"

"No, I don't know that. But I cannot say. I suppose you knew him?"

"No. I was recently posted here from Lima, like you."

Cori caught herself biting her lip and stopped.

"Are you surprised I know so much about you?" he asked.

"Well, I imagine the Education Ministry would tell you whatever you asked." She forced a laugh. "I don't think teaching assignments are state secrets."

"You are exactly right. Whatever I ask. We know the name of every teacher in this zone and where they are from. But that is all that the ministry provided. Our military intelligence goes much further than that."

"Oh?"

"You are friends with this American, for example."

Juan, she thought.

"The priests try to get to know the teachers out in the campo because we are their link to the children, and religious instruction is part of the curriculum," Cori said.

"And your good friend, Señorita Lucero?"

Cori balked. The lieutenant noticed. His eyes seemed to darken and his gaze to grow more penetrating.

"What about the señorita?" Cori asked. "She is not such a good friend. Just one of the women of the village."

Osorio didn't answer. A vein pulsed on one side of his neck.

"Well, I have spoken to her, no more," Cori continued. The lieutenant's silence pressed on her, squeezing something more out of her.

"She and I rode into Huamanguilla once with Padre Steven."

Cori swallowed so as not to say more. She pressed her back teeth together. Another unguarded word and she would mention the climb up the hillside with Lucero. That would open a whole new round of questions. Had his informant seen her with Lucero that day? She shrugged, and smiled.

"Well, lieutenant," she said, "I'm not sure what more I can do for you."

"Would you know where she is?"

"No, I'm sorry. She wasn't on the plaza?"

"I don't think so, but then I don't know what she looks like." He raised his eyebrows and forced a smile, broad but lacking any warmth, like a child grimacing for a camera. "Her mother says she is in Ayacucho and doesn't know when she'll be back. That seems strange in such a little place as this."

Cori considered saying Lucero was very independent, except even that would have revealed more than seemed prudent.

"A mother may not know where her son is, but she always knows where her daughter is," he said. "Unless, of course, the daughter is into things she shouldn't be."

With that the lieutenant ended his interrogation, seeming to give up on getting any further help from Cori. His scowl disappeared, and with an indicative purse of his lips he turned his head toward the kitchen.

"I noticed your stove. Would you have any coffee?"

"Yes, would you like some?"

"If it isn't too much trouble."

"No, I have concentrate. I can boil some water."

The lieutenant muttered some instruction to the other soldier, who left through her room without looking back. Osorio arranged himself comfortably on the settee, crossing his legs and stroking his mustache while looking Cori over again. She went to light the stove.

She put water on to boil. So presumptuous! She wanted to

236

tell him that wasn't his seat, yet it was the only inviting place on the patio, more so than the rough bench outside the kitchen wall. She wondered where he thought a smile would lead, and she hoped she hadn't misjudged the situation—or her own vulnerability. While she waited for the water to heat, Cori remembered her mother's admonition about men, and her own defiant response. She wished she could forget the whole ugly scene, replaying now with painful clarity and a hint of foreboding. Had the barracks now come to her?

What would her mother say about a priest? The same, Cori mused. The same.

The water reached a rolling boil and she took the pan off the stove and poured it into the thermos. The lieutenant entered the kitchen behind her.

"Your coffee will be ready in a second, Lieutenant." She turned around and found herself trapped.

"Please," he said, moving closer. "Alejandro."

"Well, Lieutenant Osorio, if you'll let me—"

Stepping up to her, he took her arms and pinned them to her sides. He leaned forward and tried to kiss her. She pulled her head back and tried to loosen her arms but couldn't. He wrapped one arm around her and used his other hand, like a powerful vise, to hold her head from behind as he kissed her. She returned nothing, and soon he stopped and stood back. His lips curled into a sneer. Grabbing her wrist, he yanked her out of the kitchen. In the courtyard she tried to dig in her heels, but she couldn't physically prevent him from dragging her.

"Please, Lieutenant," she pleaded. "Please, I'm not interested."

"Just come with me," he said, now at the door to her room.

"Please, don't. Please!"

She tried in vain to keep him from forcing her into the room. He slammed the door behind them, still holding her wrist tightly. He dragged her to the bed, and with his free hand pulled the

237

mattress to the floor. With both hands he pushed her down onto it.

Cori looked at the open classroom door, her only hope of rescue or escape. The lieutenant stepped over and pushed it closed. Cori tried to get up, but he was over her before she could get to her feet. He pushed her back onto the mattress, not roughly, but deliberately and mechanically.

She could scream, but for whom? No one in this village had more power right now than he, and no one would get past his soldiers. She wanted to cry, but she felt no tears. She was scared, and getting angry.

The lieutenant grabbed her blouse and Cori gripped his thick wrists as best she could.

"Lieutenant, please, I'm begging you. Stop. Please. Okay? Stop!"

"Don't worry," he said calmly. "I won't hurt you. I have many girlfriends in the campo."

He twisted his wrists free as if her hands were a child's, and started pushing her blouse up. Instinctively she caught him full across the cheek with her palm. The loud smack was followed by a frightening silence. The surprise in his eyes narrowed to rage.

The force of his openhanded counterblow left her vision fuzzy, and she squinted tightly, as much from the pain in her head as the dizziness. She raised her hands to ward off another slap, only partially deflecting the next one, and a third before he stopped. She could hear him seething above the ringing in her ears and her own tremulous breathing.

"Need some more?"

"No," she whimpered.

He thrust her blouse up over her arms and head and broke the snaps on her bra with a single yank. He squeezed her breasts hard until she whined, and then dropped his hands to her pants. She closed her eyes and kept them closed.

Afterward, the lieutenant tucked a blanket around her shoulders, stroked her hair, and stood up. She kept her eyes closed, but could hear him buttoning his uniform.

"Are you all right?" he asked.

She nodded without opening her eyes and kept them closed until she heard him leave through the patio door.

She tore the blanket from her shoulders and kicked it off completely. She lay naked on the mattress. Tears swelled in her eyes and she balled her hands into fists. She pounded the floor. "Maldito! Maldito! Maldito!" Her nails dug into her palms. She hated herself. How careless she had been! How stupid and foolish! She wished she had never come to this place. And Steven? Not coming here would have meant never meeting him. Her anger flared again, and she hated even Steven. He hadn't been here to protect her. A foreign priest could have stood up to this lieutenant. She could have called to him. Had he been here, this wouldn't have happened. It couldn't have. But he wasn't. She wasn't even sure he would ever be back.

Cori only left her room as dusk fell over the village, just long enough to wash in the kitchen sink and carry a knife back to bed. She locked herself in her room and repositioned her mattress. The book of Cesar Vallejo poems still lay on the table and she opened it and read:

There are blows in life, so strong, I don't know!
Blows like the hatred of God, as if before them,
the undertow of everything else suffered
welled up in the soul... I don't know!

Blows like the hatred of God. Not those of the lieutenant, but blows worse than that. Like the hatred of God. What would God's hatred be but the withholding of love? She cried, and stayed in her room for the rest of the night.

The platoon bivouacked on the plaza, mostly under the roof of the veranda, an unnecessary precaution, as the dry season had already overtaken the mountains. She heard the soldiers complain that the lieutenant had drawn quarters in a little house just outside the square. Most likely it was the room Señora Eulalia had prepared for Steven. At dawn she heard them rise, and by the time the children assembled in the school at eight o'clock, the soldiers were gone.

27

Cori sat on the plaza wall, unable to break the depression that enveloped her. She had told no one about the lieutenant, and she realized she had no one she dared tell. It seemed that the villagers, already diffident by nature, had withdrawn even further from her. Their wariness in the days after the army's intrusion followed logically from the countervailing threats of the military and the guerrillas. How could they possibly please both? For that matter, how could they possibly please either? That she felt herself in the cross hairs made her feelings of isolation worse. The usual banter at the wall that had eased her passage into the community ceased, and she once again found herself treated as an outsider.

Cori had failed to make even one close friend since her arrival in February, and it was now nearly June. Lucero fled after the soldiers trooped through—or at least Cori hoped she had fled. Juan's feigned disinterest had grown almost menacing, and Steven had broken her heart. A moment of tenderness offered her no claim on him, naturally. In the course of a normal relationship such affection would have been more defining—either as the beginning of a romance or as an admitted, and embarrassing, wrong turn. Either would be better than the limbo in which Cori now found herself. Steven hadn't been back, and she had heard nothing from or about him. Had he fled the country because of the Shining Path? Had he been scared off by her desire? Maybe he was guilt-racked. What did he think of her now? A temptress luring him to ruin? A needy neurotic, mindless of the consequences of her actions? A disposable woman? The hardest question she continually asked herself: Did he think of her at all?

Lost in her own sad thoughts, Cori at first did not notice Angel enter the plaza. His appearance now didn't cheer her, either. She didn't know the catechist well, so could not confide in him, and trying to put on a cheerful face to a mere acquaintance would take more energy than she felt she could muster.

Angel grinned before he was close enough to speak to her. His lips turned up so high his eyes became slits, exaggerating his nose and making him look impish.

"I have something for you," he said in singsong when he got close, bending at the waist and bringing his face close to hers.

He smiled so effusively that Cori pulled herself out of the slouch into which she had sagged. Before she could ask what he meant, Angel drew an envelope from behind his back and waved it in front of her.

"From someone I think you want to hear from," he said, proffering the envelope.

It was obvious from Angel's cockiness that it had to be from Steven. Who else? She took it and set the unopened envelope on her lap. Whatever Steven had to say, she wasn't going to risk sharing it now with Angel. She feared the worst.

"Thank you," she said.

Disappointment seemed to extinguish Angel's smirk.

"Are you okay, señorita?"

"Sí. Gracias."

"But worried, no?"

"Sí, Angel. Aren't you?"

"Sí." He appeared to think it over. "Sí, I am."

"Have you any idea what happened to Lucero?"

"Only that when she heard the soldiers were looking for her she left the village. Her mother and sister have gone to Ayacucho, too. I don't know if she's with them or has gone somewhere else."

Angel sat beside Cori.

"I'm happy you have a letter from Padre Esteban," he said. "I'm sorry things are turning out here the way they have. The children need a teacher like you. They have a right to that."

"They're all good kids, and many are so bright," Cori said. "We are just beginning to make progress."

"It's unsafe for you here."

"It is unsafe for everyone, Angel, even you. Everyone is worried. You might even say panicked."

"I hear people talk about moving closer to Ayacucho or even going down out of the sierra to Lima, Arequipa, or Tacna. You can't blame them. Who knows where the violence will lead or how much crazier it will get?"

"The murder of the Pachari family has terrified them. The soldiers are as much to blame for their deaths as the terrucos."

"Of course," Angel agreed, "and they've only made it worse by coming here. People are afraid they'll be accused of collaborating either with the guerrillas or the army."

"I used to think of the military as the protector of the nation," Cori said. "I don't think they offer much here. Not now."

"No. Better they weren't here at all. With just one or the other, maybe we'd be all right. But when they both demand you take their side, you end up being the enemy of both."

"Why don't they just leave us alone?"

"The problem is that this is the way to the jungle," Angel said. "Until now the communists were free to move about the sierra because the government wasn't too concerned about them. But the army keeps sending more soldiers, and with helicopters, so these guerrillas are taking cover in the forest. We're right in their path. That's the way to the coca, too. So it's not just ideology. It's money, big money, cocaine money."

"Will they bring troops back here to keep the guerrillas out?" Cori asked with an involuntary shudder.

"Where? Urpimarca? We must hope not. That would be the end of our community, worse than the hacienda days. And it won't work. There are too many paths to the jungle. The soldiers don't respect us, or our way of life. Even if they were once campesinos, the uniform changes them."

That is what was at stake for Angel, a system of beliefs and a way of life. With his indigenist philosophy, he was a walking paradox, opting consciously for a life that his smarts and education should have encouraged him to leave behind.

Whether it would be destroyed by the army or by the terrorists, this Andean way of life Angel loved was in great peril of disappearing. The violence would get worse. The rebels would show themselves, or the soldiers would return, or both. Cori remembered with scant comfort the kitchen knife she now slept with every night.

"So, maybe all we can do is pray," she said. "Maybe we should pray to the apu here for protection, or to Pachamama."

Angel looked off to the hill that rose up from Urpimarca, the summit hidden above.

"Neither apu nor Pachamama have jurisdiction in these matters," he said. "Pachamama is our mother, la tierra santa who nourishes us. She's also our lover, whom we open up and in whose furrows we put seed so that we may live well from her abundance. The apu, the spirit of the mountain, takes care of our animals, our houses, our health. Here we pay homage to both, make offerings to both. If you forget the apu, or Pachamama, you will be punished."

He stared off at the hill again, seeming to find some natural resonance there with his own spirit. Cori looked too, and sensed the mountain's presence, its strength, its power, its determination not to be trifled with—especially if everything you were and had depended upon it.

"Punished by soldiers or murdered by guerrillas," she said.

Angel shook his head from side to side. "I don't think so," he said. "Pachamama can cause drought, or maybe she sends one of the three lazy brothers—the wind, the hail, or the frost—to rob the best of our crop. But that is all she does. If you skip your offering to the apu, maybe your sheep die. No, Señorita Cori, in this matter our prayers need to go to God. This war goes beyond Madre Tierra and the spirits of the hills."

"Between good and evil?" Cori asked.

"Only which is which?"

"I'm not sure even God has the answer for that."

Angel leaned over and stretching his long arm around her shoulders gave her a strong hug, shaking her hard as if to emphasize the brotherly nature of his gesture.

"Listen. I brought you that letter. Maybe that will cheer you up." He stood up and strode a couple feet away before turning back to address her again. "You know, in the Bible, God is the creator who makes everything, which means he makes good, but he makes evil, too. No? I've never been able to truly understand that. For the Quechua, God imposes order out of chaos. Now so much is happening in the world, I think maybe God is just too busy somewhere else."

Cori watched Angel amble back down the road the way he had come. Maybe it was not the hatred of God so much as the indifference of God.

Cori opened Steven's letter with trembling hands.

Dear Cori:

Please excuse the long time that has passed since I saw you in Urpimarca. I'm sending this letter with Angel, who is here in Ayacucho for a couple of days. He told me the army went through the vil-

lage and people are worried about being associated with the military and provoking the rebels just like with the Pacharis. Please be careful.

I will be in Urpimarca in a few weeks for the feast of Corpus Christi and I'd like to talk with you before then. Could we meet in Huamanguilla? I'll be there Friday at Judy's house. I'll wait for you there until eight o'clock that evening.

Fondly,

Steven

Friday after school Cori walked to where the road was drivable. A group of señoras had contracted a pickup truck to meet them there and take them and their goods to market in Ayacucho. It had taken Cori a while to learn the informal transportation system serving Urpimarca and how it depended on word of mouth. The village wasn't so isolated if you knew who was going where, when, and how, and conversely who was coming from where, and when, and how willing they were to bring supplies, packages, or correspondence.

She would get to Huamanguilla in plenty of time to meet Steven and had until then to steel herself for what she expected him to say. The wait until Friday had been a mix of anxiety and anticipation. The letter sounded to her like a summons. And why include Judy? Cori liked her very much, but why couldn't they have met in Ayacucho—alone? Or was that too public? Or did he need a chaperon? Probably. Or perhaps a witness. Maybe she had overreached, asking more of Steven than he could give. The past weeks of silence had spoken volumes. This would be her official termination notice.

The señoras wanted Cori to sit in the cab with the driver, but she refused. They had arranged for the truck, and it seemed only right to her that one of them should ride in comfort. Besides, that would separate her from them, and she needed, in as many little ways as possible, to make them understand that she didn't think she was superior to them. Bundled against the wind with a manta lent to her by the señora who took the seat up front, Cori wedged herself among hard sacks of potatoes and burlap bags bulging with kernels of dry corn. An hour later, she arrived in Huamanguilla, her hair snarled by wind, making her look, she imagined, as wild and carefree as she now felt. Maybe it made her look all the more the seductress. Good. She wouldn't make it easy on him. All's fair in love and war.

Steven's Volkswagen was in front of Judy's house when Cori walked up from the plaza where the truck dropped her off. He answered Cori's knock at the door.

"Hola," she said. "How are you, my friend?" Just seeing Steven warmed her and she felt her uneasiness about him falling away.

"Good," said Steven. "I'm so glad you came."

"You summoned me, Padrecito. What else could I do?" she said with a smile. She stepped in, gave him a perfunctory peck on the cheek, and looked around the room. Near the door were a couple of cardboard boxes, one empty and the other half-filled with small objects wrapped in newspaper. "And Judy?"

"She's overdue. She's off saying her goodbyes. I expected her an hour ago. She's packing, as you can see."

"She's going home?"

He nodded. "Her group has been targeted by Sendero, and her supervisors are worried about her safety. I'll let her tell you more." He walked Cori to the sofa and motioned for her to have a seat.

"Is that what you wanted to talk to me about?" she asked.

"I needed to see you."

"You said talk," Cori said sitting on one side of the sofa.

"I guess I did," he said taking the other side of the sofa, leaving an empty cushion between them. They sat in silence and Cori took in the room, noting the empty places where Judy had removed things from the walls. How Cori had wanted to emulate Judy's decorative touches—before the market attack. She still had the broken ceramic musicians and condor in a bag in her room.

Steven spoke first. "I didn't know what you thought about the last time when we were together."

"I didn't think anything. I was feeling—as I am now." Cori surprised herself at her bluntness.

He looked into her eyes, and she watched his expression as what she had said sank in.

"Cori, look, you're beautiful and you know I have feelings for you, but—"

"That's right, Esteban," she interrupted. "And sometimes you just have to follow your heart instead of your fat head."

Cori scooted across the empty cushion, took his head between her hands and kissed him. It took a while before he joined her. They kissed for a long time. They stopped, breathed, looked into each other's eyes, and kissed again. They collapsed on the couch, side by side. They stayed that way, kissing softly, then passionately, and finally tapering off to whispering.

"If you're going to try to break it off, you should wear that white thing," she said in a hushed voice, poking him playfully in the hollow of his neck.

"It's complicated, Cori. So complicated—"

"I know. Hug me. Just hug me, please." She pulled him to her, and the last of her words were muffled against his shirt as she tried to mute her sobs.

He held her as she cried, rubbed her shaking shoulders and cooed to her, "It will be all right. Everything will be all right."

Her weeping subsided to sniffles.

"Just don't tell me you can't care for me," she said, dropping her head back to look at him. "Don't pretend you can't love someone, because I can't pretend. You know I'm falling in love with you."

248

"I'm not pretending anything now. Am I?"

"No. I don't think you are." She kissed him, and then settled comfortably onto the cushion as he kissed her back. She squeezed her arms tightly around his back and held him to her.

The click of the key in the lock resounded like a gunshot. They sat upright and sprang apart.

The door opened and Judy came in carrying a woven bag that clinked of glass.

"Hola, amigos," she said, with an exaggerated squint of suspicion. With her free left hand she seemed to steady herself on the arm of the chair.

"You know, I can get lost again if you two want to be alone."

Steven and Cori glanced at each other, rumpled and red-faced.

Steven slid closer to Cori. "That's okay," he said. He took Cori's hand and settled into the sofa beside her. Cori rested her head against his shoulder.

"Hola, Judy," Cori said.

Judy nodded, setting the bag down with a hard clunk on the glass tabletop, and winced. She took out two bottles of beer and set them on the table with strained care, but still managed to make one wobble enough that she had to grab it again.

"I already had a few of these at my sendoff with the señoras."

She grabbed three glasses out of the back of the wooden box supporting the tabletop, fumbled with an opener to uncap one bottle, and poured beer for each of them. She passed them each a glass and lifted her own into the air.

"This," she said, waving her glass at them, "calls for a toast."

Steven and Cori raised their beers.

"To you two—"

"And to you," Steven interjected.

Judy frowned and lowered her glass, then swayed and set a foot back to steady herself. She plopped down into the chair and spilled a bit of her drink onto the floor. She looked at the splattered beer and shrugged. "For Pachamama," she said, reaching across the table and clicking her glass with theirs.

"I don't know if you two know what the hell you're starting," she added, "but you both look so happy."

"Salud!" Cori said.

"Cheers!" Steven said.

"To love in dangerous times," Judy offered, and downed her drink in one long draft.

28

The feast of Corpus Christi was celebrated in Urpimarca as nowhere else in the campo, according to Father Jaime. He advised Steven not to expect the least orthodoxy around a procession that bore all the trappings of a patron festival: part religious, part civic, and part commercial. The solemnity of the feast day tended to be overshadowed by the carnival atmosphere of the celebration. Patron festivals in other communities came after the harvest, usually beginning with the day of St. John the Baptist, near the end of June. Most were held between July and October. The Corpus Christi festival was the only time of the year that Urpimarca rose to notoriety, and even that only among the nearest villages. Yet, the old priest said, it transformed the hamlet.

Steven had been advised by fellow priests in Lima not to miss the Corpus Christi observance in Cuzco, a sixteen-hour bus ride to the south. The procession of statues around the plaza that had once been the center of the Inca holy city mimicked a time-honored ritual of parading the mummies of Inca kings around the square. But for this year's feast of the Body of Christ, Steven had no intention of being anywhere but Urpimarca.

The American priest's presence at the festival had been expected since his first visit to Urpimarca. Now, the threat of more violence made it all the more imperative for him to walk with the people, to accompany them as Christ would have done, despite

251

the danger. That the guerrillas would target Americans, as they indicated they would do in their disruption of Judy's seminar, added an unequivocal measure of risk to what Steven did now.

Could he really believe that being a priest would shield him from the rebel ire, obsessed as they were with the unwanted influence of foreigners? Maybe it would if he were from another country, not a Yankee. While Don Javier believed it was the rebels' protocol to issue personal warnings before striking, Steven drew little solace from that notion. But not going to Urpimarca simply wasn't an option he would consider right now.

He didn't calculate the risk as especially high just yet, and his presence would support the open and unashamed expression of faith by a people for whom the divine was ever-present, not confined to an obligatory hour a week at Mass. Their faith ran far deeper than the vestiges of ethnic devotions he had glimpsed back home, where the old European immigrants were allowed on rare occasions to make public, anachronistic displays of their faith. Here in the Andes, Catholicism was infused with a radiant Quechuan vision of the mysterious, a syncretic unity of the contemporary and the ancient, where Christian saints functioned like apu spirits, not just models of pious behavior but powerful and active minor deities—watchful and alive. So Steven felt he had to be there. It was his portal to the Indian cosmos, to their traditional approach to God.

It was also where Cori would be.

Since Cori had come to him a few weeks earlier in Huamanguilla, Steven had struggled to find words to express what was happening to him. For some time he had come up with nothing more insightful than that it was a time of transition for him. Finally, he just admitted it to himself. He was in love. For the first time in his life, he was in love, and to just say that to himself bolstered his spirits and gave him a surge of joy. His ideas of love and of Cori were hopelessly entwined. He had felt affection for other women in the past, but nothing compared with this. His feelings for her didn't negate any other love—for God, for the church, for the people, for his family, even for himself. It was new, overpowering, and compatible with every other love he felt. He thought about Cori constantly. If God was love, and this was love, then God must be present in his feelings for Cori, and in their relationship.

Steven was deliriously bemused in trying to sort out his love for Cori and his love for the priesthood. How could anything that so completed him be wrong in any sense? He would no longer deny his feelings for her. That much was clear. He wanted simply to be with her, Shining Path or no, military patrols or no, anti-Americanism or no.

The festival began on the afternoon of the eve of the Corpus Christi observance, the day before Steven could get there. Not to worry, Angel had told him, the priest is only needed on the day of the celebration. The catechist was a perfectly acceptable stand-in on the first day. So Steven had missed the inaugural luncheon among the organizers and sponsors, the small candlelit procession that kicked off the public celebration, the vespers that evening in the chapel led by Angel, and the music and dancing that night on the plaza.

Steven arrived the second morning in a huff. He was late, with no time to prepare for Mass or the procession, after being delayed two hours at the military checkpoint outside Ayacucho. At first the soldiers refused to let him pass, saying the area was under a state of emergency because of the violence. They couldn't guarantee his safety, they told him, especially because he was a foreigner. It took his implacable insistence, and several phone calls by the soldiers to their superiors, before he was allowed to continue. Then he came upon a band and dancers in his path after leaving his car. Four men and two boys played instruments as they walked—flutes, guitar, drum, and trumpet. A dozen women and girls swayed and twirled to the beat and sang in the falsetto of highland huayno music. They laughed and nodded and waved to the priest as he hurried past them, alternating between a fast walk and a trot.

When he reached the village he found it had turned into a street fair. Stands shaded from the sun with blue plastic tarps lined the main dirt road up to the square. People filled the street, smiling in the festive air. Many tables offered food and drink. One man roasted a pig, glistening brown in its crackling rind on a spit over a wood fire just where the road turned toward the square. He tried effusively to wave Steven over, pointing to the pig with the blade of a long knife.

"Le invito, Padre," the man said, recognizing Steven even without his collar. "The first piece for you, Padre." He turned to a woman and said something in Quechua. She produced a plate.

"No, no thank you," Steven protested. "I have to say Mass. I'll come back later." The man looked disappointed.

"We'll save some for you, Padre," he said.

"Return, please, Padrecito," the wife called after him.

Steven made little headway before a tipsy man offered him a drink of beer. He recognized the man as Juan, the gangly fellow who had been watching Cori's patio, the hacendadito, Angel's half-brother. Laughing good naturedly, the priest thanked Juan, patted him on the back, and said it was too early. A few steps farther along, a woman offered him a tamale from a tray she carried.

Steven eventually threaded his way to the plaza, where he saw Cori, as usual with a group of schoolgirls, standing in the late morning sun, pulling the cotton-candy-like fiber out of pods of the pacay tree and eating it.

The sound of a band and singers behind him clashed with the music of another group on the plaza, catching Steven and Cori in a cacophony of competing melodies and rhythms. Steven paused and caught his breath. Cori, apparently inured to the noise and commotion, kissed his cheek primly in customary Peruvian style.

"Ay, Esteban, I've been waiting for you for days."

"I've been looking forward to this festival for weeks," he said, raising his voice to be heard over the warring tunes. "And to visit my favorite village and my favorite teacher."

"And you are my favorite gringo," she said, not so loudly and glancing around to see if the girls were listening. They were, and waiting to greet the priest.

"Buenos dias, Padre," three or four girls greeted him in unison, though without kisses, which Steven by now had come to understand was a mestizo practice, not a habit of the shy campesinas. The girls waved goodbye and melded into the crowd.

Steven would have liked to linger there with Cori had he not been immediately swept up in a group that included Angel and Señora Eulalia and hustled off to the chapel. As if reading Steven's thoughts, Cori promised to be along shortly. So little had they spoken of her faith, that Steven was surprised that she planned to join the liturgical celebration. He felt it as affirmation of everything else about them.

Steven celebrated Mass from the altar in the chapel and, when he stepped outside, discovered the largest crowd he had seen in any small pueblo. It seemed as if everyone who had come to the village for the festival was there. Worshippers spilled out of the tiny chapel and extended seamlessly from the small courtyard at its door and across the newly mown hayfield, fanning like the train of a gown behind a royal bride. The chapel faced south, where the land opened across the wide vista of the Ayacucho plains under the cerulean sky. It was for Steven, and would always remain for him, an impression of incomparable beauty, all the more so for its enigmatic, even deceptive, quality.

Steven, wearing white vestments, stepped out of the chapel to where a skirted bier was flanked by eight men ready to carry it on their shoulders in the procession. On it the painting of the crucified Jesus had been arranged, surrounded by flowers and candles burning in clear glass holders against the wind. Steven held the real body of Christ, the Holy Eucharist, in a simple monstrance. He took in the crowd and then the countryside and then the mountains. Ayacucho, he remembered, meant Corner of Death in Quechua. He regarded the image of the brutal execution of a rebel two thousand years ago and this celebration of the paradoxical humanity and immortality of that body of Christ, of his sacrifice in a time of political upheaval and occupation by a foreign power. How many more would be sacrificed in this insurrection going on here and now? Who, like the murdered Pachari family, would meet some grisly end, some senseless slaughter in the struggle for power? How many of them would he know? Or would he be among them?

A breeze caught a banner held by one of the standard bearers behind the litter, flapping it sharply in Steven's face. He turned and followed the cross bearer, the candle bearer, and the thurifer with the censer of incense to the front of the bier. The crowd parted as the procession began and then closed in behind Our Lord of the Hacienda to make the round trip to the plaza and back again.

Most of the people fell out of the procession after they reached the square and before prayers were finished at a temporary altar there. Then the revelry of drink, music, and dance resumed once more. The solemnity of the occasion was largely dispensed with, and only Steven and the most devout accompanied the Lord's image back to its customary niche behind the altar in the chapel. Steven saw Cori in the crowd that followed him, and it pleased him in a way he could not name. He would be a guest of honor in the village for the rest of the day, and he planned to make sure the school's teacher was honored as well.

Before long, they gathered at Don Javier's house, among the guests sitting on adobe platforms running along the walls. The room was lit only by a window and light streaming through the open front door. The sounds of music and dancing continued, where the two bands pressed their rivalry, one playing huayno music on the plaza and the other a kind of marinera on the saddle just below the house.

Steven sat with Don Javier on his left and Angel on his right. Cori sat next to Angel. Beside her was an elderly former mayor. A group of señoras sat along the shorter wall perpendicular to them and nearest the kitchen. A few younger men and women, apparently wanting to establish themselves as leaders in the community, sat across the room, drinking chicha, listening to the elders speak, and looking very much like they would rather join the party outside.

One of the younger men near the open door got up and looked outside. He stood in the doorway watching the festivities of the visiting musicians. He seemed annoyed and occasionally looked in to say something in Quechua.

"He says the village where that band comes from is full of Senderistas and they shouldn't have been invited," Angel told Steven.

"It doesn't seem like everyone agrees," Steven said.

"Some tell him he is too suspicious."

"What do you think?"

"It's not so simple," Angel said before he was cut off by an exchange between the young man and Don Javier. Angel translated what each said.

"Young Elias says they have always coveted our land because our fields are not so hilly," Angel explained. "They are going to take advantage of politics to get what they want. That's why they're all going over to the side of the communists. Don Javier says he has no proof. Elias says two men from there were killed in a battle with soldiers near Cangallo last month. His cousin's wife is from there and told him many men and women fled and hid when the soldiers came. Don Javier retorted that it is easy to accuse even the innocent."

Elias responded loudly and forcefully.

"He says Don Javier is being too slow to organize the militia the army lieutenant ordered us to form. That we should be preparing to defend ourselves against the Shining Path, not letting them dance in the square."

The old man next to Cori spoke.

"He tells Elias that we have always quarreled with people from there. Some of them even rustled our cattle. This feud they are talking about goes way back," Angel explained to Steven. "He thinks it's very dangerous now to be putting these kinds of names, like 'cattle rustler,' on people. It could have unintended consequences. And who's to say they might not do the same to us?"

Elias responded, now pleading his case to the entire group.

"He says that's just his point. Having these people here risks getting us associated with the Senderistas and in trouble with the army."

Don Javier spoke in a conciliatory tone.

"He tells Elias these people always honor Our Lord of the Hacienda by coming here for the festival, the same way that we will go to their village's celebration next month. Don Javier says to drop it and enjoy the festivities."

Those in the room seemed to side with Don Javier, and a young woman said something to Elias, who crossed the room and stood beside her sullenly, brushing off her attempt to draw him onto the bench.

"I'm sorry, Padre," Don Javier said in Spanish.

"That's all right. I imagine it needs to be discussed."

"Perhaps. But this is not the time."

An awkward silence settled over the room. Abruptly Elias walked to the door again.

"It's a good thing you have your gringo priest," he said angrily in Spanish. "He will soon be saying a funeral Mass for all our miserable souls." With a dismissive wave of one arm he stepped through the door and out onto the road.

"He is very young," Don Javier said by way of apologizing. "I just hope that it is we who are right, and not this rash young man."

29

Steven and Cori left Don Javier's together well into the evening. They had stayed and sipped shot glasses of harsh cañazo, while listening to stories of life in Urpimarca, of the time of the hacienda, of the founding of the village afterward, and of the alliances and rivalries with neighboring communities.

Outside, most of the stalls had closed and the activity was now centered on the musicians and dancers. People milled about the street. As he walked with Cori toward the plaza, Steven was troubled by suggestions that campesinos might use the current political violence as a cover to settle old scores.

"Are you upset, Esteban?"

"No, just thinking."

"About what Elias said? Did he frighten you?"

"A little. It's just the crazy onion layers of this violence. People don't know exactly who to fear, so they're seeing the worst in their old enemies, maybe using the troubles to get something they want. That would be human nature. Uriah to the front."

"What's that?"

"In the Old Testament, King David seduces Bathsheba and sends her husband, Uriah, off to war."

"Oh, and her husband gets killed in battle or something?" Cori interjected.

"Right. So if even kings in the midst of war succumb to petty weaknesses and use the conflict to their own selfish ends, what can we expect of average people? Why should anyone here in the Andes be different?"

"I hear you writing a homily."

"I probably am."

"That's okay. It's your job. Maybe to people in the other village, Urpimarca seems too well off?"

"Is it? I don't see lots of differences among the villages I go to."

"Envy is a big problem here," Cori said, recalling Lucero's story of how her father died, poisoned because he was getting ahead. "If few people can really improve their lives, I guess most figure it is better if no one does."

Cori wore her hair pushed straight back from her forehead, held in place by a wide red band so her face was clear and open and radiant in the light of the festival lamps. She had never seemed more beautiful to him. He wanted to kiss her, but remained mindful of the people all around them. Nonetheless, he pulled her to him and wrapped her in a strong embrace.

Cori hugged just as hard. They leaned back to look into each other's eyes, momentarily oblivious to everyone else.

Juan crashed between them.

They broke apart and Juan teetered, almost falling over, only to be grabbed and held up by Steven. Juan wheeled and glared at him, tripping backward over his own feet. He clutched a plastic jug.

"Tha's nah right!" he bellowed at them.

Cori stepped back while Steven kept his arms raised, ready to catch Juan's fall again or repel another charge. Juan, pointing the finger of his free hand, leveled his eyes on Steven, squinting to focus.

"You! You priessst!" He sputtered. "Pa-dre! You're a pa-dre. A grin-go pa-dre." His voice trailed off and his gaze darted to Cori. "And you, tea-cher. In the arms of this priest."

Juan's head sagged on his shoulders and he jerked it up

again, struggling. His face slackened as he stared at her. His eyes drooped and his lips quivered. He opened his mouth, as if to say something, and lunged at Cori.

She jumped aside. Steven caught Juan by the lapel of his jacket and spun him aside. The two men tumbled to the ground.

Steven felt someone else grab him and help him as he got up. Two other men lifted Juan to his feet, staying between the priest and the drunk. They pushed Juan away as he tried again to charge Steven.

"Ya! Hacendadito, ya! Enough!" one of the men yelled.

"You're crazy," said the other. "What are you doing attacking the priest?"

Juan said nothing, wobbling where he stood. A small crowd had gathered around them, and on the plaza dancers stopped in mid-step and looked toward them. The band continued its rapid huayno rhythm.

Cori came to Steven's side as the men tried to steer Juan away. He pulled free of his handlers and turned and stumbled toward the square. The two men caught him as he reeled and he mumbled something to them.

"La casona. He wants to go to the hacienda house," one of them said.

"Let him," said the other. "Let's take him. He'll be out of the way there."

As the people dispersed, a few apologized to Steven and asked if Cori was all right. Reassured that all was well, they returned to their celebration. Steven caught a glimpse of Señora Eulalia on the edge of the light, away from noise and festivities of the plaza. She turned toward her house, shaking her head disapprovingly.

"Did we create a spectacle?" Cori asked when it was just the two of them again.

"Maybe." He brushed the hair that had fallen across her face, sweeping it neatly behind as it had been. "I should walk you to your door and say good night," he said. "It's been a long day."

"I'll never get to sleep. There's too much noise."

The band on the plaza took a break, and the musicians passed among them the same kind of cañazo jug Juan had carried.

"Let's go to the field near the chapel and look at the stars," Cori said. "It will be quiet there."

The hay stubble they crossed was dewless in the mountain air and the ground was hard where they sat looking toward the sloping plains of the wide Ayacucho valley below. A few blurs of light marked villages in the distance. Steven leaned back and found the Milky Way arching over them. He tilted his head to pick out the Southern Cross, so bright and high above the horizon this time of year.

Cori leaned on her elbow and looked at him. He propped himself up and kissed her, then stretched out comfortably on the ground again. Cori leaned over and kissed him, then pulled herself back to rest again on her elbow.

"Do you love me?" she asked.

He sat up and looked into her face.

"Yes. Yes, I do."

She smiled.

"Good. Because I love you."

They kissed with great tenderness for a long time. Cori turned and looked for a while at the sky, then toward where Ayacucho lay.

"What does it mean for a priest to be in love?"

"I really don't know. I find myself in a place I've never been before. I don't know what I can offer you for a future. I only know now how I feel, like you said once."

"I don't need promises. I just need you to love me."

They kissed again.

"So tell me what love is," he said. "I think you know more about it than I do."

263

"I know more about love that can't be." She gazed across a landscape dimly illuminated by the profusion of stars. "That's my lot—things that can't be."

"Why do you say that?"

She smiled at him. "I'll explain another time, mi amor. Not now. I'd rather just enjoy this moment."

Cori rested her head on his chest, nudging him onto his back, and they stayed that way a long time, staring at the stars above. It grew cooler and she snuggled up even closer to him. He took off his jacket and draped it over both of them. They slept.

Steven awakened at the first calling of the birds. The dark sky was a slightly lighter shade along the eastern horizon. He felt Cori stir and he sat up slowly, to avoid waking her. He tucked the jacket around her shoulders.

It was light enough to see the hills when Cori awoke.

"Is it time to go?" she asked without sitting up.

"I'm afraid so."

They rose stiffly and brushed dust and yellow blades of grass from their clothing.

"I have a sick call here in Urpimarca with Angel's mother-in-law, then another Mass. Can you join us for lunch?"

"Of course."

"Then I'll be free to leave. Will you come with me? Tomorrow's Saturday. We could visit some ruins. I'll bring you back tomorrow afternoon. Please, come with me."

Cori hooked her finger into his shirt just above the last button and pulled him to her. "Esteban, I would follow you to the end of the world."

They walked back to the school, and onto the school patio, and Steven kissed Cori goodbye at the door. A red and black fly-catcher on a wavering branch of a sapling sounded a few high-pitched notes, welcoming the new day and whatever it might bring.

30

Cori was exhausted. Except for dozing on the chilly ground all night, she had slept little since the first night of the festival. Most of the visitors would be gone by this morning, but the villagers would celebrate for a third day. The idea of slipping away to escape the musicians and dancers would have been enticing on its own. Knowing she would be with Steven made the intervening hours almost unbearable.

She lay down on her bed to take a nap before the revelry resumed. She imagined herself with Steven and lapsed into sleep with a picture of them cuddled together somewhere warm, clean, and comfortable.

Cori stirred at the sound of voices on the plaza. She awakened fully to noise on the patio, then someone pounding at her door. She sat up in bed. Who would do that? They pounded again, hard, as if with something heavy. She swung her legs out of bed.

"Abre la puerta!" Boom, boom, boom.

"Ya voy," she said, getting up quickly.

Cori pulled the door open and found herself looking into the face of a young campesino who stepped back and pointed a rifle with a long curved clip at her midriff.

He led her at gunpoint to a group of women standing outside the school and looking out across the square. Three men she did not know sat on the ground on the lower half of the plaza, just below the cement wall. Their hands were tied behind their backs and they kept their faces down. Their clothing was like that worn in Lima, dark trousers with dress shirts opened at the collar. The front of one man's shirt was stained with fresh blood. Villagers crowded around three sides of the square, leaving open the side that led to the main road. Musicians clutched their instruments and dancers stood uncomfortably, still in their party regalia. The plaza was largely silent. Cori could see a half dozen other rebels, some holding short rifles with the long clips and others with heavy pistols. Among them were two women, who looked like any other campesinas in their braids and polleras, except one carried a rifle and the other a revolver. Those two stood guard over the bound men. The others kept their weapons pointed at the assembled villagers.

Down the road, a few campesinos straggled in. Farther behind them came the mayor and his wife, pushed ahead by rifles in the hands of another man and a woman in blue jeans. Beyond them in the distance a few other gunmen guarded the crossroads. As the four reached the plaza, a murmur arose among the villagers. Cori startled when she recognized the woman. Lucero.

Others in the crowd identified the man. "Teacher," whispered a señora beside Cori. "Señor Cespedes," said another. The word "teacher" was repeated around the square.

Lucero did not acknowledge her former neighbors. She made no eye contact. Cori watched Lucero's face, drawn in a tight grimace with her lips pressed firmly together. The former teacher looked around the square with a disdainful air, allowing his gaze to drift over the faces of the villagers as if they were strangers, seeming to dare any of them to address him.

Behind her Cori heard voices, someone complaining, and another voice giving orders. She turned, as did others, to see Juan come over the knoll at gunpoint, followed by the same young rebel who had rousted her.

"Hacendadito," the former teacher said loudly, with an amused expression. Juan's face blanched.

The rebel youth pushed Juan onto the square and over to the prisoners, where Cespedes—apparently the guerrillas' commander—stood.

"Take a seat with these miserable wretches," he told Juan.

The lanky man balked and stammered an unintelligible appeal that was cut off abruptly by a rifle butt hammered into his back. He fell to his knees, catching his fall with outstretched arms. He sat on his haunches, arching his back and wincing up into the face of the man in charge. Cespedes gave him a dismissive glance and walked to the center of the upper square.

"We're missing the American. He wasn't anywhere?" he asked. Several of the rebels shook their heads.

"Where's the American?" he yelled. "Where are you hiding the priest?"

No one answered.

Cori looked into the dirt. How could this be happening? Her heart raced. How quickly bliss turned to nightmare. That Steven was gone from the village was her only hope. She prayed. God, please, protect him. Fly away, Steven. She imagined him in the hut blessing the sick woman, ignorant of the rebels' search. Would he stumble innocently out of the adobe's darkness into tragedy? Maybe he had been warned about them, and someone was watching over him somewhere.

Cori pictured Steven in an image born of a children's tale, lowering himself into a huge, empty crock used to ferment chicha. Campesina hands covered it with a board and a señora whispered, "Padre, stay there until it's safe to come out." Cori looked then for Angel and when she didn't see the catechist in the plaza her hopes soared. Maybe Steven had escaped into the hills with him, away from these maniacs. A feeling of abandonment suddenly gripped her. But would he leave me? How she wished she were with him, hand-in-hand sprinting—as if she could—through the forest to find help, bring someone, anyone, to end this travesty before something terrible happened.

Señor Cespedes, the teacher who abandoned Urpimarca, spoke again. His voice was calmer and matter-of-fact.

"We know the American is here. He left his car on the road outside the village and it is still there. Who saw him last?" He turned to Lucero. "Translate." She repeated in Quechua what he had just said. No one responded.

"Search again," he told his followers. "This miserable pueblo is too small for him to hide." The youth who had brought in Juan and another man ran out of the plaza and along the road toward the cluster of houses up the hill. Cori shivered.

Her predecessor began to lecture, a lesson in Marxist economics and Maoist revolution, in a deep baritone drone echoed in Lucero's alto syncopation. Cori tried to focus on what he was saying, if for no other reason than to keep her mind from running to all the horrible possibilities that might unfold, to find something redeemable, some way to forestall the impending violence. Cespedes' voice came to her like sound blaring out of a cheap amplifier at a large assembly. Patches of words and platitudes faded in and out of her awareness.

"Here in Peru...the class struggle...the incessant struggle of the campesinos...That is you!...heroic. The campesino proletariat even more so...without your help, your support...will accomplish nothing. This is...Gonzalo Thought, applying Marxism-Leninism-Maoism to our concrete reality."

Cori looked at Juan, who kept his head down now, like the others. Guilt rose in her as she recalled how she had rejected him, dismissing him as the others did. She might have tried to talk to him again, to be the bigger person, to reason with him, to reiterate her offer of friendship. Instead she had been all too willing to cast him aside because it made everything simpler for her. Yet, she had been a little afraid of him, of his ludicrous fantasy. She had felt she couldn't deal with him, and maybe she had feared if she did she would somehow lose Steven. She had opted for the easiest response, not the kindest.

"La guerra popular!" Cespedes' diatribe flowed now in an incoherent porridge of clichés. "Revolutionary violence is a universal law…one of destruction, the other of construction…the people take up arms to destroy the old order…create a new order…humble dynamite…weapon of the people."

She caught her breath at the words, which brought to mind reports of the Senderistas killing people by blowing them up. Against her will she saw Steven hurt, lying wounded on the ground, his bright hazel eyes looking to her, and someone's thick fist wrapped around a sparkling stick of dynamite and tossing it at him.

How could this teacher, who had stood in the same classroom as she, speak like this? How could someone who had taught these very children advocate such acts? The perversity of it baffled her. She looked more closely at him now, to discern what in him was different from her and what was the same. Where was there some commonality? Wherein was the soul to which she might appeal for Steven if they found him. Cespedes' mestizo coloring and features ran on the darker and angular side. He favored the Indian more than the conqueror, yet was taller than most of the villagers. His bearing reminded her of Angel. It occurred to her that Cespedes had more in him of the classic teacher than she herself, more of a sense of pedagogy, the arrogance of one who spoke expecting to be listened to, and whose certainty wasn't to be challenged.

"Why are we looking for the American priest?" he asked rhetorically.

Cori tuned in sharply. He was looking at her. It was as if her blood sank to her abdomen, leaving her lightheaded, feeling as if she might faint. His gaze moved on and settled on a woman near her and then onto another. His eyes interrogated each in turn. He lectured as he went.

"We must end the domination of Yankee imperialism in our country. Not only is this man an agent of that exploitation, he serves the old theocracy that since the time of the Romans has repressed popular struggles and defended the interests of the oppressors and exploiters. We aren't opposed to the people's religiosity, which isn't an obstacle itself to popular struggle. Religiosity is acceptable under freedom of conscience. But that too will dissolve as people advance in the new order and replace it with a scientific, transforming consciousness of the world!"

His triumphal finish was met with blank stares.

Cori wondered if she alone on the plaza understood these big words spoken in Spanish. How had Lucero translated them? She was probably just reciting a prepared text. Cori prayed again, God, please, don't let them find Steven.

The guerrilla commander composed himself, assuming again the demeanor of a patronizing lecturer, smirking at the faces around him. He was like a conquistador reading fiats to illiterate natives who could not possibly have understood.

"That! Is! His! Crime!" The former teacher threw down the words one at a time.

"The job of this American, this priest, is to defend this corrupt ecclesiastical hierarchy, the papacy, and North American imperialism. Just as it is the job of these three foreigners to validate the corrupt establishment by pretending to improve your lives here in the campo."

He still got nothing but blank stares from the crowd.

The Senderista's face tensed at the ineffectiveness of his tirade, and Cori sensed that he was struggling for another way to make his point. When his face relaxed and his eyes widened, she knew he had hit upon something.

"Oye! Can't you understand? This gringo is the *pistaco!*" He screamed the last word.

The villagers around the plaza stirred as if awakened. The accusation that Steven was a monster perhaps disturbed them, yet no one rose to contradict the commander lecturing them from the trigger side of a gun.

"This priest, like all the gringos, is stealing the fat of Peru to grease the machinery of imperialism. They will leave Peru as desiccated as the mummies of the ancestors, the way grave robbers carry off the riches of the tombs and leave nothing but scattered bones, dried skin, and useless rags."

Cori couldn't read the people. Cespedes' fury was so terrifying that even she dared not raise her voice in protest, although she felt she betrayed Steven by her silence. Again she placed her hope in prayer. Please, God, don't let them find him.

The two men sent to find Steven returned to the plaza—by themselves. Cori let out an inaudible sigh of relief. The guerrilla leader just shook his head.

"We're here for a trial," he announced to the villagers. Some gasped. Others moaned.

"We're going to try these three foreigners as agents of exploitation, no better than the American priest. He will be tried in absentia. This hacendadito will be tried as a revisionist and the mayor as a stooge for the illegitimate government in Lima and as a collaborator with the military."

The mayor's wife screamed and clutched her husband's arm before one of the rebels grabbed Don Javier and shoved him to the ground with the others.

Villagers called out in his defense, some in Spanish, some in Quechua.

"The mayor's a good man," said one.

"He's done nothing but work for the village," said another.

"He's innocent."

"He's done nothing."

"Let him go," people cried out from around the square.

The guerrilla commander raised his rifle to silence the crowd. A few murmurs echoed the same refrain with waning conviction. Cespedes waited until they were all silent.

"They are all guilty," he said.

The people interrupted again, more forcefully, raising their voices in anger. The younger rebels shifted and glanced around them, readying their rifles. One with a pistol extended it toward a yelling and gesturing campesino Cori recognized as Elias, the young man who had argued with Don Javier the day before.

"Where's the trial?" Elias yelled.

"Those aren't crimes," called another.

"This isn't justice," screamed one woman. "The priest too, he's innocent. We have done nothing. Let them go."

"Silence! Shut up, all of you!" the rebel leader commanded. "They're all guilty and they're all condemned to death."

Cori closed her eyes to steady her balance as her head spun. This was madness. She opened her eyes to see Juan sitting up wide-eyed, throwing his gaze in panic to one and then another of his neighbors. The campesinos protested again.

"They've done nothing."

"Why must they die? Why?"

The rebel raised an arm to quiet them. "You want them spared?" he asked in a placating voice. "You want them freed?" he asked, glowering around the square. "Then take their places."

The silence that followed was broken only by weeping.

"Who among you wants to take the place of one of these miserable wretches? Who?" He stared into their faces.

"You? You want to come up here?" he demanded of Elias, who shrunk back into the crowd. A young woman gripped his clothing, as if fearing his impulsiveness.

"You?" he snarled into the face of a señora. He moved on.

"You? Or you? Or you?"

He stepped back, a smirk on his face.

"Perhaps, Mayor, you want to choose someone to take your place? You're the jefe of this hamlet. Order someone to die for you."

Don Javier, his hands clasped between his knees, raised his head to look the rebel leader in the eyes. The mayor's face showed nothing, neither fear nor hate. He said nothing. To Cori the two of them looked like predators squaring off—still, breathless, waiting for the imperceptible signal to strike or flee. The former teacher blinked. He turned on Juan.

"Hacendadito, won't anyone sacrifice themselves for you?" He waited, as if expectantly. "Of course not."

"Wait, wait," Juan pleaded.

"For what?"

Juan had no answer. His faced screwed up in a frantic contortion, but only a desperate stuttering came out of his mouth. "Uh, uh, uh..."

"Uh, what? Have you someone to offer?"

Juan spun around on his knees and looked at Cori.

He glanced at the rebel and then settled his eyes on Cori again. The guerrilla leader lowered his rifle toward Juan's head.

"The teacher is his lover," Juan stammered. "She is the priest's lover—and the army lieutenant's whore!"

Cespedes looked down at Juan, sneering. He moved away and signaled with his hand for Cori to come forward.

Her steps were heavy and her lagging hip never felt so stiff, nor the distance so long to the wall bisecting the plaza. No one spoke. Most heads were down or turned aside. Lucero stood as if covering the villagers with her rifle, but her head was down too.

"Is this true?" he asked Cori.

She looked to Don Javier. Give me courage. Share your courage with me.

"Is it?" the rebel demanded.

She looked him in the eyes and held in her mind the vision of the mayor doing the same. The eyes of the guerrilla were like those of an animal that hunts, his pupils but black points because of the bright sun, the dark irises like the inside walls of a well. This time he didn't blink.

"Where is the priest?" he asked.

She struggled to keep from trembling, to stay dry-eyed, to remain implacably silent, for fear the least word would become betrayal.

"Teacher, be smart," he said quietly, so only Cori and those closest to her could hear. "You've much to learn and much to give these children. Don't toss your young life away for that ungrateful American, who's only exploited you, too."

Cori could no longer keep from blinking. She was otherwise still. She was not so much defiant anymore as inert, as if her will had ceased to exist. This wasn't lost on the Senderista leader, who sighed. He looked at Juan, then at the soldier standing over him, and jerked his head to the side.

The soldier drove the butt of his weapon into Juan's face with a loud crack. Juan fell back and lay sprawled out, arms splayed. Blood flowed from his nose.

"Get out of my sight." Cespedes hissed.

Juan rolled onto his hands and knees and crawled a few yards before pulling himself to his feet. Stumbling to the high end of the plaza, he ran through the crowd toward the manor.

"Sit," the rebel leader ordered Cori, pointing to the concrete wall.

Cori sat on the wall where she used to rest with her students at recess, where she had chatted with the señoras, and where she had first met Don Javier. She looked again to the mayor and saw him staring at her. She wished she could thank him for giving her strength, and she hoped her eyes conveyed as much.

"We've wasted enough time with theatrics," the rebel said. "There's no revolution without violence and no new order without purging of the old."

"No killing," yelled someone among the villagers. Others repeated it. "No killing." Wailing arose from some of the señoras and children.

"Enough!" roared the rebel. "We didn't come here to talk. We came here to kill."

Cori bowed her head, slumped to her knees and cried. She summoned an image of Steven. He's not part of this. He's not part of this. He's not—

Her hair was yanked up, her head pulled back, and she looked into the face of a braided campesina. Cori closed her eyes as the pistol barrel touched her forehead. Take care of Steven, she prayed.

31

A gunshot echoed across the hillside. Steven startled in the darkness where he crouched, his nose filled with the odor of eucalyptus, damp llama wool, and sweat. Then another shot rang out. The priest squinted out of the shady lean-to into bleaching sunshine that radiated off the sandy path.

"From the village," Cesar, the campesino beside him, said. Three more shots spaced a few seconds apart reverberated through the otherwise still mountain air.

Steven dropped his forehead to his folded hands. No doubt they had killed their prisoners, and he asked God's mercy on their souls, whoever they were, and for whatever they had done or failed to do in this life. Then he prayed for the safety of the rest of the villagers and for a softening of the hearts of the killers.

"Don't worry, Padre, they won't come here," Cesar said. The strain in his voice contradicted the comfort he tried to offer. "I'll go to where I can see down the hill. I'll be right back."

Steven counted the shots. One per person? He prayed he was wrong. Who else? Maybe the first shots were only warnings, a call to attention. Speculating was futile. He would know soon enough—if he wasn't found and killed himself. He could think of no reason why they wouldn't continue to search for him if they wanted him badly enough. And what if they threatened the lives of the villagers if they didn't betray him? If that happened, what choice would he have but to surrender? But he didn't know that to be the case. Perhaps he should run, get away, even from Angel and Cesar, circle the mountain and come out on the other side where the road came up the ravine, and make his way back to his car. He could return with the military.

Was that cowardly? Just to run? Follow his animal instincts to flee? He doubted anyone would really blame him. His family, friends, and colleagues would be grateful for his escape. And Cori? The villagers? Would they understand? Perhaps the campesinos would expect nothing more of him, an outsider. Wouldn't they do the same if they were being hunted? But what of Cori? Shouldn't he just go down and face whatever fate awaited him? He didn't know anything for certain, so what could he do but wait?

Cesar came up the path and spoke into the lean-to.

"Nothing. I think we should wait for Angel. I'm going off just a little way. I will warn you if anyone comes."

Steven decided he couldn't run away, because the only place he wanted to run was to Cori. Even now he felt he had abandoned her. The terrorizing possibility that she too had been targeted suddenly struck him. He couldn't see why they might single her out, yet he longed to cradle her head, stroke her hair, and soothe her as one would a child. It's all right, he told himself. Everything's going to be all right. He put on the poncho and chullo and went out to watch with Cesar. The lean-to now seemed vulnerable.

Cesar lay on his stomach at the top of an arroyo from where they could see the hillside below them. Cesar nodded and Steven crouched beside him.

"If Angel is not here by dark," Cesar said, "I will slip down and see what's going on. You should wait here. If I don't come back by dawn, Padre, get away as best you can."

Steven patted the man's shoulder reassuringly without replying.

They waited for hours in nervous silence as the sun dropped beyond the hills and left them in the cool shadow of the mountain. Late in the afternoon a condor swept down the hillside and over the open valley below until its black profile was lost in the gathering darkness.

Angel returned at dusk. He explained how the terrucos had swarmed into the village with hostages in tow, three foreign engineers. The leader of the terrucos railed against foreigners and said the three men had been brought to Urpimarca to receive justice.

"We have dead to bury, Padre."

"Who?"

"They killed those three engineers. They shot Don Javier. And, Padre, they killed the teacher."

Steven rose and descended the mountain like a man slogging through water. He wept silently. His throat closed and he struggled to breathe, and he didn't care if he took his last breath on this rugged mountainside. He imagined, with an odd sense of hope, that at any turn they would meet the Senderistas. The symmetry would be complete—and justice delivered.

They came to the eucalyptus woods and then to the cemetery, and he was aware he still wore the poncho, the one they said was for funerals. He wondered if they had come this close in their search. Had they found him here, might Cori have lived? Past the graveyard, the first outlying houses stood dark and fireless, even on this cool night. Normally families would have been busy with the evening meal and end-of-day chores. Only the livestock seemed to stir. Udder-bloated cows moaned for milking. A few sheep scattered from the road as they approached. Past the curve the village rose into view. Perhaps there was still hope. Maybe Angel had been mistaken and Cori was merely wounded. Yet people in the campo aren't queasy about death. No miracle lay ahead. He knew that in his heart. They walked on.

The lights of candles glowed on the dark plaza like stars trembling against the night sky. A vigil had begun. The weight on Steven's heart hung more heavily the closer he trudged. He approached as mourner, utterly lacking the will to minister to the suffering of others.

He didn't want to continue. He didn't want to get to the plaza. As long as he didn't get there it wasn't truly real. Cori remained alive as she had been when he left this morning. Yet neither could he stop. Neither could he fall and wail and pull his hair and rend his garments. Not yet. He would have the rest of his life for lamentation. Even now his legs felt as though they couldn't carry him. He had but to let them go and they would buckle, and he wouldn't be able to get up. Instead, he willed them on. Step after step, the three men drew closer to what lay ahead.

They walked on to the flat now, passing the road that ran across the top of the ravine and back to Huamanguilla, back to a time and place before this nightmare had begun. Angel put his arm around Steven's shoulder, and they walked on together. Up the road the figures of mourners were silhouetted by candlelight on the plaza. He stood up straight and shook off Angel's arm to walk the last twenty yards to the square.

People were crying. The sound of weeping at first rose so softly that it was almost a soothing sound, a rhythmic murmur. It grew louder, and as it grew he heard choked and labored breathing, gasping sobs, low moaning.

"Padre," a woman's voice said in the dark.

"Padre," said another voice, and then another. "Padre. Padre." With that the crying became profuse, as if his presence gave the mourners permission to grieve more openly.

Sheets of blue plastic covered three unattended bodies, a single candle marking each. Striped mantas draped another, beside which sat Señora Huanta and several other women. A gray wool blanket outlined another form in candlelight, surrounded by a small group of schoolgirls, as if they expected the one beneath it to be just sleeping and to awaken with the dawn.

Steven remembered that he had left his prayer book, holy water, and oils in the old woman's house, where he had been when the rebels arrived. It made no difference. There was no sacrament for the dead. He made the sign of the cross over the body of Don Javier, knowing as he did that he acted only because something was expected. At that moment he lived only in the heaviness in his chest and the swelling ache of his heart, not in the sanctuary of prayer or the providence of a loving God.

Steven knelt beside Cori. The flood of grief he had expected didn't come. Rather, the dread subsided. Replacing it was a numbness he hadn't expected, a dullness that steadied him, some insensate state between sorrow and fury where he could still function rationally.

He tucked the end of the blanket beneath Cori's body and pulled her to him. As he wrapped the rest of the blanket around her, his hand brushed a moist knot of hair, blood, and sand. He covered it with the makeshift shroud. He stood, lifting her.

"They said not to move the bodies," a voice said.

Looking into the aura of darkness, Steven could make out the face of Elias, the young man from the mayor's house. The priest turned away without a word and headed across the plaza with Cori in his arms, oblivious to Angel, who still walked silently behind him.

"We should wait for the military to arrive," Elias called weakly after them.

In Steven's arms Cori's body felt more like that of a child than of a woman. He barely shifted his weight as he stepped up the embankment past the school and headed toward the chapel. As he approached the small building, one of the young girls darted past him and opened the door to the dim sanctuary. Several others slipped in before him. He stepped into the chapel and waited while they lit more candles. He set Cori on one of the benches and pushed it to the altar. There he knelt beside her. He heard the school girls kneel behind him, and glimpsed Angel off to the side.

Above them, on the wall over the altar, hung Our Lord of the Hacienda, the sorrowful and suffering Christ, with its somber patina cracked with age. Steven looked at it through tears that blurred his vision, and it seemed to him that Jesus' eyes glistened too. Bowing his head, Steven found himself praying for a miracle. Lord, I beg you, show pity on this lovely and innocent woman, whose only sin was to love and whose life mirrored your love of little children. On what better life could you bestow mercy? Pardon her, Lord of the Andes, and pass this punishment on to me. Then he said aloud, with a breaking voice, "Please, Lord Jesus, me instead of her! Undo it and take me instead!"

Then he cried bitterly as he had needed to ever since Angel had returned to the mountain. He didn't hear the others enter the chapel, and his tears receded only when they pushed a bench with the mayor's body next to Cori's.

Breaking glass shattered the midnight silence of the wake. The mourners turned, looking for the source of the noise. Steven, who had remained sitting on a bench near the bodies, rose and went to the door. If the Shining Path wanted him now, he had neither a place to run to nor the will to do so.

Outside, the stars accused him, and he couldn't bear their gaze. He didn't dare look upon the night, to profane the space where just one rotation of the globe before he had enjoyed the happiest hours of his life. He turned from their silent reproach and followed the sounds, down the path beside the chapel and up the other to the manor. It roared in flames. In the yard, a dozen villagers watched the blaze, one with an axe in hand, another with a fuel can.

With walls of adobe and a roof of clay, the house burned like an earthen oven. Everything combustible inside seemed to have ignited. The air smelled of kerosene and eucalyptus, and an ember-red glow traced the outline of the last vestige of the hacienda. The draft from the flames drew the air from around la casona, sucking at everything faintly within its grasp, like some fierce spirit indiscriminately sweeping everything, good or evil, true or false, into the inferno. The fire rose and howled as if some demon within fought for its very existence, and Steven thought of the pistaco. He wondered if this beast of the Andes might not dwell in such abandoned places and if fire might not be its antidote, its silver bullet, its wooden stake. Some spirit seemed to screech in fury and pain, and Steven struggled for a rational explanation of the sound, until he saw the dark figure inside.

In a balconied window on the second floor a human shape writhed in firelight. Thin and long, it flapped at flames riding up its legs and battled the locked frame that imprisoned it in the conflagration. Steven stepped back in awe, a witness to evil incarnate, to the reality of the Peruvian fiend, the pistaco, and to the tangible existence of the devil.

"Oh Prince of heavenly hosts, by divine power, thrust into hell Satan and all evil spirits who prowl the world," Steven prayed aloud.

A sharp scream of human agony brought him up short.

He recognized Juan only when the man threw himself against the window, just as the roof collapsed. His figure disappeared in billows of smoke as the house caved in atop the flames.

32

They sat together at a table in a café tucked beneath an arched colonnade on the Plaza de Huamanga. Steven picked coca leaves out of his tea absentmindedly. He hadn't bothered to drink more than a sip. Angel nursed his tea with the same languor.

Since the incursion at Urpimarca, Steven had been back to the village only once, for Mass on the eighth day after the murders. He had not visited any of the other communities on his regular circuit. Angel had been his emissary, going from pueblo to pueblo to tell all what had happened. These rugged people needed little explanation. A few of them had come to see Steven, and he had spent the last few days saying goodbye.

"Maybe I should have my future read in these," Steven said, setting the leaves on the palm of his hand. "What do you see?" he asked Angel.

"Soggy coca leaves," Angel answered. "I'm not a diviner, and if I were, I wouldn't tell you. You lack the predisposition to believe. We can go to the market and find someone to do it if you want. But for them, it is probably just a game to make a little bit of money."

"I should have done it when I got here."

"The leaves would have told you maybe that you would find love and lose it, and you would have been amused. Perhaps tragedy would have been foretold. The old brujas who prognosticate never seem to know any details."

Steven added sugar to the now tepid tea.

"The devil is in the details. Or is it God? I've heard it both ways."

"Padre," Angel said, "you didn't bring tragedy to the village. This reign of terror was starting before you got here."

"They were looking for me."

"Sí, but Don Javier and those technicians who died had nothing to do with you. Either way, the Senderistas would have come and people would have died."

"Don Javier at any rate, I guess."

"And my brother would have found someone else to scapegoat. Me probably."

"But not necessarily Cori."

"Not necessarily, but we don't know. They were looking for excuses to kill, to make examples of people, and she was an outsider. The old teacher never liked the hacendadito. Only he and God know why he set Juan free. Juan shamed the whole village by betraying her. Killing is very rarely a punishment for us, but expulsion is common. Burning the manor was meant only to run him off forever."

Steven shuffled the coca leaves around on his saucer, making patterns out of them. "Angel, this thing about the pistaco—what was going on with that? Connecting it to me just for being American? I feel like that's kind of crazy."

"Not so crazy," Angel said. "The pistaco is a shape shifter. It takes on different forms at different times. Other than saying it's pale, like a gringo, its description is always vague. Some say it goes back to the conquistadors, but it was surely something else before then. Timeless. Everlasting. Some say now Sendero is the pistaco."

"So you don't believe in it literally?"

"Do you believe in the devil, Padre?"

"What's the word for devil in Quechua? Supay?"

"The pistaco isn't the devil, but in a way it's the same. I am asking, do you believe in the reality of Satan?"

284

"With horns and tail and pitchfork? That's just an artistic rendering. It's a way of conceptualizing—"

"Do you believe in the personification of evil? Yes or no?"

"In short, yes."

"And I believe the pistaco steals our fat and leaves people to die emaciated. It doesn't matter how literal you want to get."

No, it didn't matter. The details may not really matter after all. "You should leave too, Angel, with your family," he said.

"And go where? Become a refugee? Like others who are fleeing? Take part in a land invasion in Lima for a scrap of sand hardly big enough for a house?"

"At least your children would be safe."

"Padre, I have more faith than you," Angel said. "You people think we're fatalistic, that it's our culture. Really we aren't. God isn't random nor is our destiny part of a great plan. Bad things happen because someone has broken God's law or hasn't made their offering to the apus or Pachamama. You can't run from what you've done or from what you didn't do that you should have."

"These Senderitas don't give a damn about your offerings. We're talking twentieth-century political ideology here, not indigenous customs."

"We're Quechua," Angel said. "A tiny village or the entire Quechua community, we must examine our conscience, because what has gone wrong here is something only we can fix. Blessings will return—when they are balanced by duty and respect for God, for Pachamama, for the apus, and for the saints."

Steven looked at the coca leaves drying now on the saucer. In Angel's Andean vision, reckoning came during this life, not after death. Heaven and hell were here and now.

"I'm sorry. I couldn't stand to see anything else bad happen."

"It's not in your hands, and you're doing what is best for all of us, including yourself. I'm doing the same."

A taxi pulled up outside the open door of the café. From the back of the cab, Judy leaned over to talk to the driver, who got out and came into the restaurant looking for them.

Steven left some money on the table, and he and Angel went to the cab, where Judy got out and greeted them both with hugs. Steven and Angel embraced, this time without the display of comradely backslapping.

"Be well, Padre, and God bless you," Angel said.

"You too, and may he keep you safe." Steven got into the taxi.

"I'm going to miss Ayacucho," Judy said to Angel. "I'm going to miss the people."

"Will you stay in Peru?"

"Somewhere in the Andes, I hope. Maybe Bolivia. I don't like big cities, so Lima isn't the option for me that it is for Steven."

"Bueno. I think we will see you in Ayacucho again someday."

They hugged. She kissed his cheek, turned, and got into the car. Steven looked at his Indian friend, stared into his dark, resolute eyes, and nodded farewell.

The taxi pulled away from the curb.

"Do you think he feels we're abandoning him?" Judy asked

"No. He's grounded here in a way I could never be anywhere."

They looked back. Angel was crossing the street to the plaza.

"Are you okay?" Judy asked.

Steven nodded. "I don't know if I'll stay in Lima or not."

"Because you don't know if you'll remain a priest or not?"

Steven shifted to get comfortable, his knees pressing the back of the driver's seat in the compact sedan.

"Technically, you're always a priest, but I've got a lot to consider right now."

He looked out the window as they passed one of the many churches he never had a chance to explore.

"The bishop asked about my relationship with Cori," he said.

"What does that mean? Are you in trouble?"

"Not really. He wanted some answers about what happened. I told him she was a friend who had helped me connect with the community."

"Which was true enough."

"He was looking for a martyr. I didn't give him one, but I didn't deny him one either."

They drove past the Temple of the Good Death, and the irony of that name brought back a swell in Steven's chest. A quick death wasn't the same as a good one, a peaceful one. He didn't know what was in Cori's heart when she died, but he assumed it was anguish. He recalled the brave young woman on the bus with the pistol to her head, and the villagers' account of how she refused to answer the guerrilla leader's questions about him. Why hadn't she just denied it, rebuffed Juan's accusation, and dismissed him as loco? He had asked himself that question over and over again. It would have been the easy thing to do, to deny him, but she had not done so. They probably wouldn't have believed her anyway. "Scared stiff" was how she had described herself after the bus holdup. He didn't believe that. The Good Death was reserved for the purest of hearts, and perhaps it was as much about how one faced the end as it was about any enduring Christian tradition.

They pulled up to the old monastery. Judy stayed with the taxi and her luggage while Steven went inside to get his bags. He had said his farewells earlier in the morning to all but Father Jaime. The old priest sat in the dining room, drumming his fingers on the tabletop.

"Father Jaime," Steven said.

"Ah, Steven, I was waiting to wish you a safe journey." He tapped the table sharply with his index finger and Steven took a seat next to him. "You know, I'm sorry things didn't work out for you here."

"You've been a big help, Jaime, and I owe you thanks for your faith in me."

"Did you love her?"

"Yes."

"It's awful to lose someone, and worse when it is so brutal, so senseless." Jaime's big, age-spotted hand patted and covered Steven's. "I'm very sorry for your loss."

Steven was going to miss the old man.

"Thank you, Father."

"I hope we don't lose you. It's never easy. I found the mountains were a good antidote to desire and loneliness. I was so tired from traipsing up and down those hills it blunted temptation. At some point in life, of course, the urges fade, but the loneliness remains. You just get used to it...." He let the sentence trail off, sat back, and balanced his fingers on the edge of the table.

"Well, young man, this I know with all my soul: God didn't put us on this earth to suffer. No, sir, he didn't. If you grow to recognize that, you'll know what to do." Jaime pushed himself to his feet.

"Let me give you my blessing before you go," he said.

Steven stood up and bowed his head before the old priest. Laying both his palms on the top of Steven's head, Jaime bowed his own head and prayed silently before speaking his blessing.

"Merciful Lord," he said, "please guide and protect your servant Steven in his travels, and give him the wisdom to discern his journey forward and the courage to walk the road you show him." Opening his eyes, he made the sign of the cross with one hand over Steven. "Vaya con Dios, Padre," he added.

Steven hauled a large duffle into the hall outside his room, and before he could turn back for the rest of his things one of the young caretakers was there, hoisting the bag onto his shoulder.

"I got it, Padre," he yelled and headed off toward the monastery entrance.

God didn't put us on this earth to suffer, Jaime had said. And what was human happiness if not finding love? For God is love and there could be no contradiction in that.

For the first time in his young life, Steven understood the expansiveness of love. Wasn't that the great commandment, simply to love? He had allowed himself to love a woman, true, and in doing so had met the paradox of love, its endless power to bring us both joy and sorrow. What had changed in him? He had listened to the deepest voice within him, the one crying to love and to be loved. How he ached with the loss of the love he had found. He ached for Cori. Yet through her he understood something deeper about love. The human heart expands infinitely to give it room.

Was it any different for a priest, even a disobedient one? He couldn't see how. For what voice should he listen to but the one deepest in his soul? Because in the end, what voice is that? What voice did Jesus obey? And in the name of that voice, what other voices did Jesus refuse to heed?

Steven put the last of his personal items into the case on his bed, looked around the room to make sure he had everything, and started to close the lid. His black shirt with a Roman collar was folded to one side, under his shaving kit. He recalled Cori jabbing him where his collar would have been, admonishing him. He looked at the heavy green flannel shirt he was wearing. The weather in Lima would be warmer. He remembered houses built on sand, the devotion of the old señora at the pachamanca, the straw men burning to ashes with the birth of the new year. Love had been brief, and at the same time would remain forever. He had tried to avoid love and found he couldn't. Of course he couldn't.

He changed his shirt, snapped the white collar into place, and left to catch his plane.

Acknowledgments

In recognition of those who contributed in some way to this book, I would like to thank Maria Chemi Hilares for her trust and confidence in me; the late William D. McCarthy, M.M., for generously lending me resource materials to guide me on Andean spirituality, as well as David Molineaux for advising me on conscience, James Christiansen and Joseph R. Veneroso, M.M., for advising me on prayer, and Margaret Gaughan for advising me on faith; Carlos Gutiérrez Bilbao for helping me set the village scenes and for a copy of *Recuperando Nuestros Cuentos*, from which I drew inspiration for the story of the tomb robbers; Lili Salcedo Guillen for her guidance on Quechua and life in the campo; John Herman at Manhattanville College, without whose guidance this book might never have been written; my early readers Edith Milton, David Link, Cheryl Roberto, Ted Kuhn, the late Frank Termini, Frank Maurovich, Scott Wolven, Dr. Kenneth Emonds, Richard Luchansky, and Michael Leach; my editors Michael Coyne and Greg Pierce; and Carmen for her love and support, Abby for her optimism and enthusiasm, and Mariana for her humor and insight.

Glossary of foreign words and phrases in *Pistaco*

abrazo — a hug
Abre la puerta. — Open the door.
Acha chau — Quechua interjection of consternation, like "Aye-yi-yi."
Allimllam kachkani. — Quechua for "I am fine."
ambulante — ambulatory street peddler
amiga — friend, specifically a woman friend, or girlfriend
Año Nuevo — New Year
anticucho — skewered and grilled meat
apagón — blackout
apu — mountain spirit
atentado — attack
avenida — avenue
ay or ayi — an interjection to mean ouch, alas or woe, often extended, as in "Ayiii!"
ayllu — originally a clan in Inca society, now a social structure in Andean communities
barriadas — neighborhoods or shantytowns
Bienvenido — Welcome
brujas — witches
Buenas tardes. — Good afternoon.
bueno — good or well
campesina — woman of the country
campesino — man of the country
campo — countryside
cañazo — a Peruvian rum, like moonshine
capitalista — capitalist, specifically a woman
casera — a favored vendor
casona — big house or mansion, used with article "la", as "la casona"
chica — girl or young woman

chicha, chicha de jora — corn beer, usually homebrewed

chichería — an establishment that serves chicha

choclo — fresh corn

cholo or chola — mestizo or mixed-race person, sometimes pejorative

choncholi — grilled pork, beef or lamb intestines

choza — hut or shack

chullo — knit cap with ear flaps common to the Andes

chullpas — Aymara burial towers in the Andes

chuspa — small bag or pouch

ciudad — city

Ciudad de Dios — City of God

Cono Norte — the northern cone, refers to northern part of Lima, Peru

costeña — woman from the coast

criollo — a person born in Latin America of primarily European descent, or of such culture, particularly along the coast of Peru

curandera — healer, folk doctor

cuy — guinea pig

desayuno — breakfast

Dile al padrecito que ya vienen los terrucos. Que no salga! — Tell Father the terrorists are coming. Don't come out!

dinero — money

Dos desayunos, por favor. — Two breakfasts, please.

emoliente — a tonic made with toasted grains and herbs

empleada or empleado — an employee; empleada usually refers to a maid

en vivo — living

Está bien. — "That's okay," or "That is good."

Feliz Año — Happy New Year

Glossary of foreign words and phrases in *Pistaco* (Continued)

garúa — drizzle or light rain

gringa/gringo — North American woman/man

hacendadito — little lord of the manor

hacendado — lord of the manor

hacienda — a country estate or ranch

Hermanos Mantaro — Mantaro Brothers

Hoc est enim corpus meum. — Latin phrase spoken during the consecration of bread and wine during a traditional pre-Vatican II Mass: "This is my body."

hola — hello

huayno — a style of Andean folk music

huayro — one of thousands of varieties of potato grown in the Andean highlands

inquieto — restless

jefe — boss

jirón — street, particular to Peruvian Spanish

joven — young

la guerra popular — the people's war

ladrones — robbers

Le invito. — "I invite you," or "Have some."

Limeña — woman from Lima

loco — crazy

madre tierra — mother earth

maestra — teacher, feminine form

Maldito! — Damn!

mamá — mom

mamita — diminutive for mother

Manan kanchu — Quechua for "There is none."

Manan kanchu wilto. — Quechua for "I have no change."

manta — a blanket or traditional shawl

marinera — a Peruvian folk dance

marmakilla — an aromatic herb

masacre — massacre

mate de coca — coca leaf tea

mestizo — polite term for a man of mixed race, especially Spanish and Indian

Mi casa es tu casa. — My house is your house.

mi amor — my love

miski — Quechua for candy or sweet

Mucho gusto. — "Very pleased," a common expression when first introduced to someone

muy bueno — very good

ojotas — sandals fashioned from old tire tread

ollucos — sweet, slender Andean tubers

olluquito con charqui — stew of ollucos and dried meat

Oye! — An interjection meaning "Hey!" or "Listen up!"

pacha — "world" or "earth" in Quechua

Pachamama — Mother Earth in Quechua

pachamanca — a way of cooking food on hot rocks in a covered pit

Padre, quiero confesarme. He pecado. — Father, I want to confess. I have sinned.

Padrecito — diminutive for Father, used affectionately

paico — a pungent herb used in cooking

papá — dad or daddy

paqo — shaman, mystic, or traditional priest in Quechua culture

peor — worse or worst

pisco — popular Peruvian brandy

pistaco — mythical figure in the Andes, often a pale man, believed to feed on human fat

pollera — full skirt favored by campesinas in the Andes

Glossary of foreign words and phrases in *Pistaco* (Continued)

por favor — please

profesora — teacher, specifically a woman teacher

Provecho. — short form of "Buen provecho," meaning "Enjoy your meal" or "Bon appétit!"

pueblo, el pueblo — village, the people

pueblo joven — young town, a Peruvian term for informal settlement or shantytown

puka picante — regional dish made from potatoes and beets

puna — high treeless terrain in the Andes

Qanchu kanki musuq yachachik. — Quechua for "Are you the new teacher?"

Que nadie se mueva. — Nobody move.

Que te vaya bien. — A farewell, wishing good fortune

Quechua —indigenous people of the Andes, their language and culture; pronounced "ketch-wah"

Rimaykuyki. Imaynallataq kachkanki? — Quechua for "Hello. How are you?"

Recemos — Let us pray.

saltado — stir fry

Salud! — "Health" or "To your health," a popular drinking toast

Senderista — a member of the Shining Path (Sendero Luminoso)

Sendero Luminoso — Shining Path, armed Maoist insurrectionist group in Peru in the 1980s and early 1990s

señor — term for a man, or an honorific prefix, Mr.

señora — term for a married woman, or an honorific prefix, Mrs.

señorita — term for a single woman, or an honorific prefix, Miss

señora de campo — woman of the country

servinakuy — Quechua term for a trial marriage, still practiced in traditional communities

sí — yes

soroche — altitude sickness

supay — Quechua for demon

suyos — political/geographical regions of the Inca empire, the four suyos

tallarines — noodles

té piteado — hot tea spiked with alcohol

Tengo que irme. — I have to go.

terrorista — terrorist

terruco — Peruvian slang for terrorist

tierra santa — holy land, or sacred ground

Todo está bien? — Is everything all right?

tumi — a pre-Columbian ceremonial knife with a semi-circular blade

valeriana — valerian root, brewed as herbal tea for sedative effect

Vámonos. — "Let's go." More emphatic than "Vamos."

Vamos. — "Let's go," or "We're going."

Vaya con Dios. — Go with God.

vicuña — smaller, undomesticated relative of the llama, prized for its wool

viva — long live

Ya voy. — I'm coming.

yanqui —an American, a Yankee

zampoñas — panpipes or pan flutes

Other Books from In Extenso Press

ALL THINGS TO ALL PEOPLE: A Catholic Church for the Twenty-First Century, by Louis DeThomasis, FSC, 118 pages, paperback

CATHOLIC BOY BLUES: A Poet's Journey of Healing, by Norbert Krapf, 224 pages, paperback

CATHOLIC WATERSHED: The Chicago Ordination Class of 1969 and How They Helped Change the Church, by Michael P. Cahill, 394 pages, paperback

CHRISTIAN CONTEMPLATIVE LIVING: Six Connecting Points, by Thomas M. Santa, CSSR, 126 pages, paperback

GREAT MEN OF THE BIBLE: A Guide for Guys, by Martin Pable, OFM Cap, 216 pages, paperback

THE GROUND OF LOVE AND TRUTH: Reflections on Thomas Merton's Relationship with the Woman Known as "M," by Suzanne Zuercher, OSB, 120 pages, paperback

HOPE: One Man's Journey of Discovery from Tormented Child to Social Worker to Spiritual Director, by Marshall Jung, 172 pages, paperback

MASTER OF CEREMONIES: A Novel, by Donald Cozzens, 288 pages, paperback and hardcover

NAVIGATING ALZHEIMER'S: 12 Truths about Caring for Your Loved One, by Mary K. Doyle, 112 pages, paperback

SHRINKING THE MONSTER: Healing the Wounds of Our Abuse, by Norbert Krapf, 234 pages, paperback

THE SILENT SCHISM: Healing the Serious Split in the Catholic Church, by Louis DeThomasis, FSC, and Cynthia A. Nienhaus, CSA, 128 pages, paperback

THE UNPUBLISHED POET: On Not Giving Up on Your Dream, by Marjorie L. Skelly, 160 pages, paperback

WAYWARD TRACKS: Revelations about fatherhood, faith, fighting with your spouse, surviving Girl Scout camp…, by Mark Collins, 104 pages, paperback

WE THE (LITTLE) PEOPLE, artwork by ISz, 50 plates, paperback

YOUR SECOND TO LAST CHAPTER: Creating a Meaningful Life on Your Own Terms, by Paul Wilkes, 120 pages, paperback and hardcover

BAPTIZED FOR THIS MOMENT: Rediscovering Grace All Around Us, by Stephen Paul Bouman, 168 pages, paperback

AVAILABLE FROM BOOKSELLERS
OR FROM 800-397-2282 • INEXTENSOPRESS.COM
DISTRIBUTED EXCLUSIVELY BY ACTA PUBLICATIONS